A Woman's Story

Also by Francine Rodriguez:

The Fortunate Accident

A Woman Like Me

A Woman's Story

Francine Rodriguez

MADVILLE
PUBLISHING

LAKE DALLAS, TEXAS

FIRST EDITION

A Woman's Story is a work of fiction. Names, characters, places, and incidents either are the products of the author's imagination or are used fictitiously. Any resemblance to actual events, locales, businesses, companies, or persons, living or dead, is entirely coincidental.

ACKNOWLEDGMENTS
Thanks to these publications where stories were first published: "I Still Like Pink" first appeared in *Taboos & Transgressions* (Madville 2021); "Smiley and Laughing Girl" first appeard in *Fleas on the Dog*, Vol. 7, 2020.

Cover Design: Jacqueline Davis
Cover Art: Created by DaisyArtDecor for International Women's Day. Licensed through Shutterstock.

ISBN: 978-1-948692-60-1 paperback, 978-1-948692-61-8 ebook
Library of Congress Control Number: 2020941275

TABLE OF CONTENTS

Ten Days in May

I tried to ignore the terrified look in the old man's eyes as I threaded the plastic tube down his trachea, while he lay in the narrow white bed with his head positioned so he stared straight up at the ceiling, and his eyes running with tears moved frantically from side to side. I hoped I was on course, because I couldn't tell if the laryngoscope was working, and I couldn't see the upper portion of the trachea the way I'd seen it done before. I could hear myself mumbling as I pulled it partially up and tried to hold his tongue aside while I inserted the tube again. Before this week, I wouldn't have been doing anything like this, a procedure for someone experienced and trained in sticking tubes down people's throats.

I'd only done it once by myself with Dr. Shirvani watching, but there was nobody to supervise or guide me now. If something went wrong, this man would be breathing in the contents of his stomach. If I went too fast, I'd mess up and have to start again, but if I was too slow, he'd get even less air in his lungs and they wouldn't be able to use the mechanical ventilator. "Damn," I muttered to myself, and patted the skinny arm with its translucent white skin under the worn hospital gown, and hoped it was some comfort. I wasn't sure how old the man was, because like many of the patients here, there was no mention of family in his chart, and even if there was, they wouldn't be allowed in to visit. Nobody had been allowed since the quarantine was imposed by the government.

Intubation was not something we normally did at this facility. We were really just a storage facility, where patients came to finish healing or to finally die, and we only had a couple of ventilators, and I wasn't sure if they even worked. It was a horrible

1

process and the only reason we went through it is because we couldn't move the patients anywhere else. There was no more room in the city's Intensive Care Units. I hooked up the patient's catheter and put a wet towel under him to bring down his fever. If he lasted through this round lying on his back, we would turn him over to ventilate the rest of his airway. I loaded up his IV with enough meds to knock him out. It was such a miserable and uncomfortable process that this was the only way the patients tolerated it. I checked his catheter again and wondered how many people he'd exposed before he got here.

"Okay, there you go. They'll be in to hook up your ventilator real soon, you'll be okay," I told him.

He didn't give any sign he'd heard, just lay there, tears streaming, eyes moving. He must be in a lot of pain, I thought, wishing that he was like the other one I'd handled who had been unconscious by the time it came to this.

I started out the door as Tyson, the orderly, on loan to us from County, wheeled in another bed with a young man lying on his side, his legs in casts, his breath raspy and choking.

"Help me move this over," Tyson pointed to the bed.

I pushed the old man's bed further into the corner so they could squeeze the young man's bed into the remaining space. The room was not really set up for patients. It used to be for storage, but now with no space left on the floor, the custodian had cleaned it out, and we kept the COVID patients there. If they crammed the beds together, it would hold two patients. I didn't see how all the equipment would fit, but it wasn't up to me.

I checked the young man's chart quickly. He was here at Culver Convalescent to recover from two broken legs. He was a county patient, from the city. No mention of an accident. Standing next to him I could see the tattoos on his chest and upper arms: FIRM 22 in large black lettering with something that looked like a badly drawn swastika on his forehead. He was a member of one of the local white neo-Nazi type hate groups.

I used to think of them as skinheads, but now I guess they call themselves something else. They were really right wing, anti-immigrant, anti-Black, anti-Hispanic, anti-you-name-it. Anybody who wasn't white was their enemy.

I moved closer and studied his face. Bad teeth and grayish skin. Probably from speed. He must have been transferred here because they ran out of room at the last place he was hospitalized. His chart said he tested positive for COVID. He probably didn't come into the system with COVID, but he must have picked it up along the way. His breathing was raspy, and he held onto the sides of the bed as he forced his breaths. His eyes met mine for a moment and I saw him glaring as he watched me. He was young, too, I thought. His first name was Ryan, so I figured he must have a nice white family somewhere wondering about him. But maybe they gave up on him like my mother gave up on my younger brother Fernando. Fernando had gang tattoos too, but his tattoos said "*M13*," a violent Latino gang that was gaining new members every day. You probably heard on the news about how they lured a rival's girlfriend to the woods and took turns stabbing her to death.

I haven't seen Fernando since he got sent up. At first my mom visited him every week, making the three-hour trip by bus, but now she only goes once in a while. She says Fernando has more jailhouse tattoos and complains if she doesn't put enough money on his books. I looked back at Ryan giving him my best "mad dog stare," to show him I was nobody's bitch, as I rang for Dr. Shirvani to authorize the LVN to set up the ventilator if he thought it was necessary. Personally, I wouldn't waste one on him if I had a choice. To me, he was just trash. The same trash that called my brother and me names and threw rocks at us when my mother sent us to a white school in a neighborhood where we were out of place. She had this idea that if we were with white kids, we'd be taught something and not just passed through. I got through school because I started fighting back. Those white girls were no match for me. I pulled hair, scratched, and punched, whatever was necessary. I spent a lot of time in the principal's office, but they started leaving me alone.

Fernando wasn't like me. Tender-hearted from an early age, he cried a lot, and I ended up fighting some of the kids for him, just so they'd get off his back. I guess that just made it worse for him, because they called him a sissy through elementary school. Fernando had trouble reading and stopped school in the ninth grade. He was an exceptional artist, though, and liked to sit at the kitchen table drawing for hours while I got into fights in the street. I still have a couple of his drawings at home. There's one he did of my kids in charcoal before they sent him up. It looks like something you would see in a museum. I don't think he draws anymore where he is now.

Culver Convalescent isn't a perfect place for a nurse to work. Located on the island of Bridgeview, it's a ferry ride away from the city, but the ferry only runs at eight o'clock in the morning and five o'clock at night. If you miss the ferry leaving the island, the only place to stay is the ratty Motel 8 off the main highway, unless you want to drive the badly lit and crater-ridden main road to the decaying bridge that connects to the city. The bridge is mostly pockets of crumbling concrete linked together to form a deck without guardrails that connects the island to the city by a thin finger of land. Since the tax base moved from the island long ago, there's no money to repair the bridge and most people bypass the road. Too many cars have veered off and ended up in the deep water filthy with chemicals from spills or dumping at the tire factory. I make the journey slowly every night across that bridge on my way to work, worrying that one dark night it will collapse and throw me into the dark putrid water that sits so still I don't think I've ever seen even a ripple—like it's waiting for me.

Nobody with anything going for them lives on the island. The white population started leaving in the early eighties and thirty years later the residents are more than ninety percent Black and Hispanic. The ones who have jobs mostly do assembly work at the factory that manufactures truck tires at the far end of the island. The smell of burning rubber rides on the breeze during the day and you could swear you taste rubber in your food every time you swallow.

The residents here who don't work at the plant work at the local market or the several liquor stores, take-out places, government offices, the two schools, or the bank. The remainder work as CNAs, LVNs, cooks, or janitors who double as orderlies at Culver. That's about all there is in the way of legitimate work. Those who want to make better money sell drugs. There's a lot of meth around if you're interested and of course the favorite, opiates. Young people sit by the water or in the park most of the day staring blankly at the few cars traveling by. If you want to buy something to wear or get your hair cut or have a baby, you have to travel to the city. I always get the feeling that a lot of these people have never even crossed the bridge to see the other side.

I ended up at Culver when I answered an ad looking for a nurse to work the graveyard shift. They wanted someone bilingual, and they didn't say anything about experience. That was a good thing, because even though I'm over forty, I haven't been out of nursing school very long. That diploma was a long time coming, because I first had to get my GED and then pop out a couple of kids with their father who was a player and eventually left me for a twenty-year-old he met online. He wanted to try again for the kids' sake, but I didn't trust him. My gut told me to keep walking before he noticed my graying hair and dumped me again. Meanwhile, I worked everywhere and anywhere, from restaurants to cleaners to a real estate office.

After I got dumped, I was so depressed that I didn't want to get out of bed. I stopped working and started drinking and left the kids with my mother until she finally told me she was too old to raise another family and that she would have to send the kids to County if I couldn't figure my life out. I don't think she would have really done that, but it got my attention. I joined a rehab program and started over, this time taking school seriously, and not just killing time like before. A counselor suggested nursing school because it would get me a job with a future. I think the counselor looked at me and figured the most I could achieve was a CNA certificate, but I'm the kind of person that likes to take a risk, go the whole route. If you trip, you should always get up. It was tough, but I finally graduated with an RN license. My kids were so proud when they first saw me in my work scrubs. They went without a lot so I could finish school and I wanted to make it up to them, make sure the rest of their young lives would be better.

Sometimes when I'm sitting at the nurse's station I look down at my hands, rough from years of hard work, fingers bent from the instruments and implements I've used. I don't think they'll ever be idle or unwanted. I can't imagine just sitting and holding them in my lap like my grandmother did. She ended up in a place like Culver, discarded and unwanted. I could still see her rage and frustration at being shelved and ignored. My hands will keep working until their life drains away.

The graveyard shift was perfect for me, I got off in time to get home and see my kids off to school in the morning. They were fifteen and sixteen, so they stayed by themselves when I was gone. They were used to it, I waited tables plenty of nights when they were younger, while they stayed behind a bolted door alone, huddled together on the couch in front of the television. It couldn't be helped.

Culver takes in mostly Medi-Cal patients, indigents from other convalescent facilities that need some kind of medical care or nursing that they can't get in other places, or patients who are too difficult to handle, like Mrs. Fortier on the second floor who screams day and night, or Jesus Calderon who is partially paralyzed from a gunshot wound to the spine. The patients here are the least healthy, all fragile, and all with chronic health issues. There's nothing to help them: no diet or medication management. Community care doesn't exist for them, and preventive care is a joke.

Sometimes, when they were awake late at night, I'd talk to the old and delicate patients, the ones who were with it, and ask them what they used to do. Many were in the military, some were teachers, or janitors, or they drove a bus in the city, and now they're bedridden. It sucks that they contributed their whole lives, and now there was no support system for them.

Culver advertised that it had a medical staff on duty twenty-four hours, but in reality, there is only one RN on each of the shifts and a couple of LVNs. CNAs do the day-to-day care, and Dr. Shirvani shows up a few times a week to review charts and prescribe new medications or renew prescriptions. The rest of the time the CNAs and the service staff do their best. The patients don't complain much even when they wait more than an hour for a drink of water, to be turned in their beds, or to have their diapers changed. They're used to waiting endlessly for any kind of help. They've done it all their whole lives. Dr. Shirvani is on call, but nobody calls him unless one of the patients dies. He had made it clear he didn't want to be here any more than he had to be. God help anyone who bothered him for what he called "nonsense."

"Get me a new gown now. Move!" Dr. Shirvani burst into the room swinging the heavy entry door and shrugging his soiled white gown off his shoulders. His mask was pulled below his high-bridged nose, and his graying beard stuck out of the bottom portion. He glanced at his watch and I knew he was getting impatient to leave. He'd come in around noon and it was now after six. I knew he worked at another hospital during the day just like many of the CNAs who struggled to work two shifts, usually at two different facilities.

That particular night when they brought the young man Ryan in, I was working a double, because the swing nurse called in sick and they couldn't find a replacement. It had become standard operating procedure during those days in early May to work a double. They kept bringing in new patients, a few of them with COVID, and there weren't enough CNAs to handle them. I heard it was worse in the city, where they said beds were now set up in the halls, and the dead bodies were overflowing in the morgues. I even heard they had trailers outside the medical facilities to hold all the dead bodies.

I hurried over to the storage cabinet and pulled out a clean gown. There was only one left. Gowns and masks had started running low a while back, and so far nothing was being delivered. I brought Dr. Shirvani his clean gown, which he grabbed from my hands, and stepped back to see what he would want next. While I waited, I glanced down at my name tag pinned to the front of my uniform top, "Nettie Cardoza RN." Sometimes I need to check the title and remind myself who I am, and what skilled things I can do, especially when I have to do CNA work like taking temperatures, hooking up IV's and cleaning up vomit because there is nobody else to do it.

Dr. Shirvani doesn't bother to use anybody's name. He directs us around by pointing and grunting. If you were across the room, he would shout out, "Hey you!" I could say that Dr. Shirvani is not well-liked at Culver, but that wouldn't be exactly true. He is hated by everybody that works here, and by the patients too, at least the ones who are with it enough to hear him yell at the nurses and the janitors. I know I hate him myself, and I wonder why he works here in the first place.

The staff doesn't like him because he's arrogant and rude, like a lot of doctors. But Dr. Shirvani makes a point of looking down at all of us, like we're peasants, and he talks to us like we're morons. Even without that, the staff wouldn't like him because he is Muslim, and most of them have no idea what that means or think it's something bad like being a devil-worshiper. He's dark-skinned and heavy-bearded, and he wears a particular round cap on his head all the time. I was curious about the cap, but not curious enough to ask him why he wore it. Who wants to be regarded with a sneer or yelled at? The staff referred to him as "The Arab," and "The Towel Head," when he wasn't around. If he ever found out, I would have told him not to feel so alone in being disliked because the Blacks and the Latinos here didn't like each other either. The Latinos complained that the Blacks were "lazy," and looked down at anybody who spoke Spanish. They said that the Blacks thought they were superior to them, calling them "stupid wetbacks," and saying they should go home to their own country. It didn't help that Culver hired a lot of women as CNAs, who probably were illegal and paid them less than the others. The Black employees claimed that the Latinos here called them "niggers" and "monkeys," and talked about them behind their backs in Spanish. The derision went both ways.

About fifteen minutes after Ryan's bed was set up and the old guy next to him was intubated, the code lights went on and the alarm sounded. I stopped in the middle of my rounds and ran toward the room I'd just left. Dr. Shirvani was leaning over the bed, and Connie, one of the CNAs, was pacing in front of the ventilator.

As soon as she saw me, she started crying, "He's not breathing. It's too late for the ventilator."

I looked over and Dr. Shirvani was trying to find a pulse, but he was shaking his head. "Damn people. You take so long! This guy's gone!"

Connie gave him a dirty look. The kind that meant she'd spit in his face if she could.

"Call the orderlies," Dr. Shirvani snapped looking in my direction, and walked away.

I bent over the bed and felt tears coming. I blinked and covered the old man's body with a sheet. There was no FaceTime video call like on the wards of some of the hospitals in the city, where the family could at least be with the patient through a video call. It was a shitty substitute, but at least the patient's family got to say goodbye, even if the patient didn't know they were there. We weren't set up for that here even if this old man had any family I could contact. His chart didn't have any next of kin or neighbors listed. He might have been homeless. He looked indigent. So Manuel Rojas died alone in his narrow hospital bed while Connie hooked up his ventilator. Maybe he heard me talking to him, telling him that it would be all right. Probably he didn't, I told myself. He looked out of it, struggling to breathe in his world of pain while his eyes tracked me as I left the room.

I called for the orderlies and one of them told me they were moving another body now and would be up soon. There were two deaths today, counting Mr. Rojas. There were five bodies now, stored in the cold locker where bodies were usually kept overnight until they can be picked up by the morgue. Nobody had come out to pick them up for the past four days.

"It's okay." I told Connie, reaching out to hug her. Her head was bent, and her Afro peeked out of the scrub cap.

She just stared at the figure on the bed and kept shaking her head. "It's not right. None of this is right. My father died on the sidewalk by himself up in San Francisco. They said it was an overdose. All of these people ..." She gestured down the ward and wiped her tears with the back of her hand. "And that asshole," she looked toward Dr. Shirvani and gestured by extending her middle finger, "doesn't have an ounce of compassion for nobody."

I agreed with her. Totally. But it wasn't a good idea to talk about anything like that with the staff, to make them think I was taking their side against the doctor. It could get back to the wrong people. I murmured something and stood back as the two burly men who worked as custodians and helped with orderly duties came in and wheeled the bed out the door. Now Mr. Rojas was just another patient I would think about when I was angry at Dr. Shirvani. I would blame him for Mr. Rojas dying because he didn't care about any of them. It would make it easier to hate him.

"Hey, I want water."

I looked over at the remaining bed. Ryan had raised his head slightly off the pillow and directed his demand in my direction. "Water. Get me some now."

I looked at his chart set in the bracket at the doorway. "No water," I told him. "Your breathing is bad, and it can cause aspiration. I can give you some ice chips if you like. We're waiting for this special water. It's thickened so you can't choke on it."

"I need some fucking water! I'm thirsty! Can't you see?" He squinted as if he was first seeing me. "I don't want you to give me anything. Where's the white nurse? I want the white nurse!" He yelled and immediately began to choke.

I walked over to the bed and started to crank it up a little to help with his breathing. He flung out his arm in my direction, nearly hitting me in the face.

"Leave me alone. I don't want no greasy border hopper touching me. I told you get the white nurse." He started to cough harder.

I could feel my cheeks redden and my heart start to beat faster. I touched my mask to make sure it was in place picturing his germs flying through the room. "It looks like I'm the only nurse here. No white nurses on this shift." I thought about telling him there were no white nurses here period, but he was coughing too hard to hear.

Exhausted, he finally stopped choking and leaned back against the pillow. "Was that sand flea that was in here supposed to be the doctor? I don't want him touching me either!"

I turned away so he couldn't see the little smile at the corner of my mouth. I couldn't help it. Everybody was so afraid of Dr. Shirvani, but nobody called him any funny names. Nothing but "asshole" or "motherfucker." It felt good to hear him called a name just like I was.

"If you're talking about Dr. Shirvani, he's the only doctor here too," I relayed the news a little gleefully.

Ryan gave me a dirty look. "Well that's why I'm getting out of here. I got my brothers coming for me. They're coming to take me outta here. Nobody better get in their way!"

"I don't think you're going anywhere," I told him. "Not now, anyway." I checked his IV and looked at his vital signs.

They were poor. He was lying down now, spent from the exertion. "I'll be back later," I said.

He turned his face to the wall and didn't answer. He was concentrating on getting a breath in and it was taking all his energy. The wheezing sound coming from his chest told me that his COVID was more advanced. Like a lot of the people who ended up here, he didn't go to the doctor until it was almost impossible to breathe.

Trailing behind Dr. Shirvani, while he made his rounds, I entered notes about procedures and medications in the patient log. Dinner was over for the patients who were able to eat, the trays had been removed and feeding tubes had been adjusted for the rest. The air was still with the exception of the faint humming of breathing equipment and the low drone of a television coming from the visitor's lounge, which was empty. The squeak of my rubber-soled shoes reminded me that my daughter needed new tennis shoes and that I'd forgotten to give my kids a call at home to check on things.

"We need tests for these people, I don't understand what is going on in this country," Dr. Shirvani suddenly walked over and spoke to me. "In this country with every advantage. You know they're all going to die." His voice was low, and his shoulders slumped.

I looked up shocked. He never addressed me without yelling out a command, usually followed by a curse. He didn't sound angry the way he usually did. I hesitated, trying to remember what I heard on television. People were wearing masks and social distancing. That seemed to be all you could do. "But they say the curve is flattening." I answered. "I mean most people will get over it, won't they? These people just happen to be sickly to begin with."

He shook his head and reached into his pocket to pull out a pack of cigarettes. He opened the stairwell door and stepped through it. I followed as we started up to the second floor. "That's just propaganda. Most of these people here won't make it. Not in places like this one. This thing is going to spread like wildfire. All those people crowded in there like that."

"But there's nowhere else to put them."

He stopped and leaned back against the railing. "Yes, that is true, isn't it?" He flicked his ashes down the stairwell and leaned against the railing, massaging his beard. "I don't understand the way things are in this country. It's not a third-world country like mine, but people suffer and die here just the same. Nobody cares."

It really bothered me when he said that because as far as I could see he was the most uncaring of anybody there. I looked up at the cap he always wore. Maybe I was wrong, but his eyes looked sad. "Where are you from?"

"Where?" He looked confused.

"Yes, What country? What place?"

"Oh, my family was from Iran, but my mother came from Pakistan originally. Did you know that the name Shirvani is the most common name in Iran?"

"No," I answered, wondering why I'd know a thing like that. "How did you end up in the U.S.?"

"Nowhere else to go. I never planned to come here. My wife wanted to, but not me."

"You have a wife?" I could hear the shock in my voice. As far as I'd imagined, Dr. Shirvani's life consisted only of working here or some other medical facility. The fact that he could have a life outside of that, and a wife too, never occurred to me. He was just a miserable person, a fixture at Culver, like the straight-backed chairs in the lobby.

"I had a wife. She's dead now. My little girl too."

I looked over at him and felt my mouth drop open. Moments passed while we climbed the remaining steps to the second-floor.

"I'm sorry," I blurted out.

Dr. Shirvani nodded slightly. "I don't tell many people. For a long time, it was too hard to say it to myself. Finally, I accepted it. Coming here helped, I think. I put some distance between the memories I have. They never lived here in the U.S. with me. So, it's easier here for me."

"An accident?" I heard myself ask automatically and then bit my lip. "Sorry. It's none of my business."

"It's okay. No, it wasn't an accident, it was Ebola."

"Ebola? Oh my God! But how?"

"My wife was a doctor and she worked for the Health Ministry. When the first outbreak started in Afghanistan she volunteered because that's where her mother was from. She thought she could do the most good there. She took my little daughter with her because I was working twenty hours a day and couldn't take care of her. She planned to come back as soon as things stabilized, but we didn't understand Ebola then. It just grew worse every day and people were dying in the streets. They're so poor, so desperate. Not even clean drinking water. Nothing to feed the children." He looked down at the last of his cigarette and stubbed it out on the metal landing. "Then it got worse and nobody could travel out of the country. She was stuck there working day and night. They took precautions, but in the end all the health workers were exposed. My daughter got sick first. She died in a few days. It took longer for my wife." His eyes clouded over, and he stared at his feet.

"I'm so sorry," I said again because there was nothing better I could say.

"She died alone there. People moved the dying to one area and left them. Everybody was afraid to go near them. It's a horrible death I've heard." He looked at me for a moment, "And I wasn't there with her."

I thought about old Mr. Rojas, dying alone in his strange hospital bed. "I'm sorry," I told him again.

"That's why I don't understand why things are like this here. It's happening all over again! I thought it was so modern in the States, the latest technology, people all healthy, a good life for everybody. But look …" He pointed down the hall. "Nobody can stop it. Explain it to me. How does this happen here?"

"Life's just unfair." I repeated what my mother said every time something bad happened to someone.

Dr. Shirvani glanced over at me. "That's not an answer. That's just an excuse. With all the power this country has, we shouldn't be fighting this thing the way they do in the villages back home." He looked over at me. "What do you think we need to do? From your perspective?"

I felt my face turn red, not so much because of the question, but because I was embarrassed that he was speaking to me so directly in front of the other staff. I noticed a few of the CNAs staring at us. I picked my head up and stared them down. To them, I was conspiring with the enemy. "These people had health problems before the virus hit," I answered. "Everything about their health is bad. No preventive care, bad diet, bad living situations. It's all bad here."

Dr. Shirvani stopped suddenly in front of the second-floor lounge. I was out of breath trying to keep up with his long stride.

"I need a cup of that awful coffee." He smiled just a little. "I'll buy you one too."

"No thanks," I said. I wanted to finish making the rounds and leave.

He chuckled. "Do you hate me too? You know it's hard to keep living with all this hate coming at you. All these women here hate me, talk about me behind my back, call me a terrorist or a dirty Arab. It used to make me sad, but now I'm just angry. I never planted any bombs. I'm not a terrorist. Maybe my grandmother could be one. She hit all of us kids with a broom. We were terrified of that broom." He laughed a little and held the door open for me.

I didn't know what else to do so I walked into the lounge with him. The night shift LVN and a few CNAs were on their break. They sat eating graham crackers from a store-brand box and watching a soap opera rerun. They stared at us, their mouths open as we took a seat at the small table by the coffee machine.

Dr. Shirvani glanced in their direction and looked at me pointedly, "I hope being seen with me doesn't make you an outcast here."

I blushed again but could feel some of the tension in my shoulders relax. For the next ten minutes I told Dr. Shirvani about the health problems the patients at Culver had and how the poor people in the city had the same problems. The infrastructure was broken. Dr. Shirvani sipped his coffee and stared down at the table while I talked.

He interrupted once to tell me that he chose to work at Culver because there was so little in the way of medical resources for the people here. He asked me if I'd been tested yet, and I told him I hadn't. There were no tests available at Culver. He told me he'd tested two days ago at the other facility where he worked. He didn't know the results yet. He told me that as soon as his contract was up, he planned to leave the U.S. and go back to his country. "I don't see hope in these people's faces here. I don't see a future anymore," he said, after I told him that I raised my children to believe that the world is full of goodness in spite of how bad things could seem. He looked around the room and then turned back to me. "What they don't realize is the same people that hate me, hate them too. Maybe they're too blind to see it."

I thought about Ryan. He was so clear in his hatred. He hated everybody who wasn't white. I wasn't so clear. I walked a lot faster when I saw a group of Black guys hanging around a corner. I held tighter to my purse and looked the other way. I'd grown up in a part of the city where we didn't see many people who didn't look like us or speak our language. It was comfortable that way, but it made me feel uneasy around Black people, because the only ones I ever saw were getting arrested on *Cops* or in lockup doing time. White people didn't come around the neighborhood unless you counted the police or people who worked for the government. They lived in a different world I only saw in the movies. They were always well-dressed, polite, and lived in beautiful homes with all the money they could ever want. Even Asians were rare here except for the store owners I saw daily. I think they're all Korean. Probably I've never met any other Asians except for them. The ones I saw usually didn't talk to me, avoided my eyes and lived somewhere else away from us, where they went every night when the day was over. I didn't know any Muslims, but like most people here, when I heard the word mentioned it was because some terrorist had blown up a building. That was probably the one thing that the Blacks, Hispanics and probably the Asians, agreed on: they all hated the Muslims.

After Dr. Shirvani finished his coffee we slipped our masks back on our faces and finished the rounds on the second floor. Another patient, an older woman who was recovering from pneumonia started showing symptoms, and we moved her into the room with Ryan. He wasn't awake when we did it and he was going to be surprised when he woke up and saw his room-mate was Black. Then I drove home just like every early morning, praying that the bridge didn't collapse and send me into the water below.

That night I thought about Dr. Shirvani losing his wife and daughter and then coming to a strange country to try to forget. It was a tough thing to do, I thought. Especially when you knew you were disliked everywhere you went. I decided I couldn't blame him for being so short-tempered and rude. Maybe he was just giving back what the others put out.

I was scheduled back on graveyard the next day, but they called me in early to work a double because they were short of CNAs and LVNs. Another LVN got sick that morning and two other CNAs said they weren't coming in anymore now that Culver had patients with COVID. I gave my kids some money so they could order pizza for dinner and reminded them to wear their face masks if they went outside. I had to admit they were adjusting pretty well to their school being closed and not seeing their friends. As far as I could tell, they were following their schoolwork and only going out to get takeout during the day when I slept. When they weren't doing that, my daughter was occupied on FaceTime and my son with his video games.

While I was driving, the radio announcer said that the ferry to the city had stopped running due to the COVID epidemic. Several of the operators had tested positive and most of the others were calling in sick. We still had the road, I told myself, as my car bumped along bouncing through the potholes I forgot to avoid. The sky was getting darker, clouds blowing across the horizon and covering the thin rays of light that remained. I could hear the wind whistling against the window glass, pushing my small Toyota from side to side. As I crossed the bridge onto the island, the sky opened with a huge crack of thunder that flashed an electric current of blue light across the sky. Huge walls of water gushed down, as if someone had released the gate on an ocean that had been locked away somewhere and was churning anxiously, waiting to be freed. By the time I walked from my car to the building, I was soaking wet and felt a bad mood coming on.

I stood drying off at the nurse's station, while checking in with Shayla, the RN on the day shift. It was a bad day all around she told me. Another two bodies were now in cold storage. They were a couple of older residents and nobody was sure if it was because of COVID, but since it happened so quickly, they thought it probably was. A truck was supposed to be coming out by ferry to pick up the bodies but now that had been postponed again. Ryan, the white boy, she told me had ripped out his IV and his other hook ups and started bleeding like a fiend. Dr. Shirvani, the son-of-a-bitch, was called and he had gotten into an argument with Ryan. Two orderlies had to restrain Ryan while she gave him a shot to knock him out. Ryan was sleeping now, and Shayla was grinning from ear to ear.

"It did my heart good to see that dirty white boy call the doctor every bad name in the book. He thinks he's so much better than us," she said primly. Then added, "but I'm not taking any more shit from that kid either. It'll be a cold day in hell before I knock myself out for him. He can sleep in his shit till he dies for all I care."

I watched her grab her lunchbox and stuff her uniform into a plastic bag. As soon as she stepped out, she turned around, her eyes wide. "That's a monster storm. No way I'm driving now. I'll wait it out." She headed for the lounge.

I checked the call log and calculated that more than half of the swing and graveyard shift had called out. I didn't bother to call the agency for replacements, nobody wanted to work all the way out here, especially now.

After another hour, I helped collect dinner trays and followed the CNAs checking vital signs. I hadn't seen Dr. Shirvani yet, but I knew he was there because of the whispered complaining I could hear from the staff.

Connie pushed open the patient's room door and leaned in next to me as I applied a dressing to the feet of an old man lying quietly in his bed in the corner. The poor old guy worked as a *paletero*, selling popsicles from the small metal hand truck he pushed around. He had to be over seventy, I figured. They'd brought him in when he had a heart attack in the park, and while he was on the ground, somebody stole all of his popsicles and his cart. His shoes were so worn that the blisters on the bottoms of his feet had burst and gotten infected. He squeezed my hand when I put on the salve.

Connie reached over me and poured a glass of water, but the old man was too weak to hold it. "I'll get a straw for him," she offered, then remembered something and turned back to me. "He's on the warpath. He told the new orderly, Alberto, to get a move on, and Alberto told him to fuck himself and go back where he came from. Boy, you could see he was furious, but he just gave Alberto one of his looks. Now he's jumping down all our throats."

"Alberto shouldn't talk to him like that. He's a doctor. Nobody talked to Dr. Moore that way." I didn't have to add that Dr. Moore was white.

"Well, anyway, you were getting real cozy with His Highness yesterday in the break room, I heard. What were you talking about?" she asked suspiciously.

I sighed. "Nothing important. Please get this man a straw, okay?"

She gave me a long look and turned away.

My cell rang as I started out of the room. I picked it up on the second ring. My mom was sobbing into the phone. "Fernando's got COVID! He just called. They're moving him with some others to one of the wings they don't use anymore."

My heart heaved in my chest. I thought about how tightly packed the prisons were and how there was no way to isolate anyone, and Fernando, always finicky about germs, constantly complained that there was never enough soap or hot water to keep clean. And that was before the virus hit.

"They say nobody can see him," my mom started crying again. "Is that true?"

I told her it was. Nobody was allowed to visit here either, and I wondered if she was feeling guilty for all the times she didn't go and see him. "You couldn't go anyway. Older people are at a higher risk." I assured her, hoping that might ease some of her guilt, though it didn't ease any of mine. I called home and told the kids to stay indoors and order something to be delivered. They didn't argue. The rain had progressed to a full-blown storm and the streets were flooded.

I turned on the television and scrolled through the channels until I found the local news which was all about the storm. I sat alone at the nurse's station, stared at the television and thought about Fernando and how he was so tender-hearted as a child. How he cried when an older neighbor boy lined up garden snails on the sidewalk and ran over them with his bike. That boy ended up on Rikers, and after Fernando got out on parole this time, he would probably end up there too. I was pretty sure there was another prison sentence right around the corner in Fernando's future, if he lasted through the virus. His fate was to enter life through jail doors, and he knew each time how harsh a penalty he was looking at if he tried to plead not guilty. He gave up a long time ago. It was easier that way once you were in the system.

The call lights were going off along the board, and I looked around for someone to cover them. The CNAs who'd reported in were running back and forth between patients. Lydia, the senior LVN, was checking equipment. I tightened my mask and jogged across the hall. Dr. Shirvani was finishing his rounds on the first floor.

He looked up at me blankly for a moment, as if he didn't know me, then pointed at my eyes. "You're crying. What happened?"

"It's just allergies," I told him embarrassed. I couldn't see myself explaining Fernando's situation to him.

"Okay." He said shrugging in disbelief. "I just heard that part of the bridge closest to the city washed out." He pointed to the flat screen on the wall. The sound was turned off, but the camera was trained on familiar streets now flooded with water.

"I won't be able to get home!" I heard myself saying.

"Nobody will. Not now. They're sending in a crew to fix it. But the rain has to slow down first."

I ran out to the hall and called home. The message said that my call couldn't go through at this time. Cursing, I ran back to the room where Dr. Shirvani was yelling that he needed help with CPR, but nobody was coming to help him.

Three hours later, the staff sat in the break room waiting for me to direct them. Lydia was running equipment checks and monitoring the patients on ventilators. I stopped counting the number of times I tried calling home. Dr. Shirvani finally stepped behind the counter and took a seat. "The rain has almost stopped," he pointed out.

I stared past him at the darkness on the other side of the small window visible through the break room. "Are you waiting for the repairs on the bridge?"

"Looks like it'll be another couple of hours until the crew

gets here." He popped a stick of gum into his mouth and stared at the patient log. "You know that young boy in the back isn't going to make it. Poor kid shouldn't have to die alone."

"You mean the Nazi?" I asked. "I can't say he'll be missed."

"He's a human being too. That's what my religion teaches."

"Your religion also keeps women down in every possible way, so I don't see why this guy is more of a human being than the women who have to live by your rule."

Dr. Shirvani chuckled. "They don't see it like that."

"How do you know what they see?" I was feeling irritated and frightened at the same time, and I didn't like the idea of spending the night here. I wanted my kids to call me, and I wanted to talk to Fernando. I wanted to tell him everything would be all right and I was sorry it seemed like I'd abandoned him. I hoped I could still tell him that. I'd write him tomorrow and put money on his books. That's what I'd do.

The light started going off in Ryan's room and I took off down the hall. Dr. Shirvani followed me. Lydia had placed Ryan on his side, and he was struggling harder to breathe than he had yesterday. I didn't have to ask; I knew there were no more ventilators. His eyes were open, watching Dr. Shirvani, and his face was gray. He flailed his arms weakly, mumbling something, but I couldn't understand what he was saying. It didn't matter; his time was counted. "We need to contact his family. I saw a number in his chart," I looked over at Lydia.

"Why bother? Good riddance to bad rubbish. That cracker told me to go to hell," Lydia snapped at me. "Called me an ugly ape too."

"Just do it. Act like a goddamn professional!" I yelled back.

I noticed she'd pulled the curtain around the old Black woman's bed. I wondered whose benefit that was for.

Dr. Shirvani walked over to the bed and examined the IV drip. "Refill his pain meds, and add a sedative," he barked at Lydia. "When did you last check him?"

As Dr. Shirvani stepped toward his bed, Ryan raised his

head just enough to shoot a stream of spit in his direction. It landed thick and viscous on Dr. Shirvani's mask near his nose and slowly rolled down. Ryan fell back weakly on his pillow, overcome with the effort.

"You know what else he was saying?" Lydia had stepped back into the corner and was watching wide-eyed, looking back and forth between us her eyes narrowed, full of hate.

"I'm sure you're going to tell us." Dr. Shirvani hesitated and wiped his mask with the hem of his gown that was already filthy from two days of rounds. The mask couldn't be thrown away and the gown couldn't be changed. Everybody was using the same ones as long as possible. Supplies still hadn't come in.

Lydia looked pointedly at Dr. Shirvani. "He said he hopes you die of COVID because you fucking yellow geeks brought it with you from China in the first place to infect everybody else."

Dr. Shirvani flushed. "Sorry. Wrong country. Wrong nationality."

"Oh, I told him all that, but he said all you apes are alike to him. You ought to be wiped off the earth. He said it'll happen one day because Hitler had the right idea." She looked at Dr. Shirvani expectantly. "He got tired after that and shut up. He's just mumbling now."

My cell rang, and I grabbed it instantly. "Why are you up at this hour?" I bit my lip as soon as I heard my words. "Are you okay? The storm scared me. I was worried."

My kids were fine, and the only reason they called me was because my son saw all the calls I'd made to them. I felt my stomach unclench, slowly. I looked over at Ryan now lying still, a hoarse wheezing sound coming from deep in his chest. "I love you guys," I told them before I hung up.

Dr. Shirvani went to the break room and closed the door behind him. Nobody followed him there. I went back to the nurses' station and poured myself another cup of black coffee to get me through till morning.

At six-thirty, I jerked upright, picking my head up from

where it was cradled on my arms. I had dozed off sitting at the desk. The regular shift was due in, but they wouldn't be coming until the road was fixed. I rubbed my eyes and wondered how I could get all these people, numb from exhaustion, through another shift.

I woke up the remaining kitchen staff. They had spent the night on the lobby floor as far away from the patients as they could get sleeping on extra bedding from the linen storage. I asked them to start preparing food and located the rest of the CNAs to start making the morning rounds. Typical of the weather here, the rain had disappeared this morning as suddenly as it came, leaving the sky clear and cloudless. Once the sun came out, the air would become choking thick and it would be a scorcher of a day. Someone had turned on the small television at our station, and I stopped to see what had happened in the past few hours. The blond woman in a short form-fitted dress standing in front of the courthouse was my first inkling of what the day would bring. She was broadcasting live, trailing after lawyers as they left the courthouse, asking them to comment on "the ruling." I vaguely remembered that some police were on trial for killing a young Black man—again. The issue was the use of deadly force. "The officers were acquitted," she spoke to the camera in a breathy voice.

The acquittal wasn't a surprise, there was nothing different about the outcome of this trial. It had all happened before. Over and over. Within the last year, the police killed a young boy of thirteen flying his kite in the park. They said they thought he had a gun instead of a kite spool. They also killed two other young men they stopped for questioning with chokeholds, and a young woman who failed to stop for a traffic light had her taillights shot out before one of the bullets struck her in the head. She died instantly. The police in each of the cases were acquitted. In my head, I ramped up my "you better watch your back when the police are around" talk to have with my son, and how he should behave if, God forbid, he was ever stopped. I tried to forget that that advice didn't work most of the time unless you were white. So far, I haven't heard if my talk has come in handy. My agonizing worry every time he leaves the apartment won't really begin until he starts driving next year.

The TV station then interviewed representatives for the ACLU and the Black Brotherhood for Justice who still insisted that the police were murderers and then condemned the state government and the governor. The governor was calling for an investigation into police tactics. It all sounded familiar. There had been an investigation a few years ago and one before that. Nobody ever heard the outcomes. Nobody really cared because it wouldn't change anything for people like us.

All of the television stations reran the film clip of the young man's mother sobbing into the camera. "He was a good boy," she kept saying. "He shouldn't have died like that. He was scared. He was just trying to get away."

I sighed and turned away from the television. Just then, someone threw a trash barrel though the ground floor window of the city government building. The sound of smashing glass drew my attention back to the screen. More people moved toward the building's courtyard and began throwing things through the windows. Rocks and chunks of wood started to fly. More trash barrels were dragged to the site, and men were lifting them and tossing them through any windows they could reach. People were gathering so fast; the crowd was now out of the camera frame. The reporter hurried away toward her news van, yelling into the microphone that her audience at home was witnessing a riot.

"Thank God it's over there," I whispered to myself. All of a sudden, I didn't mind being stuck here for a little while, away from all those crazies. People were marching in the square carrying signs saying, "No Justice No Peace," and "Police Are Dangerous Criminals." I switched to another channel, and the staff started gathering around my desk to watch. Crowds were starting to run up the street, like a herd of bulls in heat. Only a few wore masks. There's no social distancing in a street mob.

One by one, as the windows were smashed in the shopping district, groups of people ran in and came out carrying armfuls of clothes and what looked like shoe boxes. Others came out balancing television sets and computers. One of the CNAs complained that by the time she got back into the city, all of the good stuff would be gone.

And then the police arrived. I watched as they came into focus on the screen, a mass of dark uniforms and shields descending like a hoard of dark, shelled insects, their equipment bouncing against their bulletproof vests as they advanced. An army anxious to partake of a war. Their voices boomed over bullhorns and the protesters and the looters advanced to meet them.

I grabbed my phone and called home. "You guys stay inside. There's no way you go out in the street."

My daughter asked if I was watching television. Her friend called her to see the looters in the shopping centers. They were picking up some good stuff she told me. "Don't even think about it!" I yelled into the phone and turned back to the television. The police were trying to push the protestors back and ignoring the looters. Smoke bombs and tear gas blurred the images. The popping sound of rubber bullets was followed by the screams of those who were hit. Emergency sirens drowned out the bullhorns and the noise from the exploding canisters.

"Looks like Beirut." Dr. Shirvani stood behind me to watch the television. "Three more patients have symptoms this morning, and your little white friend in there took a turn for the worse. I don't think a ventilator would even help now. I watched him most of the night."

Looking up at him, I remembered that I'd checked the break room once last night and he wasn't there. This morning his eyes were red and sunken, and his mask was stained a dirty gray. He scratched the gray hair that stuck out of his cap. "Change the channel to the local news," he said pointing at the screen.

I changed the channel in time to hear the newscaster announce that the bridge to the city was reopening. The road crew had just checked, and it was safe again. "Safe" was a relative term. I began to message the day crew, telling them to report in. We would be short-staffed again today even if everybody showed up.

I was waiting for the day shift RN to report and Dr. Shirvani was checking the patients for the last time when we heard the sound of smashing glass. I ran to the front lobby in time to see the lobby floor covered in glass and the front windows smashed out. A handful of young men were throwing bricks at the side windows. I looked up the street to see more people were grouped together in front of the small government center carrying metal trash cans that they pitched at the windows as I watched. "Call the police!" I screamed, running back down the corridor.

A group of four young guys were running crazily through the lobby, heading toward the nurses' station. Their faces were recognizable. They looked like the kids I saw hanging around in the park, dazed and glassy eyed. One of them grabbed me by the arm. I twisted around trying to break away, but he hung on tight. I noticed his hands shook, and the nails were broken and dirty. His face unmasked was a sickly yellow color.

"Where are the drugs? Where do you keep them?" He dug his nails into my arm. "You better tell me, bitch!"

I pulled away and felt something cold and metallic against my forehead.

"Did you hear my friend here?" The voice was high and whiny. I looked at its owner, thinking crazily that it didn't fit this large lumbering boy-child, whose shirt, struggling to cover his stomach, was missing buttons. He had long greasy hair that had come loose from his ponytail and hung in strings around his face. He pressed the gun harder against my head.

I closed my eyes and took a deep breath. "Look," I began, "why don't you just leave now so we don't have to call the police?"

The one holding the gun laughed. "We're not leaving till we get what we came for. Isn't this a hospital? We're sick too. Really sick." He snickered.

I heard the gun click. Two more guys walked over from the direction of the lobby. I thought fleetingly of Pablo Muñoz, who acted as a security guard on the day shift. Poor Pablo. He had to be at least sixty-five with a stent in his chest. He couldn't walk very far, much less run. He'd stopped coming in when the Stay-At-Home Order started. He was too afraid of getting sick. He wouldn't be any good now, I thought. He didn't even carry a gun.

I felt myself being dragged forward toward the nurses' station by the one with the dirty hands, while the one holding the gun moved along, one step behind. Once they hit the dispensary, they would kill anybody who could identify them. You just knew these things about guys like them. Just like you know all about cops where we live. "We have very sick patients here. Some of them have COVID. You're exposing yourself." I was pleading now, seeing my kids, seeing Fernando. I couldn't leave this world yet.

"Get out of here you son of a bitch!" The voice was harsh, commanding. I could hear the accent very clearly. I didn't remember hearing it so clearly before. Dr. Shirvani stood in front of the counter, his arms folded across his chest. "You heard me! Turn around and get the hell out of here. I already called the police."

The one holding the gun stepped back, and for a moment the cold pressure of metal against my skin was gone. I saw him turn slowly, looking over at Dr. Shirvani, who looked back, defiant. Then I heard the sound of the trigger being squeezed and I watched Dr. Shirvani fall, blood oozing out from the wound in his neck. He called out in pain and I watched the gun jerk back as he was shot again. Dr. Shirvani was silent then. The one holding the gun looked back at me his eyes wild, unfocused, and then turned back and emptied his revolver into the white-coated figure on the floor. A few shots connected with his partially turned chest. For a moment, it was totally silent in the corridor, except for the whirring noise of the machines that kept the patients alive, and the sound of somebody sobbing. I held onto the wall and slid to the floor as the tears ran down my face. I remember seeing faces staring down at me and then the darkness came.

An hour later, I heard voices and I turned toward the sound. I was still at Culver, lying on the sofa in the break room. I recognized some of the staff from the day shift, and several police standing near me.

"She's awake!"

I looked up at the day shift RN confused.

"You're okay. The EMTs checked you out before they left." She assured me, rubbing my arm. "I heard how brave you were. I would have hid somewhere."

I pushed up on my elbow and looked around. My hands were still shaking. "Where's Dr. Shirvani?"

"They picked up his body already. The cops arrested the junkies that broke in and shot him. You know we were really lucky that the bridge was flooded this morning, all the cops were still on duty from last night. They showed up in minutes. But I guess it was too late." Her voice trailed off and she looked over at the area near the front counter that was now outlined with yellow tape.

I stared at the taped outline that marked the spot where a man once stood. I thought about how much Dr. Shirvani missed his wife and daughter and how much he disliked this place. Before he was shot today, before he died, he already had wounds in his heart that were bleeding out. Except they were the kind of wounds that nobody could see, the kind that couldn't be treated by medical care, maybe not even by time. And all of us had dug into that wound, a little at a time with our hatred, pulling off any scab that was trying to form, not letting it heal, making it deeper. The weight of it all wrapped itself around me.

"You're not going to work a double, are you? I mean, not after this morning?" I looked up at the newest CNA. You could see she was young. Probably new and scared stiff. She twisted the hem of her scrubs between her fingers and looked down at her feet. "I want to ask, before you go, can you give us some help with that white kid over at the end of the hall? He looks like he's going to die any minute."

"Ryan," I said the name sadly to myself. Dr. Shirvani believed that Ryan was a human being too. He said that's what his religion taught. He sat by Ryan's bed last night because he knew he was dying, and he didn't think he should die alone. Fernando might die alone too, without his mother and sister, in a crowded cell block where there was no place to isolate. Fernando, who liked to draw animals with the charcoal pencil I bought him, the gentle boy who hated when anyone raised their voice. The world was too cruel a place for someone like him, so he escaped to another place that lead directly to a prison cell.

My hands had stopped shaking and lay in my lap, the fingers spread and poised to act. Capable hands that had healed others before and would keep healing. That's what Dr. Shirvani's hands would have done, because even though we were different in so many ways, he saw the same injustices I did, and he felt the frustration and rage of the same people that hated him for who he was.

"I'm doing a double today," I told the CNA, who was still staring at me and had started biting her nails. "Dr. Shirvani would have wanted my help."

All the Lonely People

Last night Laurie dreamed that a torrent of ice-cold liquid was being poured onto her face while she was sleeping. As the stinging cold deluge soaked into her skin, it filled her mouth, choking her and cutting off her breath, then ran down her jawline and onto her pillow. More water followed, until she was weighed down beneath it, trapped underwater, while long fingers stained with soft pastel paint held her head in place. The person doing the pouring in her dream was her husband.

And then something, a noise, maybe the barking of the dog next door, woke her up. She sat up straight, rubbing her eyes, her heart pounding, and touched her face. It was perfectly dry.

Laurie thought they were okay before the divorce. Maybe not really happy, but okay. But okay wasn't good enough she guessed. She didn't really know much about men. Never being allowed to date while she lived at home, before she married Steve, there was no way to measure if things were going well or not.

She was alone in her bedroom. The husband she'd just dreamed of wasn't anywhere around. In fact, according to Instagram, he was on his honeymoon in Hawaii. His new bride looked a lot like a woman she'd seen long ago from his art class. She supposed she'd never see him again.

Laurie sat up in bed that morning and took a deep breath. This place was her apartment, just hers, and it was the first time she'd ever lived by herself, shy and unsure, having moved from her mother's house to live with Steve right before they got married. Her mother approved of him, after all, he was a college graduate, respectful, artistic, once-in-a-while churchgoing. But she was divorced now, a newly freed spirt at age twenty-six, with a decent job teaching English at one of the high schools adjacent to downtown.

It wasn't a dream job; most of the students weren't interested in American literature. It had no place in their lives where iPhones occupied most of their time, followed closely by a second activity, getting high. Then there were the endless piles of papers. Papers to grade, reports to prepare, and bureaucratic red tape to wade through. Still, she knew she was lucky. So many friends she'd known from college couldn't find a decent job to save their lives. She knew she owed part of it to the fact that she spoke Spanish, and the district was looking for bilingual and bicultural teachers. She heard that fifty percent of the new teachers quit after their first year, and she could sympathize. She thought about quitting at least ten times every day.

By 8:10, she was taking roll, dressed in layered sweaters, defending against the unusual cold that had suddenly appeared in California. Her eyes moved across the rows of seats, looking for empty chairs. She barely heard him answer when she called his name, Marco Perez. He was new. A transfer from the valley. She wondered what he was doing in this part of town. Nobody wanted to go to school here if they didn't have to.

She called the name again, and this time Marco looked up or rather, through, the too long light brown hair that fell to his shoulders. "Here," he said in a voice that spoke of boredom and impatience. Then he looked back down at his desk, hair hiding his eyes.

Laurie stared at his broad shoulders covered by a white T-shirt and moved her eyes down to his faded blue jeans. He didn't wear the customary sagging pants that hung below the wearer's butt crack, like most of the other guys. She shivered just a little. It had been a while since she'd seen a male body in fitted jeans. It didn't hurt that he looked like he had a good set of abs too.

She started the lesson by reading passages from Steinbeck and having some of the students go to the front of the class and tell everybody what the symbolism in each passage was. Sometimes it worked, and you could start some type of class discussion. Mostly, it didn't. Twenty minutes later, only one student had shuffled her way to the front of the room, looking embarrassed, and offered a lame opinion, clearly pointing out that she hadn't read the homework. Laurie passed over most of the students. Their eyes were glazed, still half asleep, not caring, thinking they could pull off a low "D" at the last minute if they had to.

She almost bypassed Marco, but there was something about the way he sat with his arms folded across his chest, and his head down, that challenged her. Insolence personified. She called his name, and he looked up, surprised.

"Me?"

"Yes. You're Marco. Aren't you?"

He looked around, slouching lower in his seat. "I didn't really read anything."

"That's okay. I want you to try and answer. You heard the passage that Paula just read. One purpose of education is to teach you to think on your feet. What do you think that passage meant?"

"Don't know."

The challenge in his voice irritated her. She could get back at him. Give him a strong directive and then send him to the boy's principal when he disobeyed. But there was something about the way he sat there, an island, as isolated from her as he was from the rest of the class. She waited a moment and then moved on, calling on another student.

When the class was over, she asked him to stay behind so she could give him the rest of the outline he'd missed. He shrugged and walked to the front of the room, sitting at the desk directly in front of her. Up close, his skin was a soft caramel. He had a handsome face: anyone would agree. Nicely chiseled features, the kind you saw in *GQ*, bare-chested, advertising cologne. Good genes, she thought. Mixed-race kids were usually so good looking.

She stapled the class assignment sheets together for the semester, and as an afterthought, stuck them into an empty folder and handed it to him. "Here you go. What were you studying in this course when you were at your last school?"

Marco looked stunned at the question and shrugged his shoulders. "I don't know."

Laurie felt herself getting irritated. "You did go to school before this, I assume. I saw you transferred here."

"Yeah, I did."

"Well…" she hesitated. It usually wasn't her practice to ask the students personal questions. Humiliating a student by making them tell you their father wasn't around because he was in prison, always seemed like a way to punish them. Other teachers did it all the time, though, mainly when they talked themselves into believing they were saviors for these challenged kids, and then the kids made them look like idiots in front of the class. "What happened, did your parents change jobs and you had to move down here?"

"I don't have any parents." Marco delivered the news with a flat, matter-of-fact tone.

"Oh! I'm sorry. I didn't know." Laurie felt her face redden and wondered why she'd been so determined to find out what brought him here.

"I live in Osiris."

"The group home?"

"Yeah," he said, looking away.

Laurie felt sudden sympathy. She didn't know much about the group homes that some of the boys lived in. She just knew that the boys that lived there were usually rude and obnoxious. They got into fights and came to class high. At first, she figured it was because they had no parents at home to correct them, but then, some of the kids with parents at home were even worse.

"How is it in Osiris?"

"Okay. They're all the same, I guess."

"You lived in others?"

"Most of my life, I guess." He looked at her directly as if he expected her to challenge him.

"Well, it must be hard to change schools and make new friends."

"I don't have any friends, really," Marco answered, watching her face.

"That seems lonely." Laurie clasped her hands together. "Maybe you'll make some new friends here."

"Probably not."

Her eyes traveled to his tanned arms, taut and muscular. The underside of his forearms were covered with small white scars raised on his tanned skin. She stared until he shifted position. Now she noticed a long, jagged scar on his neck. Pulling her eyes away, she realized she didn't want him to leave the empty classroom with the comforting sound of the heat whooshing through the radiator. "It's cold out. Don't you have a jacket?"

"No, somebody took it in the last place. The county doesn't give a clothing allowance until the first of the year."

Laurie hesitated before she spoke. She and her sister had shared clothes, including a jacket, when her mother got laid off from her job at the poultry plant. It took her mother a long time to find another job, not only because she didn't speak much English, but because employers during that time had been afraid to hire someone without papers. She remembered her ex-husband's quilted parka that he never came back to get. It was still hanging in the back of her closet. "Look, I can give you an extra jacket I have. I was going to take it to Goodwill anyway. I think it will fit you. My ..." She stopped and stumbled over the words. "My ex-husband was about your size."

She saw Marco staring at her intently, as if he was trying to determine what was going on with this teacher who was so interested in talking to him. She wondered if he thought she was one of those "do-gooders," the kind she couldn't stand either because they made you feel so small. Before her mother started taking in foster kids for the extra money, they were so broke that their mother went to church and asked for help to buy food for their Christmas dinner. Women from the congregation came around before Christmas and brought cheap gifts she and her sister didn't want, like young adult books by Christian writers and boxes of plastic checkers. They always included the gifts for Laurie and her sister in the large cardboard box they delivered along with a frozen turkey, instant mashed potatoes, and canned string beans.

Laurie looked up from the memory, feeling him staring at her. She flushed red, embarrassed. "It must get lonely for you with no parents. I mean, especially on the holidays."

Marco frowned. "No, I'm used to it. Being on my own. I don't care." He looked away from her, watching groups of kids outside the door, laughing, and calling out to each other as they walked to their next class.

She handed Marco a stack of paper and several folders. "You need these if you're going to write your essays for this class."

Marco stuffed them into his torn, faded backpack with the zipper stuck open. "Thanks, I guess," he said, looking at his backpack doubtfully.

Laurie leaned back against the utility table, picturing herself going home tonight to her solitary apartment. She would eat a microwave dinner, grade a few papers, and try to watch television. Finally, she'd fall asleep, tossing around in her single bed, her body straining and feverish, until the dreams started, the way they always did. Dreams where she whirled around in a dark universe alone, trying to break free. And then Steve would tell her he was leaving, and she would wake up trembling.

"So, where are your parents?" She was surprised to hear herself asking the question. As soon as she said the words, she was sorry. "You don't have to say if you don't want to."

Marco's face colored slightly; a rosy blush crawled across his sharp cheekbones. Laurie's fingers moved instinctively, wanting to stroke the tanned skin on his arms. She caught herself and folded her hands in front of her.

Marco looked down at his torn tennis shoes. Then he stood up suddenly and shook his hair out of his eyes. "My dad died a long time ago. He OD'd. My mom's been in the nuthouse since I was a baby. She's never going to be alright. That's what they say. They let me try to see her one time, but she didn't want to see me. I never got to go in."

Laurie felt her eyes fill up. "I'm sorry, that's so sad."

Marco shifted his weight. "No big thing, I guess."

"And you don't have any other family?"

"Nope. They said I had an older brother, but the county took him, and he got adopted before I was born."

"My mother took in foster kids for a little while. We needed the money." Laurie offered.

Marco didn't answer but waited expectantly.

"It wasn't a very good idea." Laurie added. "My mother couldn't handle it. She had to work long hours in the factories. She was always tired, and the kids had lots of problems." She turned away from Marco and wrapped a rubber band around a stack of pencils. "Look," she began. "If you need any help with your work, I'd be glad to help you. It's got to be hard, changing schools."

Marco shrugged. "I guess so."

Laurie waited for him to say more, but he'd turned his gaze back to the hall again where students were hurrying along, laughing and calling out to their friends, and others were lounging against the lockers as if they had no place to go and all the time in the world to get there. She wondered if Marco felt any different from them.

"So," Laurie started again. "How about you come by tomorrow after school and we'll go over the assignment together. You'll get more familiar with the course outline that way."

Marco stared back at her, and she thought she saw something flash across his face, first a look of confusion, and then a second one of clarity. "Ok, I'll come back."

"Great!" Laurie found herself smiling, something she didn't do that often around these kids. They mistook kindness for weakness, she'd thought during her first week of teaching. She was certain that they could see past her, see that she was inexperienced about so many things. Not just teaching, but life itself. Already many of them had lived much more life than she had.

On the way home, she turned on the radio and found the local hip-hop channel that she heard most of the kids listening to now. Frowning, she concentrated on listening, trying to understand the lyrics beyond the heavy beat. The first lyrics she understood made her face flush. Lots of talk about having sex, wanting sex, and how sex would be performed. Aggressively and often, it seemed from what she heard. And the rapper was female, brash, garish, and almost hostile in her demand to be listened to. Laurie wondered what it would be like to be a teenager in these times, to be a girl with so much freedom to say what she wanted, what she desired. She shivered picturing the singer and the object of her song entwined and lusty, just the way it was described.

Her mother had always been strict about what music she played in the house. Laurie laughed to herself picturing her mother's face listening to this song. Silly comedies were the only programs her mother let them watch on television and she kept the station on a family-friendly channel. Even Hallmark was a little questionable sometimes for her. She turned off the TV and radio promptly at nine o'clock, ordering everybody to go to sleep because she had to wake up at dawn to work another long day in the factory. Laurie remembered the foster kids listened to rock and rap on the radio in their room, under the covers. They never invited her in to join them, but she knew her sister, with her easy laugh, was always invited by the girls in the other bedroom. She could hear them all laughing in hushed voices, trying not to wake her mother. They talked about boys too. Who had done what and with whom. Inside or outside the clothing was the question. They all seemed to agree that inside the clothing was better.

Sometimes Laurie tiptoed across the hall and listened outside the bedroom door, inhaling those giggling voices, as if she had skipped over that time in her life when you could snigger and brag, tell confidences, discuss the size and shape of guy's penises, compare the size of breasts. Her mother had strict rules about what you could and couldn't do as far as boys were concerned. She kept a tight hold on Laurie and her sister. That hold extended to the foster kids, some of whom weren't used to so much control. Most of the foster girls snuck around to meet boys, and a couple of them ran away. Her sister followed their example and ran away once too with a high school senior who was arrested for possession, and then expelled from school. When the police brought her back, Laurie's mother tightened her hold even more. Her sister rebelled and moved out, but Laurie stayed. There were expectations of her. She was not like her sister. She was the good child.

The next morning, Laurie woke up feeling more eager to start the day than she had in a while, almost raring to go for a change. Marco said he was coming after school. She pictured herself helping him with his schoolwork, imparting the kind of knowledge one-on-one that a teaching career had promised but couldn't deliver in the classroom.

Marco was nearly thirty minutes late when class ended for the day. She waited, sitting awkwardly in her chair. She tried to start grading papers but kept looking up at the door. Just when she was about to pack up her things for the day, he ambled in, dumping his backpack on an empty seat.

"I didn't think you were coming," she heard her voice stammer. Marco smelled like stale cigarettes.

"I had stuff to do." He looked back at her with a small smile.

"Okay, this is today's assignment." She stood up and brought him the assignment sheet. Standing closer to him, she thought she could feel the heat leaving his body and entering hers. She backed away and went to sit at her desk.

She waited expectantly, but Marco barely glanced at the sheet in front of him. Instead he turned a ball point pen over in his fingers, clicking it on and off with each turn.

"So, do you understand what the assignment is? I mean this may be new material so I can explain if ..."

"It's okay, I guess." Marco interrupted, folding up the sheet of paper.

Laurie looked down at his long frame sprawled in the seat. "I want to go over it with you. Do you understand what I want you to complete by the next class?"

Marco shifted, and looked around the room, not answering.

Laurie watched the muscles in his arms tighten. "Why don't you explain the assignment to me in your own words, so I can make sure you understand it?"

Marco unfolded the sheet of paper but kept his eyes on Laurie. "Why don't you read it to me?"

Suddenly she was confused. "You understand what I'm asking, right?"

"Don't know," he shrugged. "I don't read too much."

"Oh," She blushed, embarrassed. "Well, that's not a problem we can't fix. Lots of students don't read at high school level. We can get you tutoring for that. Did you ever get any help with reading before?"

Marco shook his head. "The school counselor at my last school told me I was years behind my grade level. Like maybe somebody in elementary school. I didn't tell him though, he figured it out because I did so bad on all those tests. He asked me to read something for him and I couldn't."

"Did he offer to get you a tutor?" Laurie wanted to know. She struggled to understand how he had gotten this far in school without reading.

"Naw. He said I was too old already. Anyway, they always pass me on to the next grade all the time, so it's okay."

"You're going to need to read one day," Laurie responded a little angrily. These counselors and teachers who only did the minimum, never taking a real interest in the students, infuriated her. Even though the work could be so discouraging, and the kids didn't appreciate it—that, and the fact she often thought about quitting herself—she still tried to do her best.

Laurie dug around in her side desk drawer and pulled out

her reading chart. "I want to see more or less what your level is. Just so we know where to go next. Maybe this class isn't appropriate."

"You mean too hard for me, right?" Marco laughed. "Look, all you have to do is pass me. They all do."

"What's going to happen when you have to get a job?" Laurie got up and began pacing. "What are you going to do then when you can't even fill out an application?"

Marco stretched his arms and laughed. "Maybe when I get older, I can be a model. You don't need to read, just look good." He pushed his hair off his face again, and Laurie found herself watching his hand, imagining the silky texture on her fingers. Then she thought of her ex-husband complaining that he wanted to follow his calling and be an artist. After all, he'd been an art major in college. Working all day would leave him no time to paint or to go to the gym, and teachers made decent money, he said. Couldn't she afford to buy a small sailboat that he could convert into an art studio?

She forced the memory of that conversation out of her mind. "Just read this for now. That's all. Maybe I can help you, find your reading level, and go from there."

"Help me? Teach me to read? That way everybody finds out I read like a little kid. I mean, things are bad enough as it is. I don't want anybody to know!" Marco frowned and crossed his arms over his chest.

"I would never tell anyone about your personal history," Laurie snapped at the suggestion. "Never!"

Marco regarded her steadily without blinking. He was smiling now, the corners of his mouth twitching. "Let me tell you something. This social worker at the other home wanted to help me too. She set me up with a student teacher just out of college. She was really hot too. Maybe six, or seven, years older than me. A blonde with big boobs, just the way I like them. We didn't get to any reading. Let me tell you that. She was crazy about me, couldn't get enough. We were doing it in the empty meeting rooms, but the custodian said he was going to report us, so we started going out to her van after she got off work. She let me do it to her for hours. All kinds of ways. Just like the stuff in the pornos. But somebody saw the van parked there at night and told the director. They fired her ass so fast she didn't know what hit her. I think she got in trouble with the cops too. That's why I got transferred to Osiris."

Laurie's face felt hot and prickly with embarrassment. Her skin was clammy and the air in the room seemed to suddenly stop moving. She could hear the humming of the heating system, and down the hall the sound of a custodian whistling as he mopped the corridor. She faltered, sweat breaking out on her forehead, not sure how to respond. Nobody, certainly not a student, had ever talked to her that way before. If Marco wanted to shock her, he certainly had. Listening to him was like intruding on some sexual predator's confession on a true crime television series. In spite of his bragging, Marco was still a child, she told herself. But picturing him with the student teacher made her heart beat faster and her mouth feel dry.

Laurie took a deep breath and spoke slowly, looking for words. "I'm sorry to hear that happened to you. You're still a minor. You're too young for that, and that's not something you should be talking about anyway."

"Oh yeah?" Marco countered. "She said I made her feel really good." He looked quizzically at Laurie, sticking his chest out, waiting to see what she'd say to that.

Laurie turned away and faced the chalkboard, trying to compose herself. It made her uncomfortable looking at him. He was just a kid, even if he had that sullen sexy quality that women's magazines said was usually found in rock stars. Better not to pay attention to that kind of talk she told herself. Don't encourage it. Maybe she should just call this off. It was a stupid idea. This kid was trouble.

Marco's voice startled her, barging through her thoughts. "So, what is it you want me to do?" He sounded tired all of a sudden, his bravado worn down, leaving his face open and unmasked. Even his voice sounded resigned.

Laurie turned back and watched him; his hands clasped on the desktop. *He needs my help*, she told herself, abandoning the idea of packing up and sending him away. Instead she stuck a plastic-covered notebook sheet in his hand. "Read the fourth line down."

Marco shrugged. "Whatever."

He sat up straighter in his seat and began reading, underlining the words with his finger, hesitating as he tried to sound them out. Laurie listened, trying to calculate his reading level. Listening to him was painful as he staggered through the simple sentences, stopping, and looking up at her for help when the words were more than one syllable long. As closely as she could calculate, his level was somewhere around the sixth grade. The aftermath of a neglected education she thought watching him.

"I can help you learn to read a lot better," she told him, taking in the long stretch of his spine as he sat back in his chair, the arduous task now over.

Marco looked up at her and then stared off in the distance. "I don't want anybody knowing I can't read. Things are bad enough. I don't want them giving me shit for this too."

"Of course not!" Laurie answered. "This can be just between us if that's what you want. Tonight, I'll prepare some materials for us to work on and we can go over them after school tomorrow. How's that?"

"Tomorrow I have Anger Management Group," Marco told her.

"Anger Management? Why?" Laurie envisioned the class in domestic abuse she had to take as part of her curriculum. She watched Marco's mouth pucker, his lips were full and moist she noticed.

"I had a bad fight with this guy in my last placement. He was going to rat me out. He was just a hater. A real asshole. He was pissed because I got to this one broad he liked before he did. So, we fought."

"Fought? You mean physically?"

Marco laughed. "That's what a fight is. Right? He was a lot bigger, but I'm quicker. I got him down. He kept saying stupid shit, like he said my mother saw more dicks in one week than the urinal at Dodger Stadium, and shit like that. You know?" He looked up at Laurie, his eyes hooded and sad.

Laurie pressed her lips together. "That must have upset you."

Marco shrugged. His eyes suddenly formed themselves into narrow slits, drawn back in his face. "I had him down and he wouldn't shut up, so I banged his head on the ground a few times and I wouldn't let them pull me off him … I guess. He was real quiet then. I had to do a little time in Youth Authority after that. It's okay now."

Laurie flinched, picturing the scene. This strange and violent world he talked about didn't match the soft settled features of his face. She couldn't, wouldn't, address it. It was something from the past, wasn't it? "Well then," she began, "The day after tomorrow. I'll have some things for you to study. Right now, look over your assignment."

"I tried," Marco told her. "I can't read it really."

Laurie spent the next few minutes explaining the homework, thinking that if Marco couldn't read, he probably couldn't write either. Still, it was worth a try. She watched him sling his backpack over his shoulder, suddenly remembering something. "You're always late for first period. I saw that on the attendance sheet. You need to try and come on time from now on."

"That's 'cause I feed Mr. Pickles first in the biology lab."

"What?" She was taken aback. "Mr. Pickles?"

"Yeah, the hamster they have in there. I like to stop by and feed him in the morning. He eats this grain they keep in the supply cabinet. Then he likes to run on his wheel. I give him fresh newspaper every couple of days. He just tears it up, but I think he likes it."

"Did Mr. Anderson in biology tell you to do that?" Laurie asked.

Marco looked surprised. "No, I like that little guy, so I volunteered to do it. I'd like a pet someday. Not a hamster. A real pet. Maybe a dog, like a pit bull. But I wouldn't fight him, just take him with me everywhere. I'd get one from the pound, the ones that have no home, so they put them to sleep."

Picturing Marco with the hamster confused her, and Laurie debated about whether to tell him to start out earlier in the morning so he wouldn't be late for class. She decided not to. At least he cared for the hamster and that was a good thing. She watched his long, delicate fingers retie the frayed laces of his worn tennis shoes, and she shivered.

A few more days went by. Marco didn't show in the morning or after school. The attendance office marked him as absent. Laurie put together two more lesson plans and struggled with what to say to one of her students who cursed her out in class when Laurie asked her to stop talking. One of the other students spoke up, "Go easy, she's pregnant, you know."

By Thursday, Laurie was worried. If he didn't show today, she planned to call the home where he lived and try to speak to him. After her last student cleared out of the room at the end of the day, she looked up from the board to see Marco push through the door and dump his backpack on the floor.

He slumped over into his seat, putting his head in his hands.

"What's wrong?" Laurie wanted to know. "Where've you been?"

Marco didn't look up right away. So, she waited, worried that anything she might say would make him leave. When he picked his head up, she could see dark circles under his bloodshot eyes. He seemed thinner, too, his face all hard angles, the last traces of baby fat gone. His mouth was set in a straight, tense line. He kept his lips close together when he finally spoke. Laurie noticed his hands were swollen and covered with scrapes.

"There was a little problem at home." Marco told her. "I kind of got into it with this guy I got introduced to online. He drove down to meet me and tried to get more money from me after I bought something off him. What a dick! I guess he thought I wouldn't know the difference. Thought I was stupid or something. I made him eat shit for it. He won't be coming around to Osiris again."

"I don't understand," Laurie said. "You look really bad. Are you hurt?"

"Nah," Marco said. "Then that night I had another fight with the guys in the home. They didn't take my side like I thought they would. They said they were sorry they ever had anything to do with me. Now they say they looked like punks because they introduced me in the first place. They jumped me too. They're mad cause they're losing their connection to this guy who can get his hands on guns," He said dully.

"Guns? Oh, my God!" Laurie covered her mouth. "Isn't anybody supervising you over there? Do you want to go to the police?"

"Police? Are you fucking crazy?" He looked at her in astonishment and then turned his head to follow the sound of something striking the floor outside the door. Laurie watched as a few members of the basketball team strolled by, bouncing a basketball, their voices booming, their laughter raucous and conspiratorial, as they passed the ball between them.

Marco stood up suddenly, and Laurie thought it was as if she saw an alarm going off in his head, reminding him of something. Whatever it was made him shove the desk away and clench his fist as the sound of the basketball moving down the hall grew dimmer.

He pointed at the corridor. "I hate those guys. Fucking ugly guys. I see them every day at lunch. They walk by the bleachers. I'm right there but they never say hi. It's always the same. Every place I go, it's the same."

"Calm down, you're just upset right now. Things will get better," Laurie looked for reassuring words, words to make the anger and hurt go away. She could never find those words for herself, but maybe for Marco. Reaching out, she squeezed his hand. After a moment he squeezed back. His grip was firm. She felt weak and unclasped her hand, stepping back. Marco didn't notice. He was lost staring past her, his face blank.

Not knowing what else to do, Laurie walked over to the overturned desk and sat it upright, her eyes falling on his ragged folder sticking out of the backpack. Well, at least she could help with this. "Come back here. I have some new folders I just bought." She led Marco back to the central supply room off her classroom, where she'd started stocking cheap school supplies from the 99 Cent Store. So many of the kids didn't bother with folders, pens, or paper. She liked to think it was because they didn't have any money, but she figured that wasn't the real truth. The truth was a lot of them just didn't care.

They'd taught her in college that all kids had natural talent, it was just that their opportunities weren't always distributed equally. She'd repeated this mantra over and over in her head when she stared at the blank disinterested and sometimes defiant faces looking back at her. But Marco was learning to read, she told herself. That proved opportunity was important.

Marco followed her into the cramped supply room, standing obediently, his arms outstretched as she handed him some folders, a few tablets, and a package of pens. He kept his head down, his hair hanging over his face, while he concentrated on the floor covered in a thin layer of dust and old wax.

Laurie turned away from the supply shelf, moving closer to Marco. From a distance she could hear the loud voices of kids on their way home. She could feel her breath quicken, and she inhaled the smell of floor polish and Lysol, and the lingering scent of Clorox from Marco's white T-shirt. Marco closed his eyes as soon as he felt her touch. She leaned in and kissed his lips, surprised at how soft and warm they were. Slowly he moved closer, setting the supplies down on the floor and kissing her back. It was a long, slow kiss, and Laurie felt the heat rise in her body. Groaning, she pulled back.

Marco opened his eyes and looked surprised. "Do you want to go out to your car?"

"No. No … I …" She ducked her head, embarrassed at how loudly her heart was pounding and how her body felt warm and slick. "No. I shouldn't have done that. I'm sorry."

Marco snorted. "Sorry? What, for? I know how to make you feel really good."

His words snapped her to attention, and the warmth flooding her body faded as quickly as it had come. "I think it's better if we leave now."

Marco stepped back, shrugging his shoulders. "If you don't want to … whatever."

Laurie hurried ahead, grabbing her purse and notebook, and ushered Marco out of the room before closing the door. *Why did I do that?* she asked herself again. *Because I'm lonely with no one to go home to at night? Am I having a breakdown or something? What if he tells? I'll lose my job because I didn't control myself. My whole life will be ruined.*

She could see the shock on her mother's face if she ever found out. "I always knew you were a little crazy, that you'd end up disappointing me. Just like your sister, but at least she's staying married, and I'll end up with grandkids. It'll serve you right if they send you to jail. You're a child molester!"

Laurie didn't stop to pick up her messages in the office, afraid she'd run into somebody. She ducked out the side door from the teacher's lounge and hurried across the parking lot feeling like she was being watched. She didn't remember the drive home. She was just there, fumbling with her key and jerking the front door open then running to pull down the shades. She curled up in the far corner of the couch huddled in the dark. By now, she thought, he must have told somebody. She started shaking again and hurried to the kitchen to open a bottle of wine. She poured a large glass and drank a good portion of it in several gulps. But the wine didn't calm her.

She kept asking herself why, and at first, there was no answer, not until she closed her eyes and relived that kiss, and how it felt when Marco kissed her back. That is when she thought she knew. She remembered the rush of energy, the power that came with that kiss. For the first time in so long, she'd felt pretty, wanted. There had been no fear of rejection. Marco wouldn't hurt her. He'd welcomed the kiss, but now she was sorry for those few moments. So guilty! She couldn't go back and erase what she'd done, no matter how much she regretted it, and pretty soon everyone would know how she'd taken advantage of a kid. She was no better than the student teacher Marco told her about. She froze with her glass halfway to her lips realizing that what she had done now made her a sex offender.

Laurie pressed her hands to her forehead. She could feel a headache working its way around her temples. Thank God she'd caught herself and stopped. What else could have happened? Her heart pounded as she saw herself and Marco together having sex. Marco worshipping her, because she'd given him something he didn't have, love and attention. She could have given him that. Sneaking around and hiding because it was wrong, and no one could know! It could have happened, she thought. Could have gone that far.

Maybe Marco wouldn't tell anybody, but he'd told her about the times with other women. Did he tell others the same things? Maybe she could talk to him, persuade him that it was best to forget what happened and start over. Teacher and student, just like before, and she'd keep teaching him to read. But no, she'd seen the look on his face. He didn't understand why she rejected him, dismissed him so suddenly. From what he told her, rejection had happened all his life. He'd have no reason to keep their secret if he wasn't going to get any benefit from it. And even if he was getting a benefit, he'd probably tell somebody anyway, just like he'd told her about the other women. That's what sixteen-year-old boys did. He had nothing to lose, and everything would be stripped from her as soon as he talked. How could she have been so stupid? She'd deny it. Absolutely. But would anybody believe her over the word of a minor?

The mad chase in her head mixed with the wine and left her

exhausted. She stretched out on her bed still wearing the clothes she'd worn to school that morning. After trying to sleep for a couple of hours, she gave up and returned to the couch in front of the television. She tried to watch a movie, but the love scenes made her flush and perspire. She couldn't help it. She thought of Marco when she saw the actor's bodies entwined, making love, or even just kissing. And each time she did, there was the nagging thought: would he tell?

The truth was she didn't know that much about him, except that his parents weren't around, and he was still learning to read. Her mother told her that the kids in group homes were born into a troubled life and caused more trouble as they got older. That was why her mother refused to take any placements that came from places like that.

She needed to find out more about Marco, she thought, maybe figure out what he was really like. Laurie turned on the computer. They all have Facebook, she thought. She clicked on and put his name in the search and waited. There were five others with the same name. She clicked on the small photos. The first three definitely were not him, the fourth was a maybe, and she clicked on the fifth profile that showed Marco standing on a beach boardwalk looking off into the distance. There he was! She scrolled down looking for anything that would give her a clue. There was nothing except his photo. No other friends or photos. Nothing. She sighed and closed the site. What could you expect from someone who was completely alone in the world?

The next morning when the alarm rang, Laurie shut it off and tucked herself back under the covers, exhausted and tense. This thing with Marco was going to cause big trouble. She was sure of that. Wondering what to do, how to erase what had happened, she struggled to stuff the memory back into some dark place where it wouldn't find its way out.

She struggled through a shower after two cups of black coffee before she admitted to herself that she couldn't face going to school today and called in sick. She checked her phone, every few minutes as she lay in bed with the covers pulled tight around her, waiting for a call from the school, telling her that they knew what happened. When she wasn't checking her phone or thinking about the trouble she was in, she pictured herself with her arms around Marco and imagined she could smell the Clorox from his T-shirt and the sweet smell of his breath. Regret wouldn't change anything now, she told herself. After it was all over, she'd never be able to teach again. Funny, just a day ago she was bitching about what a miserable job teaching was.

By noon, her energy drained, her head throbbing, she massaged her temples as she wandered into the living room and turned on the television. Every channel was broadcasting the same thing with their cameras fixed on the exterior courtyard of the high school where she taught. She watched in disbelief as the newscasters in the studio animatedly informed the public about a shooting there that had killed three students and one teacher and left another student in critical condition. According to their sources, they didn't expect the young woman to survive. The shooter had been gunned down by police.

The camera panned to a tall blonde woman with perfectly styled hair and fitted black dress. She stood on the walkway to the school entrance and spoke directly to the camera: "Police have identified the shooter as sixteen-year-old Marco Perez, a recent transfer to this school, who is a ward of the state. Following first period this morning, while the students were changing classes, he entered the main building and opened fire with a semi-automatic assault weapon. At this time, police have no motive for the shooting. Our latest information indicates that the suspect was cornered and shot by police. He died en route to the hospital."

Laurie slumped down, stunned, tears burning her eyes. She could still feel Marco's warm skin and see his eyes looking up at her, surprised when she pushed away from him. Now he was dead. Why would he do a thing like that—randomly kill other students and a teacher? Laurie replayed her conversations with him. She'd thought the things he told her covered everything she needed to know about his life. But there was more. Something she didn't know was buried, and he had unearthed it that morning.

Laurie listened to the news. They never really established an exact motive in these school-shooting cases. The experts made general statements about a lack of acceptance, bullying, resentment against other students. She hadn't known Marco that well or that long, but she supposed all of those descriptions fit, and she'd handled it all wrong and then rejected him, dismissed him, just like so many others had, when all she'd wanted to do was let him know that everything would be all right, that he wasn't alone. But she was the one who wanted to feel she wasn't alone ...

Maybe it was the guilt. Slowly the inescapable realization overtook her. She was part of it all, one of the many reasons he brought that rifle to school, to search for some kind of recognition, for somebody to see him, because nobody knew who he was. For a brief moment, he had been known, and now it was over. He would return to being unknown again. Nobody would miss Marco or remember him other than to hate him. Nobody except Laurie.

Smiley and Laughing Girl

Chavo got hit in the chest by gunfire from a passing car as he pulled up to a stop sign on Sunset, right near Alvarado. I guess he was going to get on the freeway to go to East LA. That's where his mother lives. His foot hit the accelerator. Hard. And his car headed straight through the intersection and hit a light pole. The pole bent in half, went right through the windshield, and smashed the glass. A sharp metal spike ended up cutting his body almost in half. That's what my mother told me when they called me away from the storeroom where I was stacking pallets of baby formula and disposable diapers. It was Friday, and I needed to work for eight hours at the WIC store to keep my aid for dependent children. I have my teenage daughter and two little boys.

I started crying, pulled off my apron, and hung it up in the employee break room. I always knew that *MS 13* would come after him. That's how it goes here. Chavo and some of his homeboys jumped some guys from *Mara Salvatrucha* and beat them down pretty bad. I heard it was about somebody's old lady that belonged to *18th Street* and stepped out with a guy from *MS 13*. They cut her up pretty bad cause she was just supposed to bait the guy and bring him to her homies, not do it with him. They still had to throw down with the guys. Those must be the ones that shot him.

"Are you punching out for the day, Smiley?" Mrs. Riley, the boss, wanted to know. "Who's going to finish loading those shelves?"

I shrugged. It was her own fucking problem, I thought, tears running down my face. I wasn't really with Chavo anymore, not since I stopped running with the gang. I'm too old now, almost thirty, but they still call me Smiley, just like when

I kicked it with the homies. I have a daughter, Laughing Girl. She's fourteen, and now the homeboys are looking at her. She told me she was ready to be jumped in. She laughed when she told me, daring me to say something, because she knew I didn't like her running the street with those people.

Things are different now, and the homegirls do more stuff in the gang than they used to. We used to hang around and do whatever errands the homies needed, like carrying their weed or getting them food or booze. Now some of those bitches are strapped and go on drive-bys. I hear they're up to give a beat-down to anybody, even a homeboy, and most of them at least carry a switchblade.

Out in the lot, I started up my old Impala. It's a classic, but I never fixed it up or anything. I got it from my stepfather. Lots of guys from other *cliques* stop and ask me about it. It used to get Chavo mad cause I was talking to guys that he said were enemies of *18th Street*. My stepfather never actually gave me the Impala, but when he got sent up, the car was just sitting there. My mom didn't drive and she was too scared to try because she didn't have any papers. I tried to sell it a few times, but we didn't have any title, and some numbers inside the engine had been filed down. Nobody wanted to buy it. Anyway, my stepfather stabbed a guy inside, and then with his two other strikes, he ended up getting life. So, I guess I'm keeping it.

I drove home thinking about Chavo and all the things that had happened to me since I met him. My mind ran over them one after the other, like the first time he picked me up for a ride after I met him at a party that some homie from *18th Street* had. They said, later, that he'd gone there to pick up a young girl like he always did because he liked them young. And I was up for it.

That night, we'd smoked some pretty good weed, and I was feeling proud and happy. Lots of little hood rats wanted him, but he was mine. Chavo was twenty-five when I got with him, ten years older than me. I trusted him and did everything he said. Being with him meant being part of *18th Street*, and that made you somebody.

We were riding around one night when he saw this car that looked like the one his brother had. Some guy from the *Avenues* was driving it. He thought it was stolen, so we followed it. When we got up close, he yelled something at the driver, and the driver turned around and gave us the finger. Chavo went crazy and pulled out a gun and began shooting at the car. When we turned a corner, a cop car was coming in our direction. Chavo told me to hold the wheel, stay behind the other guy, and aim to the right to force the other guy off the road. Chavo kept shooting, but only got off a couple of shots and none of them even got near the other car. The cops turned around and pulled us over. We were arrested, and I ended up in juvie, and not for running away from home like before.

When my mother finally visited me at the facility, I'd already been locked up for a while. When I saw her, I started crying. "I thought you would come sooner." I stepped toward her, hoping that she'd hug me, but she kept her arms at her sides and looked me up and down, shaking her head.

Then she started talking really fast in that whiny voice she has. "You know it's hard for me to get here. Nobody would drive me, so I had to take the damn bus. I got better things to do than visit criminals! I got other kids at home." She sat on one of the hard, plastic chairs, holding onto her beat-up old brown purse, and started to cry. "How can you do this to me? All the neighbors know you're in jail. I'm ashamed to go outside. You're just a *puta de calle*, just like the others."

I was feeling pretty bad then. I missed being home, and Chavo hadn't come to see me, even though he was out on bail, waiting for trial. "Well, if you're ashamed, don't go outside. Besides, they said if you'd gotten me a good lawyer, I wouldn't be locked up!" I always talked back.

"You know I don't have money for a lawyer," she started yelling.

The other people in the waiting room turned around to look at us.

"I don't know why you want to be a chola so bad," she

snapped. "Going with that old gangster! He's too old for you. You're gonna get pregnant. Watch and see. Then you're out of the house!"

"Like I care," I told her, trying to be tough. "How come your boyfriend isn't too old for me then?"

"You shut your mouth. Why are you lying on him all the time?"

I'd hit home. The man I called my stepfather was really just her boyfriend, and he was a lot younger than her. My friends said he liked my mother because she always gave him money when she got her welfare check, and he didn't have to work. He always licked his lips when he looked at me and rubbed up against me whenever I was around in that little apartment.

When I told my mother, she went crazy. "You're a stupid bitch! No way he'd want a skinny little thing like you! You're jealous cause you can't have him. All you can get is just some loser gangster."

One day when I was home alone because I'd ditched school, he came into the bathroom when I was taking a shower and locked the door behind him. When I heard him, I stepped out of the shower just as he started to unzip his pants. I grabbed the sixteen-ounce plastic bottle of shampoo and swung it at his head. I got him hard on the nose, and blood started squirting out and dripping onto the bathmat. I left him there like that. I knew he lit into my mother real good because she kept asking what happened to his nose. I started staying away from home after that. It wasn't such a good place to be anyway. I stayed with a few of the homegirls whose parents didn't care or weren't around much. I slept on their couches or their floors.

When I got out of juvie that time for driving the car with Chavo, I went to live with him and his family. He was out on bail, waiting to go to trial, and I was still going to school sometimes, mostly to meet my friends and ditch. I didn't have any money for bus fare or lunch, or even eyeliner if I needed it. Chavo gave me a little money sometimes when he could, like when he just sold some weed.

Finally, I got tired of school and just stopped going. It's just like Laughing Girl now. She doesn't want to go either. I was lonely living there because Chavo's mother and sisters didn't like me. They wanted him to get back together with his old girlfriend, Marta. I guess he was seeing her too, on the side, because he finally told me to leave and his sisters packed up my things in a flash. I'd run out of places to go, so I went back home. I hated it there. My mother went around a lot with a cut lip and black eyes. She would tell me to go to hell if I said anything about it.

I was feeling really bad about Chavo dumping me, so I started going out with Ricardo right away. He wasn't as good-looking as Chavo, but he had a bad cholo reputation. They said he'd killed a few guys and gotten away with it. Ricardo, or Sly Baby like they called him, was in *18th Street* too, and was super bossy and mean. Whenever we got together, he'd hit me for any little thing and make me wait on him for everything so he could just sit in one place.

I usually spent my days sleeping late and watching TV since there was nobody around to bother me. Then Ricardo would call me, so I would get dressed up and do my makeup and ride around with him going to parties to get high, smoking, doing coke, or drinking. Sometimes I went with him when he went to get revenge on a rival gang. He kept saying that it was important to protect our territory and that the other gangs were always trying to take over our area. He carried a forty-five and showed me how to use it one day up in Griffith Park, before the orange sun went down and the park was almost empty. We shot at the trees, and I imagined that I was shooting at a real homeboy from the *Avenues* or even from *Mara Salvatrucha*.

One Friday night, Ricardo parked his car and told me to go into the liquor store with him. He told me to stand at the counter and talk to the clerk, a young white guy. He told me to flirt with him. Make him think he was getting some.

"What are you doing when I'm talking?" I wanted to know.

"Just shut the fuck up and do what I say," he answered.

I went up to the counter and pretended to look at the cheap candies.

The clerk, who looked like a teenager with spiky blond hair, moved away from the register and smiled, looking at me. "Can I help you with something?"

I smiled back and touched my mouth. Then I took my finger and trailed it down the front of my blouse. My blouse was cut low, and I was pretty much falling out of it. The clerk kept watching me, following my finger. I remember he had pretty blue eyes.

While we were standing there, I heard the sound of a loud crash in the back of the store—something falling and smashing—and his eyes moved away from me to follow it. He straightened up and yelled out, "What's going on back there?"

I turned around to see Ricardo walking toward the counter, pointing his gun right at the clerk. "No cameras set up back there," he said to me, smiling. Then he turned to the clerk, "Give me everything in that register."

I stood there, listening to it all, but kept my mouth shut and just took the handful of cash that Ricardo handed me and stuffed it in my purse as we ran out to the car. But Ricardo was wrong. There was a camera. They showed the video in court where we both got convicted of robbery and assault with a deadly weapon. When the judge sentenced me, I was sent to CIW, because I wasn't a juvenile anymore.

A couple of years later, I was back out, older, but I guess not any smarter. I was staying with my homegirl, Mona, and trying to get hold of the rest of my homies and figure out what I was going to do next. Ricardo was still locked up. He was going to stay locked up for a long time.

I needed money, so I started asking around. Chavo was out on probation and he was looking for some homegirls to push weed for him. So, I went to his house, where his sisters still lived, and ignored their dirty looks while I talked to Chavo. He said he didn't trust me because I went with another guy, but he said if I wanted to sell for him and get my foot back in *18th Street*, I needed to have sex with him and anybody else he picked. I didn't tell him yes or no. I just went back to his bedroom and let him do it. I figured maybe he wouldn't make me do it with other guys because he was so jealous.

I started selling weed and a little coke for him, usually around the high school when classes were over. He took all of the money for himself, only giving me a little to spend, but he kept me supplied with weed and coke and I figured out how to sell some of that on the side for cash. I slept there a lot too when I didn't want to go home, and sometimes I helped myself to a few dollars that he didn't see. A lot of times he had his homies meet at his house, and I watched from the bedroom while he gave them the money I brought in so they could buy guns. I saw *18th Street* was growing, with new members getting jumped in all the time. Chavo wanted to make sure they were all strapped, so he pushed hard on selling all the dope we could.

I wasn't the only girl selling for him. There were about three others, but we didn't like each other, because they all wanted to be his only girlfriend. I didn't care if I was or wasn't, because I'd been with him before. Besides, I was his top pusher, and so far, he didn't hit me or curse at me the way he did with the other girls when they didn't sell enough or didn't do what he said. He usually wanted to have sex when I picked up my drugs to sell, and after when I brought back his money. After he was finished with the sex, we'd smoke some dope or do a few lines, which was, honestly, what I waited for, because it was almost like he was a real boyfriend lying in bed with me watching television. I knew he had sex with the other girls too, but he spent more time with me and took me in his bedroom instead of doing it on the couch and telling others to watch. He only made me have sex with another homie one time. The guy had some kind of connections that Chavo wanted, and he told me to give his homie a blow job and anything else he wanted. I did what he said and tried to pretend I was somewhere else until it was over.

I was selling for Chavo for a few months, trying to save up my money so I could get my own place and not have to live with my mother and her new boyfriend, who knocked her around more than the last one. Besides, she was spending her whole check buying smack from someone in *Mara Salvatrucha* and pretty much wasn't paying the rent anymore. That month we got a notice to move out.

So, on that day when I came to pick up my supply, Chavo told me to get in his car, because we were going somewhere. I knew better than to ask any questions. We drove over to Highland Park and pulled in behind a run-down stucco bungalow. In the back of the bungalow, there was a small garage that somebody was using as an apartment. Chavo had a key, and we walked into a tiny room covered with trash. In the center was a large mattress with a few sheets wadded up in the center. Chavo told me to get undressed and then pushed me down on the mattress. When he was finished, he stood up and stretched, buckling his pants. "I feel good now," he told me. "Ready to fuck someone up real good. Now, I want you to do it with this guy that's coming in. You make him stay in that bed with you, till I come in and get you. I'll be right outside waiting. You got that? He's a dead man today!"

I started to cry then, scared and sorry for myself. Chavo stood over me, pushed my face into the mattress, and held it. "Look," he said, "You better do what I say if you know what's good for you." He pulled my hair hard, and then shoved me away.

Something went off in my head then, and I felt myself getting angry. I remembered the girls I'd been locked up with, saying they would stick a knife in any man who touched them. They were tough and hated almost everyone, but especially men. Now, I was beginning to understand why. I'd never thought this way before. Just this time, I told myself, I'll do what he says. Then I'm getting away from him and his homies.

A few minutes later, the door opened, and a big bald guy covered with tattoos came in. He looked me over and then walked around the small room, checking for something. When he saw there was nobody inside, he dropped his pants and climbed on top of me. He barely had time to push my legs apart, when I heard three loud bangs, like firecrackers going off. The big guy cried out and then stopped moving. He lay on top of me so I couldn't move away. I started screaming, and Chavo and a couple of other guys came in. They pulled him off me while I laid there and screamed.

Chavo jerked me to my feet. "Get dressed; we got to get out of here."

I looked over at the bed and saw blood leaking out of the guy's body, pooling on the mattress and running down the sides of the bed. There was blood on my stomach and the tops of my legs. When I tried to wipe it off, Chavo smacked me in the face. "I said, get dressed. Don't touch anything else!"

We got back in Chavo's car. It was dark now, and quiet. I was shaking, remembering the heavy body on top of me. It was still warm when I left, and the blood was thick on the mattress. I'd never seen a dead body up so close, and I was scared, my heart was still pounding and my legs shaking. We drove in silence back to my house. I was still thinking about how I'd decided not to come back here anymore. Now I was sure.

"Is he dead?" I finally asked, seeing myself in big trouble.

Chavo laughed. "I hope so. He had it coming. Tried to be slick and suck up our territory. Nobody else sells here unless I let them. Should have stayed on his own side. But three bullets might not be enough for his fat ass."

I felt suddenly cold and nauseous, so I rolled down the window. Chavo pulled over to the curb, and I opened the door and threw up. Sitting back in the seat, I put my head on the headrest and let my tears run. "I don't want to go to jail again."

"What's wrong with you, bitch?" Chavo spat in my direction. "You're weak, that's all—just a weak sister. Not fit to be with *18th Street*. You know what? I don't want to see you coming around no more. I don't trust you. You go home and take this with you. I don't want to see you or this ever again." He slapped the gun he'd just used into my hand. It was surprisingly heavy, but I didn't let it fall.

"What do you want me to do with it?" I stared down at my hands, thinking that this gun in my hand had just killed someone.

"You stupid bitch! Little Girl!" He swore under his breath. "Hide it someplace where nobody will find it. You keep your mouth shut, too, about what you saw today or you're next. I can't be tied to this, or I'll go back and do another stretch."

I stared back at him and felt my fingers close around the gun, but I stayed quiet.

"Can you do what I tell you? Or I can get rid of you too. You know I'd do it!"

I just sat there, crying and shaking my head. It hurt having him tell me to go, even though I'd decided I was through with him before we left that body on the bed.

He stared at me for a moment, and I thought he even looked a little sad. "Look, *mijita*," now his voice was lower, almost like the way he used to talk to me before he threw me out the first time. He held my face between his hands and pushed my hair back from my forehead. "I don't want any trouble, so you need to do what I say. We had some good times, didn't we? Anyway, I got a new girlfriend now, so you can't come over anymore."

I thought he looked proud—bragging like a little kid. "She just got outta Ironwood, and she's a hard case. Been around plenty. She'll always have my back. You know how it is."

He reached across me and opened the car door. "Don't forget," he pointed to the gun.

I stumbled out of the car and ran into the apartment, which had another "Notice to Pay Rent or Quit," taped to the door. I tore it off and threw it on the table. Then I went into the tiny room that I claimed as a bedroom and stuck the gun in the bottom drawer under my bras and panties. They weren't enough to cover it, so I threw some clothes from another drawer on the top.

Over the next few weeks, everybody spread the word about how they'd found Big Blue dead, and they were looking for suspects. So far, nobody was talking, and I did what Chavo said and stayed away from him. The sheriff even knocked on our door one day, but I didn't open it. I guess they were going around the neighborhood trying to get information. Hiding the gun in the house seemed like a stupid idea. I couldn't sleep one night because I kept seeing the cops busting in and finding the gun. I understood why Chavo didn't want to get locked up again. I turned over and over in my bed until it started to get light. While everybody else was still sleeping, I got up and put the gun in my backpack. I walked all the way to Echo Park, and then slowly around the lake. I walked by the usual homeless winos sleeping on the benches and thought about throwing the gun as far as I could toward the center, imagining in my mind it hitting the water, splashing the mud hens hanging around the utility fountain that kept the lake filled with water. But in the end I couldn't get rid of it. I heard that one time they dredged the lake looking for bodies that they thought were dumped there, but all they found were a bunch of rusted weapons and empty bottles. They wouldn't find this one if they ever dredged it again.

After a while, people stopped talking so much about Chavo, but I was still scared they'd find out that I was there when he shot that guy. I could still feel the dead man's heavy body pinning me down on the mattress, and the wet sticky blood on my stomach and legs. I heard they'd questioned everybody he hung out with, but they never came back to me. Later, they said Chavo went back to jail because he violated his probation. I know he was locked up until last year for something else. They never found the gun he used, and, of course, nobody talked. That's how it goes here.

I told myself I'd never be that stupid again, and I'd never let some guy use me like Chavo did, but with Chavo gone, I was kind of lost. I missed the attention, even if it was only lying on his bed and watching TV after he had sex with me. That was kind of like love, I thought. I wanted to get back to selling dope, but I knew I had to stay away from *18th Street*. So, I started hitting the parties and hanging out with some other homies from the *Avenues*. It didn't take long until I found out I was pregnant, but I really didn't know who the father was. Most of the time, I was high on the coke and weed we used when we partied. If you hung with these homies, you were expected to give it up whenever they wanted it, so I did. I was so high all the time that I never thought about how I'd told myself I'd never let a man use me again.

Then I had some bad luck. When I was seven months pregnant, with my big stomach popping out over the top of my sweatpants, I sold some smack to an underage girl and her friends outside her middle school. She ended up overdosing because it wasn't cut enough, and her friends were able to identify me to the cops. Everybody remembers a pregnant drug dealer with stringy hair and dirty clothes, even a bunch of fourteen-year-olds high out of their minds. But before they even picked me up, I sold some coke to an undercover cop I would have sworn was a dirty street biker.

So, there you go, I got sent up again. My surrender date was five days after Laughing Girl was born. I called her Laughing Girl, because she came out smiling and smiled up at me the whole time until they took her away. On the day after she was born, a woman came into my room and said she was from Child Services. She let me hold my baby one last time before she took her. She told me Laughing Girl was going into foster care. I cried nonstop the next few days up until I checked into CIW for my second round. I knew better than to go in looking like a weak sister.

By the time I got out on parole, Laughing Girl didn't even know me. I heard her foster mother cried because she was praying I'd never get out and try to take her back. Laughing Girl cried too, she wanted her foster mom, and I wasn't her. I guess we all cried together. When I got out, I figured I'd spent enough of my life paying for my stupid mistakes, and I stopped hanging with anybody from *18th Street* or the *Avenues*. I moved back with my mother, and I'm still there. We get along better now. She doesn't drink as much, because she has bleeding ulcers.

I heard Chavo did a long stretch and then was paroled. His mother called every once in a while and checked in. Funny thing, she likes me, now that Chavo and I aren't together. I think she wishes Laughing Girl was his kid because she doesn't have any grandchildren.

So, here I am now, a few more bad relationships and two more kids to raise by myself, and Laughing Girl looks like she wants to follow in my footsteps.

I didn't cry much at Chavo's funeral. Enough tears were falling around me to make up for the ones I didn't have. I just closed my eyes and remembered everything that happened between us, our own story. It didn't hurt so much anymore. So much time had passed. I didn't even hate him. After the funeral, I went back to the house. Tonight, my mother will go out drinking with her friends and I'll be alone with my two boys unless I can get Laughing Girl to stay in with me. Lately, all she talks about is this guy from *18th Street*, Armando. I heard he has two strikes, and he's only been out for a few months. She thinks she's in love with him.

Later, after my mother went out and I put the boys to bed, I settled down in front of the TV. Laughing Girl finally came home. She pushed the door open and staggered inside. It was almost ten o'clock. I could see she was drunk or high by the way she moved before I ever got a good look at her eyes. Giggling and holding onto the walls, she started toward the bedroom she shared with her brothers.

I yelled after her. "Don't make any noise they're sleeping. Why don't you come in here for a little while?"

"I gotta get ready," she slurred.

"Ready? Why?"

"Going out riding." She answered. "Mando's picking me up."

I got up and walked toward her. Even a few feet away, I picked up the heavy smell of alcohol and something stronger and more bitter, like the stuff they used to mix paint. No, I thought. She doesn't do that anymore. I saw her a few years back, still in elementary school, sitting by the train tracks with her cholo friends, sniffing something they poured into a sock. I stared at her wide glassy eyes that moved from side to side and didn't see. Her hair was matted and tangled, stiff and crunchy from the mousse she poured on it. Her eyeliner was smeared, and most of her penciled eyebrows had worn off.

I followed her to the bedroom, where she fell against the wall, trying to find the light switch. Muttering to herself, she stepped out of her tight black jeans and low-cut blouse that didn't manage to cover her stomach and pulled out a dresser drawer. The drawer stuck, and she fell back on her butt, ending up on the floor swearing. The noise woke up my sons sleeping in a single bed. My younger one pulled the quilt over his head, trying to shut out the light and the noise.

I focused my eyes on the glare coming from the single bulb in the center of the ceiling. There was a fresh tattoo on her neck that hadn't been there the last time I'd seen her. I recognized the sign right away. And something else, a hickey, large and red, covering the space under her jawline. The hickey looked fresh. She hadn't been home in a couple of days. "Where've you been?" Chavo's death and the funeral had kept me busy the last few days, and I hadn't seen her. But, I couldn't kid myself, she didn't come home some nights. "Answer me! Where are you at night?"

Laughing Girl zipped up another pair of jeans and gave me a dirty look. "I told you before; I'm with my friends."

"You're staying with that Mando, aren't you? He's too old for you. He's just going to get you in trouble." The words felt familiar as I said them.

She glared at me. "You don't know him. He loves me."

"He doesn't love you. He's just using you because you're young and stupid."

66

Laughing Girl whirled around and picked up her hand, bringing it toward my face. I stepped back, surprised.

She dropped her hands. "Leave me alone, okay? I hate it here, you and those dirty brats!" She brought her hands to her sides and walked back to the living room. "I need some money. You're supposed to give me money. That's what you get your welfare for."

"I don't have any money, I can barely pay the rent," I told her. "You can get yourself a little job."

"Fuck no!" she yelled. "I'm so glad I have Mando. He said he'll give me anything I need not to come back here. Tomorrow I'm taking my stuff and moving in with him."

"Go ahead and do it," I yelled back. "I'll report him to the cops. You're underage, and I'll call them on you too."

"You better not call anybody. Mando's friends will come after you, and your other damn kids. Grandma too."

We stood there looking at each other.

"Don't go out. Just stay here." I heard my voice begging her.

"You can't make me stay. I hate it here. I hate you." She slammed the door as hard as she could, making the walls shake. And then it was silent, except for the low hum of the TV.

I sat down on the couch and stared at the wall. There would probably be quite a few "Mandos" in her life before she figured it out—if she ever did. But right now, there was only this one, and I wanted him gone. I'd seen the car he drove, and I knew more or less where he stayed. But all that could be figured out; I still knew a few homeboys from *18th Street*, and even a couple from the *Avenues*. It was smart not to let go of your connections, even if you didn't hang with them anymore.

Chavo still owed me even if he was dead because he never paid his debt when he was alive. I'd kept my mouth shut and "held my mud," like the homies said. It was time to reach out to them and collect. Chavo's homeboys knew how to set up a rival with guns and drugs. They even did it for some unsolved murder that the cops had given up on a long time ago. They were willing to make that snitch call that was insurance that someone would get busted and sent away, especially if that someone was looking at three strikes. They still did it all the time.

I lit a cigarette and sat back. The problem was that if I asked the homeboys for their help now, to pay back Chavo's debt, I would end up owing them in the future, whenever they wanted, doing whatever they ordered. That's how it worked. Who knows what they would want me to do for them? I could end up back in prison or worse, end up dead. They might do away with my kids too if I didn't do what they said. No, I didn't want to owe them anything. I didn't want to owe anybody. I was done with that. I'd paid enough already. Chavo's debt didn't need payment ... not to me.

I went back to my small bedroom, the one I shared with Laughing Girl when she was around. I leaned all my weight against the heavy oak dresser and pushed it away from the wall. Behind the dresser, I'd dug out a piece of the linoleum that covered the floor. The space was about a foot wide, and the shoebox that I put the gun in fit just fine. The shoebox was covered with plywood, and in case anybody got that far, I'd nailed the piece of linoleum back over the space. I'd carried Chavo's gun with me everywhere I'd lived so far, hiding it, just in case anybody came looking. Just a week or so ago I figured I could finally get rid of it. So much time had passed by now. I just hadn't got around to it yet.

Under the bathroom cabinet was my rusty hammer, the one I used to nail a board over the broken part of the window in the bathroom and to hang my son's school pictures over the table in the kitchen. I bent down next to the dresser and used the claw side of the hammer to remove the nails holding the linoleum. It took me a long time, but I kept at it until I reached the shoe box. Sitting back on my heels, I lifted out the gun and turned it over in my hands. There were enough bullets in the chamber. I unlocked the safety and examined it. It was just the way it was after Chavo used it and gave it to me.

I felt relaxed now, and I went and sat back on the couch. When I got locked up and started doing my nickel, the day they took away my baby Laughing Girl, I said there was no justice. No justice for people like us. Not unless we made it ourselves. There were a lot of things I couldn't do for my daughter, but I could do this right now, because I wanted something better for her, even if she didn't. But maybe she would someday.

Mrs. Fonseca

Every time one of those big trucks barreled down Coronado Street flying over the traffic bumps, going fifty miles an hour on a residential street, Mrs. Fonseca's entire apartment above the garage shook, and the dishes in her cabinet over the sink rattled. The trucks passed by several times a day on their way to the freeway entrance headed south or maybe east. She couldn't really tell the difference because she never drove herself.

About half of the dishes in her cabinet were cracked anyway. She kept them just because she'd had them so long. The rest of the set had long-since broken and been thrown away. Sometimes when she stared at the few Blue Willow plates left, she remembered happier times when she'd prepared big meals for her family and served them on those same plates, *mofongo, arroz con pollo*, and *rellenos de papas*. Her sons were big eaters, known for taking seconds and thirds of whatever she cooked. Her daughters were more finicky. By the time they hit high school, they had complained that Puerto Rican food was unhealthy, heavy, and greasy, and they nibbled daintily on non-fat yogurt and baby carrots and then stuffed themselves on chips and candy bars.

When the grandkids came along, they whined for pizza and soda, and she dutifully counted out the rest of the money left from her Social Security check to order it. She hadn't seen her great-grandkids for quite a while now. Everybody was always so busy, and they reminded her she'd never learned to drive.

Juan used to drive her everywhere. He insisted on taking her where she was going and watching her every move. But he had been dead now for fifteen years. It didn't bother the kids much when he died. None of them cried. The youngest ones didn't even know him that well.

"Good riddance, asshole!" Her older son yelled as he threw some pebbles on the coffin.

By then, Juan wasn't coming around that much anyway. When he died, she thought about learning to drive, but to tell the truth, she was scared of the traffic and couldn't remember the rules for driving anyway.

She practiced driving with her youngest daughter, but it ended badly with a lot of screaming, mostly on her daughter's part. "I keep telling you, you can't turn left from the right lane, and you're following that car too close." Sometimes Elizabeth would yell at her at the top of her lungs. She was sure everybody in traffic could hear, and she flushed red with embarrassment, when the yelling started, "Mom, you're holding up miles of traffic. Figure out where you want to go, damn it!"

Elizabeth wasn't the only one who didn't think she could learn to drive. "You'll have an accident and kill somebody," her son Carlos couldn't believe that she would even consider something as complicated as driving. "You better stick to the bus," so she did. She took the bus to every location of importance in her world, the Vons market all the way down on Sunset Boulevard, the bank at the corner of Alvarado, and sometimes her doctor's office on Vermont.

Usually, once a week, she traveled west on Hollywood Boulevard on a local bus to visit her best and only friend, Mrs. Akmajian. The rest of her friends were either dead now or had disappeared somewhere, and she didn't know where to find them. She walked arm in arm with Mrs. Akmajian, looking in all the shop windows and clucking at the immodest clothing on the mannequins and the novelty items for sale. When they were tired of walking, they stopped for a Value Meal at McDonald's. It was the perfect end to a perfect day.

A few times a year, she took the bus the farthest and visited her beauty parlor, which was actually in what they called "West Hollywood." Her hairdresser was a nice young man named Rene, who wore tight pants and a lot of makeup. The makeup confused her, but Rene had been cutting her hair since he left beauty school, and he still charged her the same price for a haircut and always told her how beautiful she was. Her white-domed church was close by her home on Micheltorena. She walked there every Wednesday night and Sunday morning for services unless it was raining.

She was a short woman, grown shorter over the years, and also likely from the curvature in her spine. She kept her kinky iron-gray hair cut close because it was easier that way. The years and fatty meals she cooked had added pounds to her once slim frame, and she found herself wearing larger stretchy polyester pants and a jacket to cover her stomach and hips. Back when she was in her late sixties, she started wearing orthopedic shoes—something she thought she'd never do—because up to that time, she never left the house without her stilettos. The wrinkles in her mirror still shocked her. So many of them now that it seemed her eyes had almost disappeared into the overlapping folds, and her lower jaw receded when she didn't wear her partial plate. But then, she was almost eighty.

These days, her apartment wasn't the only thing that shook, so did her hands when she counted out pills from several bottles of pain pills and one bottle of sleeping pills. She used the pills judiciously, knowing that lately her doctors didn't want to okay a refill. They cost too much anyway. She'd been saving most of the pills for quite a while, even before her daughters moved her from her small bungalow that they'd rented for years, the place with a small garden where she raised the kids. The pills were there like a security blanket. She knew when things got really bad; they'd be there waiting, the one thing she could count on.

Both of her daughters were insistent about the move to the tiny garage apartment. "You don't need all this space. Daddy's gone, and there's nobody to help you keep it up. Walking up the stairs is good exercise for you. Besides, they keep raising the rent for this house, and pretty soon, you won't have any money left for food."

The apartment above the garage was up a steep flight of wooden stairs, and she climbed them slowly, hanging onto the railing as the pain in her arthritic hip shot down her leg. The tiny space was hot and airless in the summer and cold and damp in the winter. She kept a little portable fan on the window ledge and adjusted her small rocking chair so she could watch her thirteen-inch television set and let the warm air from the fan blow on her face at the same time.

There wasn't much furniture in the cramped space besides her rocker, a green velour loveseat, and the television stand where the portable TV rested. Above the sofa hung a large picture of Jesus wearing his crown of thorns. The image was somewhat faded because of the sun shining directly on the glass that covered the print, but the eyes still stood out, and she swore they followed her and saw everything she did.

To the right, in the alcove by the window, was a circular two-seater table that her oldest daughter had given her when her husband bought her new patio furniture. Behind a patchwork curtain, there was her single bed and a miniature chest of drawers where she kept a few changes of clothes. When Carlos visited here, the place seemed even smaller. He was a large man and complained that he had a terrible time turning around in the bathroom. The stove, an ancient two-burner, and the refrigerator that looked like it had survived the 1950s came with the apartment. The tap water ran rusty into a yellowed porcelain sink.

The one thing the apartment did have was photos, lots of them, all framed. They covered every inch of available wall space and left only enough room for the television on its stand. There were pictures of all her kids as babies alongside their high school graduation photos, which hung next to the grandchildren's photos. The walls held school photos, photos taken at her daughters' quinceañeras, engagement photos, and wedding photos, photographs of family picnics, a trip to Disneyland that the family made after months and months of saving, and pictures of Juan when he was a young man, working on a boat before he came to the United States.

In the corner where the walls met, a small photo sat on a wooden shelf in a painted silver frame. The picture was of a toddler perched on Juan's shoulders. The toddler wore all white and his light hair was long and curling. She hated the photo and always planned to throw it away. The opportunity came when Juan died, but by then, she couldn't bring herself to do it. It was a picture of Juan with one of his outside children from so long ago. Somehow it seemed like a sin to throw away a child's photo.

Narrow wooden stairs ran from the rear of the five-foot-wide service porch behind the refrigerator, down to the cement walkway behind the garage. On warm days she hugged the railing all the way down to sit in the sun on a canvas fold-up chair she dragged down from her living room. She'd always liked the sun, even though it wasn't as strong here as it was on the island. She sat, turning her face upward and felt the heat burn into her skin and dive deeper until it cradled her curved spine in warmth. She sighed then, comfortable, as the ache in her bones dulled, and she let her mind slip back to the days when she and Juan were both young before they came here to start a new life.

When she closed her eyes, she could see Juan, tall and handsome, his skin glowing like polished copper, and she, several shades darker, with crisp curling hair, holding onto his arm as they strolled along *Calle de la Cruz* watching the tourists. So long ago. Where had the time gone? They'd lived in New York for a while, in the Bronx, when they first came here. Their oldest was born when they lived in that first walk-up.

Then they moved to Los Angeles because Juan's brother found him a job in a maintenance company. It was good for a while until the company closed. After that, they both hustled their living cleaning offices. They liked living in this part of Los Angeles, where they could hear Spanish spoken almost everywhere, and the rents were cheaper. Besides, they were just a short walk to the park where the paddleboats floated peacefully on the water, and the geese chattered at the people picnicking on the grass near the boathouse.

That was before the rest of the children were born, and before Juan developed "wandering eyes" that led him out of their little house and into the bars where he spent too much of his paycheck. That was before she hated to answer the phone because some strange woman was calling to let her know she was having sex with Juan. That was before Juan got "mean drunk" and beat the kids when he came home late at night and before he started beating her too.

She almost moved out of the neighborhood once, when Mrs. Akmajian's son tried to get her an apartment where his mother lived, in the tall white building with balconies, in Little Armenia, an area of East Hollywood. He explained that only older people lived in this building near Hollywood, and you had to be on a waiting list to get in.

"The place is rent-controlled. They have emergency alarms in every apartment in case you fall or hurt yourself." He tried his best to convince her. "The apartment is just ten years old. It has carpeted floors and central heating. You never have to be cold in the winter like in that cracker box you live in now. Besides, I have connections with the Armenians who own it, so you can bypass the waiting list. You can see my mother every day without taking the bus," he said, referring to her only friend, his mother, who spoke neither English nor Spanish, but always understood Mrs. Fonseca.

She thanked him but didn't take the offer. Probably not as many people spoke Spanish in that neighborhood, and she didn't know her way around the streets there. Besides, there was no park, just block after block of apartments that all looked the same. All that concrete hurt her eyes. Where would she go to walk in the early morning, or sit on a bench and feed the geese, or buy a taco from the taco lady pushing her little cart around the park? So, she stayed, even though it rained like crazy that winter and water leaked from the roof onto her thin carpet and left it smelling like mildew.

After the big rains stopped, neighbors moved into the adjoining garage apartment next door that had been empty most of the time she lived there. She watched curiously through the window, peeping behind her heavy tapestry curtain. They were very young. Probably in their twenties. The man had long hair and a mustache, and his arms were covered with tattoos. The young woman had very red hair that she wore twisted into spirals that hung down her back. She was skinny and also had tattoos on her arms and legs and even some on her chest.

Mrs. Fonseca watched them move in. They only brought a big mattress, a tall glass bookcase with glass partitions, and a giant television set. She watched in amazement as they carried it between them up the narrow stairs. She'd never seen a television set this big. It must be as big as the whole apartment, she thought to herself. As it turned out she was right. Peeking in the window one day, after making sure nobody was home, she saw that the television covered most of the wall opposite the window. "*Gracias Dios*, why does anybody need a television that big?"

They came over that night and introduced themselves. Her name was Maureen and his name was Sean. They'd come to California to be actors, or at the very least television stars. "We're both working on screenplays too," Maureen explained. "But I work at Trader Joe's part time to get money to live on until we make it."

Mrs. Fonseca listened, nodding her head. Maybe someday they would be famous, and she could say they were her neighbors. Sean insisted that they drink some wine and invited her in to watch their television. She drank a few sips of the wine. It warmed her stomach and made her feel dizzy. She could feel her face getting red. Maureen kept asking her questions about Mexico even though she explained she was from Puerto Rico, and she wasn't Mexican. Maureen and Sean looked puzzled and asked her if she would make tamales. They'd had some in

Nebraska once. She cringed, thinking about how tamales made in Nebraska would taste and told them where they could buy some in the neighborhood.

Maureen and Sean liked to play loud music. She guessed it was music, though it was unlike any music she knew. Mostly she heard somebody screaming in a deep angry voice and a clashing sound that could have been a guitar or maybe a hammer striking metal. In fact, Sean said it was called "heavy metal," and it was all he listened to since he used to be a singer with his own band. That was how he met Maureen, he explained proudly. She came backstage and claimed him as her own.

All in all, they weren't bad neighbors, except when they brought their friends over and stayed up till the next morning, playing their music so loud that you could hear it up and down the street a block or two over. On those nights and early mornings, nobody slept. They drank a lot. She knew that because she checked the bottles in the trash, not just wine, but whiskey and gin, and other kinds of alcohol that she didn't recognize.

Most of the time, a strange smell floated out of Maureen and Sean's apartment. She figured it wasn't marijuana because her son had smoked before. It made him giggly, and he said he couldn't stop laughing. Juan found the weed he'd been hiding behind a dresser and kicked him out of the house. "*Vámonos, marijuano,*" he yelled, while he pitched tennis shoes and basketball shorts out into the street late one night, and her son held his stomach and laughed hysterically. This smell was different, like nail polish remover or maybe like too much cat pee if you forgot to change the litter box. The kids had a cat once, she remembered.

On one really warm day when the temperature was in the high nineties, she saw Maureen throwing away the garbage in the covered shed at the rear of the garage. She was wearing a long-sleeve black turtleneck with a name on the front that she didn't recognize, heavy black jeans, and knee-high Doc Marten work boots. "It must be so hot in your apartment," she inquired, staring at Maureen, knowing that neither apartment had air conditioning, and even with the portable fans running all day, you could barely breathe.

"Yes, it's pretty bad," Maureen assured her, wiping her forehead with the back of her arm. Her face was red and sweaty.

"Just wondering, why are you wearing such heavy clothes in this heat?"

Maureen looked away and tugged at the high collar on her turtleneck. "Sean likes me to dress like this. He likes all black. You know, this look. He doesn't like anything else, really. I used to …" Her voice trailed off.

Mrs. Fonseca nodded as if she understood. "Oh, I see. I mean, those clothes look so hot."

Maureen put her head down and walked away.

Sometimes she saw other things when she peeped into the side window, spoons and syringes like the nurses used when they gave you a shot and tiny little glass tubes. She had her suspicions but figured it was none of her business. Maureen and Sean argued a lot. They called each other bad names like "asshole" and "fucking cunt." Sometimes they threw things. Many times, she could hear the sound of something smashing, as whatever they threw hit the wall and broke.

But still, they were some company in her solitary life, and more often than not, she turned down her television so she could hear them argue. The sound of a human voice that didn't come from a television set was special these days when hardly anyone talked to her. She told herself it wasn't eavesdropping, she was listening to a live play through the walls, and she happened to know the actors personally. Sometimes it was actually exciting, and it made her heart race as she waited to hear the crack of one of them being slapped or the thud made by a fist striking soft flesh. Sometimes she heard the sound of blows followed by Maureen crying. Then, Sean's voice, low and deep. Maureen stopped crying then.

When she saw her the next day, Maureen's face and arms were all bruised, reddish, and purple, and she wouldn't stop to say hello. A few times, she thought that maybe she should ask Maureen if she was okay or perhaps just call the police, but she was embarrassed. Nobody in the neighborhood called the police for anything. You never knew what they could do, plant drugs or arrest you for something. Better not to. Besides, by the time they'd get here, everything would be quiet. Exhausted from all the stress of the goings-on next door, she usually fell asleep as soon as she heard Maureen stop crying.

It was a Saturday morning, the best day of her week. Today she would go and visit Mrs. Akmajian in Hollywood, and they would go shopping and have lunch afterward. She prepared her morning cup of tea and dry toast and thought about eating her breakfast downstairs as the sun was coming out. Holding her cup of tea carefully, she opened the back door to the stairway and then stopped. Her hands shook too much, and she knew she couldn't navigate the stairs and hold the cup in her other hand without spilling it. She turned around and walked back in. Sitting down on her velour couch she suddenly brightened. What she needed was to hear her grandchildren's voices or at least one of her children. It had been a long time since they called her. She'd tried calling a day ago but couldn't reach anybody.

She picked up the princess phone that she'd managed to save all these years. The phone made her kids laugh. They'd tried buying her a cell phone a few years ago, but it was way too confusing, and she couldn't get the hang of using the one they showed her. Besides, it came with a cord for charging, and she knew she'd never remember to keep it charged. She flipped through her little phone book and began dialing her children, one by one. Their phone messages were all on, telling her to leave her number, and they would return her call. Sighing in disappointment, she tried her two oldest grandchildren. It was the same thing. Nobody was answering.

Her daughter told her before that it would be better if she got a cell phone and texted. Nobody answered phone calls these days. Her son even showed her how he texted on his own phone. She watched shocked. Why would somebody want to write all those words? What she wanted was to hear the voice of the person she called. When you listened to their voice, you could tell how they were doing, if they were happy or sad if they needed comfort. No, she would stick to the phone she was used to having.

She began combing her hair, dressing in one of her better pairs of black polyester pants purchased from JC Penney's. Each year her daughter took her shopping for Christmas and had her pick out a few items of clothing to charge on her card. She scurried around the sales racks, pushing things aside and pulling them away for examination. She checked price tags and only picked the cheapest items on sale. She didn't want to take advantage.

It was nine o'clock, and she planned to take a walk around the park before she caught the bus to east Hollywood, to see Mrs. Akmajian. She was washing her teacup in the sink when she heard a huge crash and the sound of shattering glass on the other side of the wall. The crash was followed by a moment of silence, and then a shrill scream of pain that ran deep into her spine and made her hands freeze in place in mid-air.

She heard Sean's voice scream, "Oh my God!"

It occurred to her that she hadn't seen either of them come out of the apartment for a few days. It didn't seem that Maureen was going to work either. She stopped drying and started across the room. Something was wrong with Maureen. She was sure of it. The pounding on the door stopped her in her tracks.

"Open up! Open up! I need to call an ambulance quick."

Sean was standing outside her door, and it took her a moment to recognize him. He seemed even skinner than last time. His skin was pale under his tattoos, and his hair and beard were wild and uncombed, standing away from his head. He was only wearing undershorts that looked like they might have once been white but were now a dirty-gray. She stared at his legs, boney and veined, the skin translucent.

"I need to use your phone now. Can't find mine. Need to call an ambulance."

She pointed to the alcove where the princess phone rested, staring, her mouth open.

He grabbed the phone, punched in some numbers, and began yelling into the receiver. "Please, I need an ambulance. My girlfriend fell and hit her head. She's not moving."

She heard him give the address and listened as he told the person at the other end of the line that Maureen didn't seem to be breathing. She watched him drop the phone and start back out the door. Without thinking, she followed him. The door to their apartment was jarred open and the shades were drawn, keeping the room in semi-darkness. She looked around in shock. It looked like someone had turned the apartment upside down and shaken everything before it fell. The television set that used to hang on the wall lay face down on the floor. The rest of the small living room was covered with half-empty food containers, pizza boxes and scattered clothes. She could see dirty dishes stacked in the sink of the tiny kitchen and on the counter more used food cartons. A reddish blood-like liquid had splashed all over the linoleum and the puddle had dried in a sticky film. Beyond the kitchen, the bathroom door hung off its hinges, and she could see the floor covered in water and balled-up towels. There was no sheet on the mattress in the corner, and in its center was a small pile of syringes and plastic bags.

And then her eyes started to get accustomed to the darkened room, and she turned to her right. Huge chunks of glass lie broken and gleaming on the floor below the remaining glass and metal poles that had once held the bookcase shelves. Maureen lay there on the glass, her back to the bookcase, her hands flung behind her, one leg twisted to her side. She wasn't moving, and her eyes were closed. There was a long bloody scratch across the side of her face.

Staring in horror, she backed away from the body. "Oh my god, what happened? She's not breathing!"

"She fell," mumbled Sean, holding onto the sides of his head. "That's all. She fell."

Mrs. Fonseca kept her eyes glued on the body. Somewhere she had a dim recollection about first aid. You were supposed to do something. What? Breathe, yes, breathe. "We need to breathe into her mouth to make her breathe." She told Sean. She'd seen it on television before.

"Just get away from here, you nosy old bitch. I don't need you here. Go!"

Mrs. Fonseca looked up, her face dropping at the outburst. "What? We need to help her. Her color's bad."

"I said, get out!" He screamed, moving close to her face.

She looked at him now more carefully. His eyes were red and sunken, and the veins in his neck stood out. His fists were balled up as he stepped toward her. For an instant, she thought he was Juan, returning from the dead, drunk, and ready to fight her.

She backed up and turned as two husky Latinos wearing white uniforms with red stitching on the breast pocket ran noisily through the open door carrying black equipment bags. She heard them call out the address and ask who was hurt. Then she turned and ran back to her apartment.

After collapsing into her chair, she sat for the next hour, shaken by the thought of Maureen lying there. She was a nice girl. Too nice to be hurt like that. She'd just seen them kissing the other day, or was that a few weeks ago? She couldn't remember. The men from the ambulance must have made a call because when she looked out the window again, another vehicle showed up that said "City Coroner" on the side. She watched while they carried a white stretcher up the stairs and then a few minutes later, carried it back down, this time with somebody on the stretcher completely covered with a white sheet.

The police pulled into the driveway about the same time the Coroner's vehicle was leaving. After talking to the ambulance attendants, two police officers, a short Asian and a taller light-skinned Black man banged on her door. They wanted to know what she'd seen. She told them she hadn't seen anything. They took down her name and phone number anyway and said some detective would be out to talk to her later. She stuck the card they gave her into her pocket and ducked her head. She hadn't seen what happened to Maureen, she told herself. Sure, she'd heard things coming from that apartment. But why get involved? It was always better to keep your head down and look away.

So many years ago, she'd pounded on a neighbor's iron security door when they lived in the scattering of broken-down shacks that stood one block over from the industrial area near downtown. She banged on the nearest door two houses over, running from her house at two o'clock in the morning in her nightgown, blood streaming from her nose, and her dislocated shoulder throbbing as she moved. "Please, call the police. My husband beat me up. I'm afraid for my kids. Help me, please!"

She could hear the inside door latches snapping open, and the porch light flicked on. A woman peered around the small gap between the door and the frame. In the background, a television played quietly, and she could see several small children sleeping in their underpants, sprawled on a couch by the door. The woman had wide-set brown eyes and dark skin. Her braid of black hair had come loose, and the wiry strands blew around her face. "*Sí?*" She asked in a heavily accented voice.

She told the woman again that she was running away, she was afraid of Juan, of what he could do. Worried, he would hurt her son. She asked her to please call the police as she wiped the blood from her face with the back of her arm.

The woman looked at her and shook her head. "*No Señora. No quiero problemas. No me moleste.*" She slammed the door hard, turning off the porch light. Mrs. Fonseca clutched her shoulder and staggered to the side of the house bordered by a patch of dry weeds and sunk to her knees, crying.

She always cried, and at first, Juan was always sorry. He held her in his arms and kissed her and blamed it all on his drinking.

He said he'd never take another sip. She prayed he would change. But a day or so later, he'd hit her again or beat one of the kids too hard with his wide belt with the brass buckle. He stopped saying he was sorry because he wasn't. He started staying away from home. She and the kids were glad. When he finally came home to stay, he was in the last stages of cancer. Her children had grown and moved on. He lasted about a month.

Shaking, she closed the door behind the police, desperate to forget how Maureen looked, all twisted up on the floor. She sat rocking herself on the small loveseat until she heard more commotion coming from next door. Cautiously, she pulled a corner of the drapes aside and peered out. More uniformed police were running up the stairs, leaving their cars with the doors open, parked one behind the other, in the long driveway. The house shook with their heavy footsteps clomping up the wooden stairs. She heard voices yelling, and watched as three police half-dragged, and half-carried Sean down the stairs as he tried to grab at the railings with his hands cuffed in front of him. She watched as the police stationed themselves on either side of him and pushed him headfirst into the first car by the stairs. She heard one of them call up the stairs, "Lock it up, Fernandez. Nobody's coming back here."

Grabbing her purse, she hurried down the stairs, moving faster than she ever did, barely holding onto the splintery railing. Clutching her purse, she moved quickly, heading up to Sunset, where she caught the bus just before it was about to take off from the curb. Out of breath and shaking, she stumbled into a seat up front by the driver. Her heart was hammering, and all she could see was Maureen's pale purple face. She'd seen a few dead people before back home, and once at a wake held on the top floor of a walk-up in the Bronx where she'd been hired to cook food for the mourners. One side of the family had removed the dead man's body from the funeral home because they wanted to conduct the service at home, and the police came to arrest them and take the body back.

Her lips moved silently as she prayed to Jesus to protect her and keep her calm. Then she crossed herself and turned to look out the window as the bus bounced along, passing Thai restaurants, taco stands, and laundromats. When a grubby-looking man stumbled on, shoeless with tangled hair, carrying several shopping bags of possessions, and sat down next to her, she moved closer to the window and held tighter to her purse. The rank odor coming from the man's dirty clothes was familiar; she'd smelled it so many times before, passing homeless camps crowded with blue plastic tents in the park and along the sidewalks. You could count on there always being homeless people and poor people, just like her, she thought. Sometimes it was nice to know what you could count on when everything was changing and going by so fast. Thank God for Mrs. Akmajian!

She tried to keep her eyes closed and not look at the man sitting next to her, who was now mumbling to himself, but when she did, she kept seeing Maureen's purple face. The bus made a wide turn onto Sunset and picked up speed. Within a few minutes, they were across the street from Mrs. Akmajian's apartment building. She stepped off gratefully, her legs still shaking.

Ringing the buzzer by the mailbox, she waited for her friend to answer. Mrs. Akmajian spoke very little English, and Mrs. Fonseca didn't speak Armenian. But they still spoke to each other by a combination of gestures and grunts, vowels, and syllables that substituted for the language they did not share. Over time they each tried to teach the other the words for things they wanted to talk about, but neither one was good at remembering the new word for more than a few minutes, so they never quite managed to exchange vocabulary.

Mrs. Fonseca was so glad to see her friend come down the stairs that she hugged her extra hard, noticing that she looked sad. "What's wrong?" she asked over and over. "You have problems? Maybe with your son?"

Mrs. Akmajian just shook her head and chewed on her lower lip. She didn't understand. They started out on their usual walk, but she didn't seem interested in the things that usually made them point and stare; the few hookers in high platforms strolling up to the cars, the man with dozens of watches for sale hanging in the lining of his heavy trench overcoat billowing around his ankles, the teenagers with spiked mohawks, dyed aqua and purple, with piercings through their lips and cheeks. She wasn't even interested in the women with their faces and chests covered with bold tattoos of birds with spread wings and evil-looking serpents that circled their necks, tattooed in reds and greens. They stopped for their usual lunch at McDonald's, but Mrs. Akmajian barely touched her Value Meal, and Mrs. Fonseca found she wasn't that hungry either.

Shaking her head, Mrs. Fonseca looked at her friend and wondered what was wrong. She wasn't enjoying herself much either; she wondered what was going to happen to Sean now, and did she really see them carry Maureen's body down the stairs or was it all something she imagined. Sean was such a nice guy, she thought. Why did he change? Why did Juan change? He'd choked her once until she almost passed out. The kids saw it too. They were too scared to do anything, but then so was she.

When the bus stopped across from the tall apartment building, Mrs. Akmajian's son was parked in front, waiting in his black E-Class Mercedes. Mrs. Fonseca knew the car was expensive because her son Carlos had once given her a ride here and talked to her friend's son. He came away saying that the family had a lot of money they made in something called "import and export," and wishing he made enough money operating a fork-lift to buy a car like that.

Mrs. Akmajian's son stepped out of his car, holding his cell phone to his ear. "Just hang on, okay? I'll just be a minute. Don't hang up." He turned to Mrs. Fonseca, "Look, I just waited to tell you, I'm moving my mom to San Diego in a few days, so you won't be seeing her here after today."

Mrs. Fonseca stared, not believing what she heard. "What did you say?"

"I said, we're moving to San Diego. I'm opening another warehouse down there. We're having my mom move with us. She fell in the shower a couple of days ago and couldn't get hold of me. It's just too far away. Anyway, I don't think she should be living alone anymore."

"But she likes it here," Mrs. Fonseca stammered. What was she going to do without her friend?

"I know," her son told her, "but it's for the better. I mean, she doesn't even speak English. I don't know how you even talk to her."

Mrs. Fonseca felt tears start to fill her eyes. "Can I have the phone number there?"

"Sure. Don't know why you'd want it. My mother doesn't speak English. She can't talk to you."

"Yes, I want it. We manage."

The son shrugged. "Well, I know my mom has your number. I'll call you and give you our new number at the house." He turned away and started talking to his phone again. "Hello, sorry. Just some nuisance business to take care of."

The tears rolled down Mrs. Fonseca's cheeks, and she hugged her friend tight. Mrs. Akmajian was sobbing and shaking her head. They stood there together, rocking back and forth, knowing they probably wouldn't see each other again. They wouldn't be talking in their own made-up way anymore.

"Well, I've got to go." Her son told Mrs. Fonseca. "I'm taking her back to my house. My wife's coming down tomorrow to pack up her things. Time's up for the afternoon, I've got to get back to work."

Mrs. Fonseca stepped back and wiped her eyes. In the end, time was always the boss. She kept her head down all the way home, feeling sick to her stomach, and thinking about everything that had happened since she woke up that morning. Maureen, the nice girl who lived next door, was dead, it seemed, and Sean ... well, he seemed sweet too, but she knew he'd done something wrong and so did the police or they wouldn't have taken him away. She shivered, knowing their living room had become a crime scene. And now, her only friend was moving away.

Her mind ran through the procession of long days to come—days she would spend alone. Nobody to talk to, nobody asking how she was. No Saturdays to look forward to when she would get to see her friend. Days when she was in bed by seven o'clock, her dinner eaten an hour earlier. Long days with nothing much to do. Might as well end that kind of day early. The sleeping pills helped.

Stepping off the bus, she started down the block, surprised to see the mail carrier still out delivering. She walked to the rear of the front house, and the man stopped in front of her, handing her a white envelope with blue lettering. She recognized her electric bill. The mailman pushed his floppy canvas safari hat back from his forehead. "Had a late start today, and this whole block was closed off, anyhow. Heard somebody got killed up there." He gestured toward the garage apartment on the left.

The sadness started leaking out of her eyes. She was going to miss her young neighbors too. They were always so full of life. Just listening to them was more entertaining than television. She stumbled up the stairs and closed the door behind her. The stillness pressed in, filling the small room and reminding her that she was going to be spending the rest of her years here. Her kids said it looked like she was going to live a long time, and it would be some time before she'd end up in a nursing home. She needed to talk to one of them now. Better if it was one of her daughters. They'd understand how she felt, and maybe they'd decide to come down and visit her.

Feeling a little brighter, she checked her pocket phonebook and started dialing. First, she dialed her oldest daughter. The call went straight to message. Still not sure how to leave her message, she yelled into the phone, and then dialed her other daughter. She didn't answer either. Well, maybe Carlos then. He might yell at her about calling during work hours, but at least she'd hear his voice. Feeling more confident, she dialed his number. Nobody answered, and the phone rang and rang. She waited for the message to come on, but it never did. He must have forgotten to set it. She hung up, feeling worse and tottered over to the kitchen counter on arthritic legs. With shaking hands, she poured out a couple of sleeping pills. She'd finish the day early. Maybe it would be better tomorrow.

God, she missed her children. Not these adults who were just strangers, always all business, making you talk to phones instead of talking to a real person. Strangers who didn't even care enough to call her and say hello. They weren't really the children she remembered. She missed the little children who stood by the sink patiently in their new shoes from Discount Shoe Mart while she combed their hair and held her hand tightly on the first day of school.

She carried her pills and a glass of water over to the couch, turned on the television, and stared at the two people reporting the news. All of it bad. But she didn't care. She couldn't help those little refugee children or cool off the earth or keep the police from shooting more Black men. She wasn't even able to help Maureen. Maureen, with her fiery hair and her tattoos of angels, devils, and flowers that covered her chest and arms. Poor Maureen. She was some mother's baby daughter. Whoever her mother was, whenever she found out, she would feel the kind of pain that never stops.

She pictured Maureen's face again, bloody and purple. The world was a horrible place, full of men like Sean, and women like her and Maureen. She was like Maureen, she thought. The only difference was that Juan and his wandering eyes had left, or she might have ended up the same way, on a stretcher going to the morgue.

She wondered if Maureen ever thought it was all her fault. She'd felt like that at first herself. She wished she'd talked to Maureen before. She could have told her about how it was with Juan, told her that Sean wouldn't change, no matter what she did to please him, and that she needed to leave, told her not to be afraid, life would go on without him. She sat there thinking about how nobody was there to help Maureen, when all the time she had been suspicious. No, more than suspicious, she knew something was wrong next door but never said anything. She felt ashamed. All the time being lonely and miserable, useless, with no real purpose anymore, and nobody to talk to, she could have helped. She saw that now. Maureen had needed somebody to stand up for her to make sure there was justice.

She dug into her wallet and pulled out the card the police left her. She turned it over in her hand and brought it close to her eyes so she could see it better, underlining the writing with her finger and whispering the name of the officer, Thomas P. Johnson, under her breath. She could call this officer and tell him what she heard through the thin plaster walls and what she saw. She gripped the card tightly for a moment and then set it face-down on the armrest. Her shoulders slumped as if the events of the day, like a heavy sack of rice, had fallen on her neck wrapping themselves around her shoulders. Her arms and legs were weighted down, too weary to move. Outside, the sun was dropping and the room was growing blurry. She rubbed her eyes that were watering from trying to read the small lettering printed on the white background of the card. Calling wouldn't be that hard she told herself. She could just pick up the phone. If only she didn't feel so tired, her head lolling, her body aching and numb at the same time.

As the sun dipped sharply into early evening, the whirling buzz of a police helicopter flying overhead and circling the streets started up. The noise, as always, shook her upstairs apartment and rattled the windows so much that they seemed to be loosening in their frames. A deep growling voice over a loudspeaker coming from the air above, called out a name she couldn't hear, instructing them to come out with their hands up and they wouldn't be shot. The noise from the spinning blades blotted out the shrill shrieks of children and the high-pitched yelling of their mothers calling them inside. The sound filled her head. She could feel it making her jaw vibrate and her ears buzz as it put down its roots inside of her.

She looked again at the phone but made no move to pick it up. Who was she kidding? She didn't want to talk to the police. Not *ever* if she could help it. It wouldn't be just one phone call to one cop, she thought. She'd probably have to talk to a lot of people from the police about what she knew. She might even have to go to court. Mrs. Fonseca shivered, thinking about facing strangers asking her questions and everybody watching her, waiting for her answers. They would want to know why she hadn't said something earlier. Maybe they'd blame her for what happened to Maureen, and she'd be in trouble.

Should she call her kids and ask them what to do? Maybe one of them was home now. She looked at the phone doubtfully. She was sure she knew what they'd say, "It's a shame, but you should mind your own business." Then they would tell her they were busy working mandatory overtime, or that everybody in the house was sick with the flu. Maybe they'd say the basketball play-offs, or the Dodgers were on TV now, and they couldn't talk. They would tell her they would call her back. But they never did.

Lately, she'd noticed that even when she tried, she couldn't quite remember her children's faces as they were now, and even less, her grandchildren's. It was only the photos of them as babies and small children that lived on, never growing dimmer in her memory. In the photos they smiled broadly: forever through time, their eyes clear and shiny, and their plump cheeks and lips flushed and rosy. She was their whole world then.

And what about Mrs. Akmajian, would she forget how they both enjoyed their walks on Hollywood Boulevard and make new friends since she was living with her son in San Diego? If she did, then they would probably never see each other again. San Diego was so far and there was nobody to take her. Her eyes had stopped watering from squinting and now thick hot tears rolled down her face instead. She felt a lump slowly closing off her throat when she tried to swallow.

The helicopter had finally stopped flying, and the children playing on the street were now all inside probably eating dinner. The street was hushed except for the faint lull of traffic traveling west on Sunset Boulevard. Headlights from cars cresting the top of the hill threw out thin streaks of light that shone faintly through the slats in the window blinds giving the apartment its only light.

On shaky legs, Mrs. Fonseca walked the few steps to the medicine cabinet and took out the bottle of sleeping pills. It was nearly full. Sighing, she wobbled over to her chair and eased herself down, hearing her knees creak under her weight. She poured the sleeping pills into her palm and added what was left of the two bottles of pain pills. There were so many pills that they spilled out of her cupped hand and rolled onto the table. She felt every inch of her body being drawn to the multicolored selection, blues and yellows, reds and whites. A few of the yellow and blue pills landed on top of the card the police had left. She scooped them back up in her palm, frowning at the card on the table.

Carefully, Mrs. Fonseca slid the glass of water nearer to her and closed her fist around a handful of pills. She was sure she could see Maureen's face in the dark room, a faint trace of her profile almost hidden by her long hair. She sat very still facing the street, like a stopwatch winding down.

Crossing

I guess it's safe to tell our story now. Two of the main characters have been dead for a while now, so they can't be prosecuted. Besides, I don't know how long the government has to prosecute people like us. I'm the only one still around, and it was a very long time ago, back when I was an ignorant thirty-two year old who had no clue about the real-world justice system and how easy it was to get locked up. Even though I wasn't white, I still bathed in the privilege of being female when patronizing females was still trendy.

It was 1979, and I had just one more semester left before taking my orals and doing my thesis for a doctorate in Chicano Studies. It was a long hard haul during those years. I learned to sit in class and take legible notes on two hours' sleep, sometimes with uppers if I could get them, since nobody had ever heard of energy drinks back then. I was cleaning office buildings at night and working as a short-order cook, flipping greasy burgers and scooping chili in the afternoons. In 1979 you could work those low-end jobs, and with a little chump change still afford to rent yourself a one-room apartment (without utilities) and even eat something besides Top Ramen once a week. Nobody knew what I did once I left the campus. I didn't invite many people to my tiny apartment near the freeways where the Californian utopia of clean white sandy beaches and wall-to-wall palm trees didn't exist. It was a neighborhood where you shouldn't really walk around at night without bodyguards or an automatic weapon, not if you wanted to be safe from the characters that lived in the buildings with the barred windows and graffiti-covered walls—especially if you were a woman.

I had the usual student furnishings of that day, a mattress

on the floor, and a few two-by-fours balanced between cement bricks to hold my books and my typewriter. I even had a royal blue beanbag chair by the window. It had a hole somewhere and leaked air, so it was flatter on one side, but it was the only place to sit besides the bed. I learned to take my cold showers in three minutes flat, which included washing my hair, and sometimes even shaving my legs. I had to build up to it because sometimes there wasn't enough money to pay the gas bill and they shut off the hot water before I could get a deposit together.

But that summer, I was feeling the best I had felt in a long time. I was almost done with the endless studying every spare minute and writing papers on topics that, by that time, were repetitious exercises in "busy work." I was looking forward to finding a real job somewhere, preferably in a prestigious university, (remember, I didn't know much then), and publishing relevant, eye-opening articles that would bring me recognition in the academic community, and, I hoped, enough money to get a bigger apartment with a pool and air conditioning.

The other thing I felt good about was Raul. So, let me explain. There weren't that many guys in the doctoral program, maybe because the only thing you could do with a doctorate was teach or do research. Chicano Studies wasn't considered an elite major, even for Chicanos like me. Lower paying jobs like teaching and research were usually considered women's jobs, just like teaching grammar school, but for less money and benefits. It was no wonder men didn't flock to those low-paid professions after suffering through grad school. I couldn't blame them. But what else could you do with Chicano Studies? Maybe work in an underfunded nonprofit.

The truth was, I'd picked that major because there was always plenty of room in the classes. No waiting list, and everybody said it was an easy major to coast through. I've always been a person who likes to get to the meat of things, do my work quickly, and move on. I wasn't looking for an opportunity to display any hidden intellect or stand out by discovering some obscure mathematical formula to help the space program or cure cancer. I just wanted that piece of paper that would let me teach or do research for some university without too much hassle on my part and weekends off.

There were three males in my program. One of the guys was from Mexico. He spoke in heavily accented English and walked with his head down. He looked like he weighed about a hundred pounds and stood all of five feet tall. He hardly ever spoke. The other guy was from Belize, really chubby, with a lot of curly black hair, like a teddy bear come to life. He was friendly enough, but he was married with three small children and an unhappy wife, or so he said. He usually reeked of alcohol.

The third guy was Raul. If you saw him, you'd need no other introduction. He'd clearly stepped out of one of those *Glamour* magazine perfume ads—tall, olive-skinned, wavy black hair, and piercing blue eyes. I know you've seen those ads. He'd traveled all the way from Venezuela to come to the school in the United States, and get this, he wanted to use his doctorate to go to Mexico and help the people by designing social programs to take them out of poverty. He thought studying Chicano history would give him the insight he needed. I don't think there was another soul in my classes all those years who had ever expressed an egalitarian goal like that. Now, I'm not so sure if that was his real intent, but he told everybody it was. Raul, like others enrolled in the program, didn't have student loans or scholarships, had money sent to him every month by his family. He lived comfortably, he said, in a home on the beach that he shared with another young male-on-the-way-up, a graduate of Harvard Law School. They kept that house as neat as a pin, he told me. Not even a stray leaf was lying on the wrap-around balcony that overlooked the ocean on a clear day. I saw it myself.

Before I go any further, let me tell you about myself. As I said, we called ourselves "Chicanos" in those days. Now, most of us baby-boomers are dying off, and I don't hear that word used so much, but I looked then, and still do look every inch the *mestiza*. All that was well and good as long as you had your book open and were reading about Chicanos who looked like you, but when you closed the book and stepped out into the real white world, it was another story—when the beauty standards called for tall and thin, with blue eyes and long, straight blond hair. I stood short and a little too chunky with frizzy dark hair, and I had a tendency to sprout a field of acne on my too-dark skin. By that time in my life, I'd accepted my status in the looks department. Guys were not lining up to knock on my door. There was no waiting line to date me. I went out with a few guys, lost my virginity early on, and I was glad to have gotten that over with. Then I settled down to finish school and spend the rest of my life working for a living since it wasn't likely that I was going to become any man's trophy.

So, back to Raul. On the first day of class, I looked twice and then a third time, when he came into the room. After that, I just stared. All the other women in the class did too, even the professor and the TA. He was that good looking, and to top it off, he didn't behave as if he was aware of it. He had a kind of casual nonchalance. He picked an empty seat next to me, and at the break, he surprised me by following me out to the coffee machine and waving my hand away when I tried to pay twenty-five cents for my own cup of coffee. We retired to the corner to lean against an empty bookcase and sip the flavored water they passed off as coffee, while the women in the class tried to pretend they weren't looking while they peeked at us from the corners of their eyes.

After class, he walked with me to my dented 1969 Volkswagen with the chipped paint, which was parked quite a distance from Campbell Hall. When we got there, he helped me pull the door open on the driver's side. On a damp night like that one, the door always jammed, and I had to open the passenger side window with a wire hanger and ease my upper body across the front seat to open the opposite door. That night, after forcing open the door, he folded himself down into the passenger seat, and we talked for nearly two hours. I learned all about his life growing up in South America, a life of leisurely tours through Europe to soak up the culture and summers cruising on the Mediterranean with his family.

I didn't tell him that the last time I traveled anywhere was when I was an undergraduate, and my cousin and I drove up to Washington to pick apples for the summer. At the time, I thought it would be an earthy and romantic thing to do, to experience the real world with *mi gente*. After a day of strained labor in the summer sun, sweating from every pore, and aching in every joint, my cousin argued with the field-hand supervisor over the proper way to dump out a basket of bruised apples, and quit on the spot. I was grateful to follow her while she cursed him, calling him all kinds of motherfuckers, all the way back to her car. We drove straight back to Los Angeles, stopping only to use the bathroom, thinking how nice South Central looked at twilight a couple of days later.

My eyes never left Raul's face as he talked that night. I couldn't believe a man, so good looking was paying such rapt attention to me. Somewhere inside me, he'd found the beautiful, intelligent woman that I was, the one nobody saw. I was a goddess; I'd known it all along. I told him what it was like to grow up Mexican here. I told him proudly that I'd been on a scholarship all through undergrad and grad school. I didn't tell him that my mother was on welfare and still raising my four brothers and sisters who were a lot younger. I didn't know where my father was, and my youngest brother spent a lot of time in juvenile hall while my middle sister was expecting a child of her own in a few months. You couldn't compare any of that to a cruise around the Mediterranean.

I even asked Raul, "Do you have a girlfriend back home?" A bold move for me. I couldn't have asked if it was anybody else, but then I wouldn't care.

He looked surprised and said he didn't.

There was hope then, I thought. I patted down my frizzy

hair, made frizzier by the damp night air, and then waited while he opened the door and said he had to go. I offered to drive him back to his car, but he said he'd walk. Disappointment hit me like a wall. Things were going so well, but he hadn't made any moves and he didn't ask me out.

Over the next couple of weeks, he always made it a point to sit next to me in class and talk to me. Sometimes, he walked me to my car if he wasn't in a hurry. I couldn't help but notice he didn't pay much attention to the other females in the class, even though they went out of their way to be seen, stopping by his seat to flirt outrageously. But after a few weeks of his curt nods and disinterest, they mostly stopped coming by and ignored him as if he were as undesirable as the other two males in the room.

We settled into a pattern of studying in the library once a week on Fridays, which was my only day off. I never discussed where I worked or what I did, and he never asked. He always bought me coffee when we took a break, but he never mentioned taking me to dinner or a movie, or anything else that would be like a real date. I hinted a few times, too shy to ask. He just smiled and nodded and changed the subject.

The others watched us at first. You could see the curiosity in their faces as they looked from his stunning perfection to my ordinariness. Still, after a while, I could see they'd accepted us as a couple and then dismissed us as unnecessary in their lives.

I'd all but given up any hope of ever actually going out in public with him. We did talk some in the library. It's hard to study for many hours without breaking up the time. I learned all about his previous life but volunteered very little of mine. I was grateful that he didn't ask, but my fragile self-confidence was slowly getting crushed. Apparently, I wasn't attractive enough for him, something I didn't dispute as I sat across from him with the sunlight streaming down on his perfect features.

I'd entertained the idea that he was gay many times, but

since I didn't know many gay men, I dismissed it, mostly because he didn't have any of those feminine traits I associated with gay men. Namely, he didn't swish, lisp, or stand with his hands on his hips. I was pretty limited then, and you have to remember I was raised among Latinos, where a gay man was only known in one form and men aggressively thrust their "macho" personas in your face every opportunity they had. Anyway, Raul was always very sweet, telling me I looked "nice" today or complimenting me on what I was wearing, which was usually a miniskirt and a secondhand army jacket that I tried to pretend made me look like an edgy hippie, when in reality, I just didn't have any money in my budget for new clothes.

As the semester wore on, they cut back on my hours at the dive where I scooped chili onto burgers. There were fewer customers because young people were starting to focus on "eating healthy" and they didn't need as many short-order cooks and counter people. Suddenly, I had extra time on my hands and I started to feel lonely. I began hanging out at bars in my off time. A few times, I went out with a couple of women friends from high school, but it was discouraging when I was the one left alone at the end of the evening after they were both picked up by men on the prowl.

Driving home one night in my wreck of a car, I reasoned that a woman could have the finest of qualities and be a first-rate mate for some man, but if no men were attracted to her, they'd never find that out. For the first time, I started to think about not having a boyfriend and wondering if I'd grow old alone, without children. That, in itself, was an unusual phenomenon where I grew up.

My ego slipped a little more as the time passed, and I found myself going home with a few guys who'd been rejected by all the other women before the bars closed. Disappointed, as usual, I decided that I'd give my future to my work and forget anything to do with the male species. Then, one Friday night, while we were studying in the library, Raul suddenly closed the peer-reviewed article we were discussing. "I have something to talk to you about," he said quietly. My heart jumped. This was what I'd been waiting for; he was going to ask me out.

He looked around, then spoke even more quietly. "I need a favor, and you're really the only one I can ask. I don't know too many people here, and none of the ones I know are Americans, you know, full citizens here."

I listened, puzzled. This didn't sound like he was asking me for a date, but then, sometimes his English failed him. I waited for him to explain.

"See, I have a friend who needs to come here to the States. The conditions in his country are terrible, and he may be in some trouble. He doesn't have a way to enter this country—not legally, anyway. So, I was wondering … since you are legal here…"

I looked at him, puzzled. His green eyes were glowing under those long black lashes. He kept sweeping his thick, shiny hair off his forehead with a lean, well-muscled arm.

"I was thinking," he said, "if he could get to the Mexican border, maybe you could help me cross him over,"

"What?" I still didn't understand what he was talking about.

"Look," Raul explained, "I've been checking this out. Lots of people from Mexico cross over without papers. They never get stopped because they come back in with family or somebody who has papers. They don't ask everybody for papers. I think they only ask if someone looks suspicious."

I shook my head, mystified. I didn't know much about legal versus illegal back then. As far as I knew, most of my family was born here, and the ones who weren't, well, however they managed to come here and settle, it happened so long ago that nobody remembered.

Raul kept talking, "I have my visa, and you, well, you have your driver's license, and so if they stop you, you're safe. You just say that this guy is your friend and you went to Tijuana together. You didn't know he didn't have papers. Simple, right?"

He was watching my face very carefully, and as he spoke he

reached across the table and took my hand in his. I was so shocked by the gesture that I stopped listening to what he was saying.

The guy's name was Emilio, and he'd managed to travel from Argentina to Mexico, where he was waiting to cross into the United States.

"You mean he's there now?" I gasped.

"Yes. He's waiting, almost out of money. One more day, and he'll be sleeping in the street."

Raul reached across and twisted one of my kinky strands of hair around his finger. "I really need your help. It means so much to me. I need to help him, and I won't get another chance. It could be dangerous for him if he stays in Mexico any longer."

"Why?" I wanted to know. Meanwhile, I followed Raul's fingers as they traced a line up my arm, stopping just above the elbow.

"Argentina's a very repressive country. Emilio was involved in some protests, and they're looking for him."

"All the way in Mexico?" I was starting to feel warm, and not just from the sun that was setting directly outside the window.

"Yes," Raul assured me. "Actually, his life is in danger. Mexicans are always on the take. Somebody there would kill him for a few pesos."

I looked up, thinking that was sort of a racist remark, but then Raul was Latino himself. I didn't know anybody else from South America, so I didn't understand the animosity between the races like I do now. South Americans, like Cubans, seem to look down at Mexicans. I guess because they have that European blood we don't have. To them, Mexicans are just *Indios*.

"So, what do you say?" he wanted to know. "It's really simple. We drive down in the morning, have lunch, and drive back with Emilio. I want you to drive, and you can do the talking. Just act like yourself, an American student. Flirt with the border patrol if you need to. Just keep the attention off of Emilio."

I looked down at my hands, Raul was still stroking my wrist. "When do you want to do this?" I asked him.

"Tomorrow," he answered, "If we wait any longer, it might be too late."

"Tomorrow," I repeated, shocked. "I was scheduled to work all day."

"Call in sick. People do that here all the time, right?"

I looked out the window, thinking I never called in sick, so it should be okay. I looked back at Raul, thinking about how he'd never worked before and didn't need to.

"I guess so," I told him. My heart was starting to beat faster. I'd only been to Tijuana a few times with my family. My memories were of dirty sidewalks, skinny dogs, ragged little kids trailing after the tourists, and short Indian women with their babies wrapped in colorful shawls with several small kids hanging on, selling chewing gum to the Americans driving back across the border.

"We need to leave early," Raul said with authority. "How about you meet me at my house at seven tomorrow? The border should be crowded on the weekend, so it will be easier to push through. Another thing, dress really American, you know, like blue jeans and tennis shoes. Casual. Okay?"

"Okay," I answered, thinking that this was getting real too fast. I took the address he gave me written on a piece of notebook paper before we packed up and left the library. I thought all night about what he wanted me to do, barely sleeping. By morning, I was yawning and my eyes burned. I had that familiar sick feeling that I got when I'd stayed up too late and woke up early, but I called in sick at work, feeling guilty when my boss sounded concerned. Then I tried calling Raul and telling him that I didn't want to do it, but he didn't answer.

Driving all the way down the Santa Monica freeway to Santa Monica that Saturday morning, I decided that when I got there, I'd tell Raul I just couldn't do it. I'd changed my mind. He'd be upset, but I didn't feel good about it. Following his directions, I pulled up in front of a modest beachfront property with a huge wrap-around redwood deck you could see from the street. I thought about the amount of money it took to live in a place like this, and I envied Raul. Of course, if we were in a relationship, I'd get to be here all the time. Envisioning myself sunning on the deck, I rang the doorbell. Maybe I would do him this favor. Why not?

Raul opened the door and showed me around. The house was furnished with a decorator's skill, dark shades of Mexican tile and stained wood. Abstract art hung on the walls, and the kitchen was full of stainless-steel appliances. Raul sat me down at the gray-tiled bar and fixed me a piece of toast. Then he poured me a large glass of champagne from a bottle that he had just opened to celebrate Emilio's journey.

"Isn't it too early in the morning?" I said bashfully, thinking that this whole thing was special. I'd only had champagne at weddings before, and then just a few sips, which was all those little fluted glasses held.

"You Americans!" He scoffed. "You don't know how to appreciate life. In my country, we drink to celebrate waking up. Have another glass."

So, I did. I had two more, in fact, and we finished the bottle together. I was feeling flushed and anxious by then, as well as a little high. I was also very nervous. I couldn't remember doing anything out of my usual boring schedule of school and work for a long, long time. The idea of calling off the trip now had faded into thin air, leaving no memory of why I'd had that idea in the first place.

After he tossed the empty champagne bottle, Raul introduced me to his roommate, a skinny white guy named Harry with large black-framed glasses. He was slightly bald, and I noticed he had a bad case of acne, which made me touch my own face instinctively. Raul said his roommate was a corporate attorney. After seeing him, I decided that he wasn't Raul's gay boyfriend. Raul would never be with somebody so unattractive.

That made Raul even more mystifying to me.

"Okay, let's go," he called out to the deck, where I stood

mesmerized as the fog lifted, and I began to see the blue gray of the ocean. Seagulls circled the small yard at the rear of the house, shrieking and sometimes landing on the railing surrounding the deck. The planters were full of red and purple flowers, and pink blossoms that looked like crushed tissue paper climbed up a trellis leaning against the side of the house. I went back inside reluctantly, not wanting to give up the view or lose the warm buzz from the champagne.

I followed Raul out and started walking toward my car.

"No, not that one," Raul said sharply.

I turned around and he pointed at a new model black Mercedes parked at the curb. "That one."

I walked over to the car, too surprised to speak. Raul opened the driver's door and motioned me to sit down inside. I slid into the cream-colored leather and touched the wood-paneled dashboard respectfully as he handed me the key. "Whose is it?"

"Mine," he said. "Put on your seatbelt."

I belted myself in feeling like I was surrounded by luxury. "I thought the Volkswagen was yours." I remembered seeing him driving an older Volkswagen a few times when he'd parked near me.

"It is," he answered, "but I prefer to drive this one on longer trips."

I watched him out of the corner of my eye as I turned the key and pulled away from the curb. Those eyelashes were just unfair, and the color of his hair! I thought he looked more handsome than ever in a dark green sweater that picked up the color in his eyes and faded jeans. Masculine. Sexy. And here I was driving a car that I could never hope to own, with a stereo system playing music that sounded as if I was sitting in a concert hall.

We drove mostly in silence for the next few hours, stopping only once for gas and to use the bathroom. Raul kept looking around and twisting his knuckles. It was close to noon when we crossed over to Tijuana. Raul lit a cigarette and pulled out a sheet of notebook paper from his pocket.

"I'll give you directions. We're meeting him at a local bar."

I turned on the streets that he called out, and we stopped in front of a rundown saloon off of an alley with a neon sign hanging on the side of the building on rusty hinges that said "*Primos*." The letters were partially lit as if some of the bulbs had burned out. This wasn't one of those tourist bars that the Americans went to. A ratty-looking blanket hung from the door frame and partially covered the entrance. I didn't see any windows. Raul gave a handful of change to a couple of barefooted, shirtless boys around ten years old, and told them to watch the car.

When we walked inside, I saw a long scarred wooden bar and a few tables. The place was mostly empty because it was still early in the day. A few men wearing hats and beat-up cowboy boots sat at the bar drinking Mexican beers. They turned their weathered faces to stare at me as we picked a table and sat down in the corner.

Raul ordered two beers and I looked around. The place looked like an old movie set from some forgotten western, with a few Mexican blankets hanging from the wall and a couple of velvet nudes of naked girls with long black hair and tiny waists. Behind the bar, an old bartender hunched over the counter combing his greased-back hair with a black plastic comb and occasionally patted his sagging stomach that hung below his belt between his suspenders.

I barely took a drink when Raul called out, "Emilio, you're really here! I can't believe it!"

Emilio stepped out from the back of the bar, reached into his pocket, and handed the bartender something across the counter. Then he walked toward us out of the shadows. He hurried to Raul and the two hugged, teary-eyed. I watched unsure as they rocked back and forth.

"I thought I'd never see you again." Raul's voice was shaky as he wiped his eyes with the back of his wrist.

Emilio answered in Spanish, and for a moment, I watched the two, realizing there was a depth to their relationship that I hadn't experienced with anyone yet.

"This is my friend, Mona," Raul introduced me.

"*Mucho gusto,*" Emilio looked me over briefly and then dismissed me, his eyes drifting back to Raul and staying there.

As soon as he looked away, I gave him the once-over. He was medium height, had dirty-blond hair and dark brown eyes with heavy lids set in deep hollows and surrounded by dark circles. He looked exhausted. There was nothing really distinctive about him, but his clothes looked somehow off, European maybe.

"Let me get you a beer," Raul offered.

"No, forget it. I want to get out of here. People watching me; I've been here too long already." He answered in Spanish, his eyes darted around the bar, even though nobody seemed to be paying attention to us.

"Okay," Raul stood up in one quick motion, almost spilling my beer, which I hadn't touched. "Let's go."

We headed out. Raul told Emilio to sit in the seat next to me, and he told him to take off his sweater. "Change the station," he directed.

"What do you want to hear?"

"Rock and roll, really loud. You know, act like an American student. You look like one."

I tuned the radio to one of the top ten stations and cranked up the volume. The sound surrounded us. I glanced over at Emilio, but he was staring straight ahead, biting his nails. I was starting to get nervous myself. "Are you okay?" I looked toward Emilio.

"He doesn't speak much English," Raul answered for him.

I turned my eyes to the road ahead. "Isn't that going to be a problem if they stop us?" I glanced back in the rearview mirror and caught Raul's eye. Suddenly, I remembered hearing that you could go to jail for smuggling. Wasn't that what this was? I could see my family's face if I ended up a criminal. My mother would want to know why I did it, and I wouldn't have an answer. I remembered Raul's warm hand stroking my arm. Maybe that was the real reason.

Raul moved up close to the back of my seat. "The only thing they'll probably ask you is if you're a citizen of the United States, and what were you doing in Tijuana. That's about all. That's why I wanted you to drive. Usually, they don't ask any more questions if you can answer those."

I wanted to ask him if he'd done this before, but at the same time, I didn't want to know if another woman had sat in the same place and drove this car the way I was doing. I kept quiet and stared ahead. The line of cars ahead of us moved doggedly along, while small children and young girls, their heads covered in shawls darted between the cars, headed for the drivers, trying to sell *chicle* and Mexican candy to everyone heading back to the U.S.

As we got closer to crossing, Raul moved up and leaned over my seat, reminding me that he wanted me to do all the talking. He gestured toward Emilio, "We should be okay, we're both *rubios*. It's a good thing you're so dark; they won't pay any attention to us. If anybody looks illegal, it's you! Anyway, you have your California driver's license," he added and jammed a UCLA beanie on his head.

This was the first time that anybody told me my dark skin was a good thing. Except it was for the wrong reasons. Usually, my color was something whispered behind a cupped hand and I learned to be referred to as "the dark one, *La Negra*," when someone was pointing me out in a group. I flushed and gripped the steering wheel hard. My crush on Raul bottomed out. All I could hear was my mother complaining that I took after my dad, while my brothers and sisters were light like she was.

Hurt by what Raul said and starting to feel my old insecurities creeping back, I turned away and concentrated on moving closer to the line of men dressed in khaki and green, who stood in front of several single-story buildings and a couple of trailers, waving cars through or pointing them toward a second line to the rear of the buildings. Looking into the rearview mirror, I saw Raul sit up straighter in the back seat while next to me, Emilio slunk down in the passenger seat looking sullen.

I turned the radio up louder, and in my best Academy-worthy performance, I began to move to the music, rolling my shoulders and snapping my fingers. I was in too far to stop now and might as well do it right. As we pulled up to the Border Patrol officers lined up, a few feet apart, I slipped on my best smile while I stepped on the brakes.

As we approached the first two officers, I heard one of them addressing the other in a deep baritone, his hands choked up on an invisible baseball bat, swinging at an imaginary baseball with a twist of his body. "You can't take it away from Ron Cey; I'm telling you, just put your money on him. You can't go wrong."

The other Border Patrol officer who was standing with his hands locked behind his back walked over to our car. He was young, one of those white guys who look like they stepped right off the tractor on the farm or off some Marine recruiting poster, with rosy cheeks, a blond crew cut, and big biceps. This one almost smiled a little, stretching the corners of his mouth for a moment and pointed at me. "Miss, do you mind turning down that radio, please?"

I turned down the volume, feeling my hands start to shake as he stepped closer to the car. His eyes were a dark blue and they stared right through me.

"Are you coming from Tijuana? How long were you there?"

"Just for today," I told him.

"Tourist?"

"Yes, I guess so."

"You're a citizen of the United States?" He looked at me intently, not taking his eyes away.

I instinctively tried to smooth down my wild frizzy hair, knowing he probably thought that I was too dark-skinned to be born in the U.S.

"Let me see your identification, please."

"I'm a citizen," I answered while I reached across the seat to pick up my purse with shaking hands. This wasn't going well. What was Emilio going to do? I was going to be charged with smuggling him across. Emilio didn't look at me, but kept his eyes glued to something far away. Glancing in the rearview mirror, I saw Raul looking off to the side, his thick blond hair covering his face.

As I reached into my purse and pulled out my license, I noticed the officer's eyes had shifted from me to the road ahead of us. I heard a loud siren go off and saw a blur of dark green and khaki running from the buildings and the surrounding trailers. Raul and Emilio kept their heads down, not moving a muscle.

"You can go." The blue-eyed officer looked at me doubtfully, hastily taking in my frizzy black hair and my dark skin one more time. He ran his eyes over my passengers without interest. I could see he wanted to spend time questioning me more. Just me, but instead, he took off running in the direction the others were going. The siren kept wailing and a few more vehicles carrying other agents pulled up near the buildings and ran inside.

Without being asked, I stepped on the gas and drove away from the officers standing near the trailers as quickly as I could. Looking back in the mirror, I saw another group of agents pulling up in their all-terrain vehicles and taking their places at the head of the line to question the occupants of the cars waiting to cross. My heart was thudding, and a cold sweat broke out on my forehead and down my back.

Raul threw back his head and roared with laughter. "I knew when I saw you, *Negrita*, you'd bring us good luck. *Gracias Dios!* Who would imagine there'd be an emergency? The gods are with us today!"

I didn't say a word. I just kept thinking of what would have happened if the border agent didn't stop with questioning me and asked Emilio for identification too. Except the only one the agent seemed interested in was me. Raul knew that already. Somehow, even though he was raised someplace else, in a place I knew practically nothing about, in a wealthy home, he knew there was a good chance that my color would be the distraction

Emilio needed. Like he said, the gods were with us. It seemed that the gods had been with him his whole life.

We drove back through Orange County, Raul leaning over the front passenger seat to talk with Emilio, who was now relaxed and leaning back in his seat, enjoying the sun on his face.

"We should stop for a drink before we get to LA," Raul suggested. "We need to celebrate. Emilio here is finally free from his wife."

"What?" I wasn't sure I'd heard right. Emilio was married?

As if he read my mind Raul answered my question. "Sometimes we do what is necessary to survive." He reached forward and ruffled Emilio's hair lovingly.

I looked back at the road ahead, feeling embarrassed that I'd been so confused.

"And you can stop calling him Emilio. His real name is Oscar." Raul laughed loudly and leaned forward to translate for Emilio/Oscar. They hugged across the seat divider.

I made an excuse about an early date and said I didn't have time for a drink or dinner when we arrived at Raul's house. I raced home and bought a bottle of cheap Kamchatka vodka, pulled the shades and did my best to drink it all. After a while, I didn't feel much of anything.

A couple of years later, I was driving east on Sunset to pick up my husband's favorite *Dulce Leche* cake at Tropical to celebrate our first anniversary. I knew he'd be late getting home from a departmental meeting, and I had a bottle of champagne chilling to surprise him. Mateo was Chairman of American Studies at Claremont College, the first Chicano to hold that position in the history of the department. He was popular with faculty and students, and his future in academia was all sewed up. We'd met at a faculty Christmas party when I had reached a place in my life where I no longer worried about being alone. In a crazy way, I felt like I'd come out of a relationship with Raul and I wasn't looking for another one. And then there was Mateo. He was holding court with a gathering of females watching his every move as he told stories about funny questions students asked him. He smiled at me, showing dimples and huge dark eyes. His hair curled over his collar in the sexiest way. He brought me a drink, and we talked through the rest of the party, then spent the next few hours at a quiet bar downtown. After that, we were inseparable. Mateo loves me just the way I am. Outside of his academic career, I am the most important thing in his life. I can look ahead and imagine us as two old and wizened beings, still in love.

On that day on my way to the bakery, I had an urge to see the Boulevard again, the trashy lingerie shops, the over-priced hot dog stands, and the endless roll-up metal gates in front of shops filled with monogrammed T-shirts, cups, and balloons. I stopped at a newsstand. There were so few now that it was a novelty to see the *LA Times*, the *New York Times*, and the *Chicago Sun* stacked neatly on display. A young man on the front page of the *LA Times* looked familiar and I stared wondering how I knew him. It was Emilio, or rather Oscar—his real name. The headline above the picture shook me to the core. "Argentine National Extradited for Murder of Wife." I read on; Oscar was being extradited to stand trial for the murder of his wife by blunt force trauma in Argentina. He'd reported her missing, but her body had been located in the foundation of a property undergoing renovation. The article said he'd made an insurance claim and forged his wife's name to get a loan and that the police had followed a paper trail that led to the United States. I reread the dates. Oscar had already been wanted for murder when I drove him across the border. I recalled Raul's comment about doing what was necessary to survive.

"Miss, are you buying that paper or renting space here? Which is it?" An old man in a pork pie hat called out to me, tapping the side of the cash register impatiently.

I looked up, guilty, like I knew something I wasn't supposed to and hastily folded the paper and stuck it back in the rack. I walked away without turning around. I'd been given a chance to sneak away without being caught, just like that time I crossed the border.

A few months later, I started teaching at state college—two classes with no benefits, but I was grateful. The first time I walked into the staff lounge, I ran into the chubby guy from my doctoral class. He hurried over excitedly and hugged me. He was working as a TA, joining the rest of the ranks in "hoping something would open up soon." We commiserated about the lack of jobs, and then he lowered his voice and looked around.

"Remember that Raul guy? The one you studied with?"

"Yes."

"I heard he died of AIDS. He was apparently sick for quite a while, but it didn't show till the end. He had some problems with not completing his units, and they were holding back his doctorate, so he went to the department head in person to clear it up. They said he was a walking skeleton, covered with sores, and bald, too. He could barely walk, they said."

I felt a chill rush over me that made my jaw clench. I could feel Raul's fingers slowly trailing up my arm, see his deep green eyes watching me, and tears came. I felt them on my cheeks, and I wiped them back quickly. "That's awful," I said. "I hope they find out how to cure that disease."

I don't think about Raul much anymore, but I am sad about what happened to him. I know he used me, taking advantage of my insecurities, but somehow, I'm stronger for having known him. Everybody needs to be forgiven sometimes, and it would be worse never to have met him. I remember that once upon a time, a truly gorgeous guy sought me out and made me feel good about myself, if only for a little while. Sometimes you do what's necessary to survive. That's what Raul taught me.

Looking for the Reason

When I got back from Iraq, everybody kept asking me what it was like there. They all wanted to hear about the body count, the blood and gore, how close I'd come to getting blown away every day. Sometimes I thought they talked to me because they felt guilty, awkward around me, or just plain sorry for me. I came back from a different world, one that they'd only read about. I hated it when they said "Thank you for your service." I smiled and tried to say something funny, tried to meet the expectation in their eyes. They didn't care, not really. They just wanted to be entertained. They didn't know that I'd left that part of me behind, that I never wanted to talk about it, that I couldn't tell them what it was really like. The memories were too hard to believe, so I said to myself that maybe what I remembered didn't actually happen. Except some of the time, the memories wouldn't stop showing up, not with time or the counseling I got through my insurance plan that came along with a temporary job that ran out a few months back. That's when they put me on the waitlist at the VA. I'm still waiting.

The screener doing intake at the VA asked me why I joined the service. I don't know if that was a standard question they ask when they take a case history or whether she was just curious because I'm a woman. I told her I joined up because all my cousins enlisted when they were young. It's sort of a tradition in our family, just like going to college is a tradition in other families, and I know it's a tradition in my community, at least with those of us who are second and third generation. Usually just the males go. I just happened to be the first female among my cousins at the time when the military finally started recognizing that women had something to contribute. Besides, I didn't care much for school and didn't have a trade. I didn't even have a steady boyfriend, who would put me on the marriage track and make my mother happy. When she complained about me not settling down and getting married I told her I wasn't like a sofa somebody bought that fit into a room wherever it was placed. That's how I saw it then. And those were the few marriages I knew that were still going on.

The memories that I just couldn't let go of weren't the rocket and mortar attacks or the ambushes or the firefights. It was the time we spent hiding out in the mountains. While we hid we planned out our ambushes, but at the same time we were making our plans for attack, we also worked on destroying any feelings of compassion or mercy for humanity.

My last assignment was in Al Taqaddum, an airfield in Iraq located in the Anbar Province. We were there as part of a task force to advise and assist the Iraqi forces. My company helped the bomb disposal technicians dismantle roadside bombs. When my team member, the new father of a six-month-old baby he'd never seen, volunteered to dismantle the first one sighted, it exploded, killing him on contact. The rest of my team ran to the site, but I couldn't bring myself to look at the pieces of his body and his blood sprayed randomly in the dirt. I hid in the corner of the framework of a building that we'd blown up to teach the Iraqis the skilled use of explosives, and I wished he'd given me the small photo of his son that he always carried. It was something that I could have given to his son, a souvenir from someone he never knew, who loved him.

The images that stayed stuck in my mind were the real problem: blood splattered on the walls, the pieces of skull and other body parts, whatever remained of the humans who lived in that bombed-out house we raided. That, and the heads that Al-Qaeda and the militant Sunnis tossed out into the street. It's better now, I hardly see those images anymore. When I did, I wondered if I'd have the courage to end the crazy world going round in my head with my service revolver, a Springfield XD .40

caliber pistol. I imagined that I'd press my thumb to the release mechanism and slide in the magazine. Then I'd cock it and jack a round into the chamber. If I didn't have the courage, I'd put my weapon back in the drawer—try again later. I worried then that I might not know when it was time before I freaked out and did something really destructive, something crazy. Carl Bergen, who was on my tour, waited too long. He lost it late one afternoon, got in his car and started driving like a madman. After nearly causing a number of accidents driving the wrong way on the freeway, he made it over to the church that his family used to attend. He poured gasoline up and down the pews and then lit some matches. He insisted to the police that arrested him that the enemy was waiting there, hiding, planning to ambush his company. He was just trying to flush them out.

Luckily for him, nobody was killed, but the eleven-year-old altar boy who was straightening up for the evening service was badly burned. He's disfigured and scarred for life I heard. Some of the guys that I keep in touch with say they're doing skin grafts since some of the burns are healed, but that he's still terrible to look at, his skin puckered and waxen. Not really looking like a human being now.

Now Carl is on psych meds for the rest of his life, meds that make him calmer, less reactive, that dull his responses, so he won't pull anything like that again. But you can't convince me that the meds will block out the guilt he's going to carry as long as he lives.

I got a job right away when I came back but lost it after just two weeks because I couldn't concentrate. Sometimes when I was moving items down the conveyor belt at Walmart, I'd forget where I was and just stopped and stared off into space. I really wasn't thinking about anything in particular; it was like my brain just came to a standstill. The customers were complaining so they put me in the back to stock shelves. I couldn't keep the merchandise in the correct order for stocking on the shelves and kept mixing up the boxes, so they let me go.

I was back living with my mother in her cramped apartment in Venice, the decaying area of a once bohemian beach town that the hipsters hadn't yet taken over. Government housing, really. I unloaded my duffel bag in the corner of her second bedroom that was empty now. My sister Lucia moved out and was living with a roommate. She was going to Cal State LA, my mother informed me somewhat reluctantly. She would rather tell me there was a wedding date set, but college counted as something to brag about. Lucia was her favorite and always had been. She was never lost, never floundered around like I did. Lucia wasn't looking for her way out. She was always on her path since she started to walk. We hadn't talked since I came home, and then not much before. We kind of ran out of conversation after I told her I didn't know what I was going to do next. I'd gone as far as the service, now I was wondering if there were no more places to run to.

My mother told me in a lowered voice the day I arrived that I wasn't supposed to be living there with her. The managers required her to take Lucia's name off the Section Eight lease and she had to move out. Unauthorized tenants were against the housing rules and my mother said she would probably be forced to move. Mrs. Garcia down the hall was forced to move when she allowed her son and her grandson to move in with her so they wouldn't end up in the street. I promised I'd be quiet and stay out of sight. Anyway, I lost my job and couldn't afford my own place, so I slept in a sleeping bag on top of her chenille bedspread and listened to my radio with headphones.

My mother said I was the biggest disappointment in her life, next to my father, but then she was always going on about how everything had turned out so badly for her, so I figured that I had a lot of competition. My mother couldn't imagine why life brought her so many sorrows and pointed out how much she had sacrificed for her children, how much heartache she'd suffered, just like the heroines in the *novelas* she watched religiously. It was just her destiny. God's wish.

She wanted me, her oldest daughter, to get married and pump out a handful of grandkids. She didn't know that one of my real reasons for joining the service was to find a new family, some stability and maybe a place where I fit, to say nothing of a break from the constant tears, complaints and sorrows that she claimed to endure. When I was on active duty, I worried about her because I wasn't there to step in if the drama got out of hand. That was my job and it had been since my father left.

My mother was drawn to drama, like those long-running television serials that have it all: arguments, gossip, back-stabbing, jealousy, and revenge. She was demanding in a whiny, passive way. Seldom content, she generally didn't get along with the neighbors and had a terrible habit of encouraging them to spill their secrets and then letting others know whatever dirt she heard in confidence. And it was even worse with our relatives.

So many Christmas Eves ended with her crying or making some other woman in our family cry. She reached out as far as Mexico to disagree with the relatives there and heap distress on them. She argued long distance with my father who lived there now or so I heard. Truthfully, I could see why he wouldn't want to come back, even though I still missed him.

Before he left, the evenings were filled with "Who are you cheating with now? Don't try and lie to me, I know better!" She'd start in as soon he sat down to watch television. She'd been waiting for him, armed with all the gossip from the neighbor women placing him with somebody younger, prettier, probably nicer too. When he denied it, tears would start running from her eyes. He would push her away, get up and leave. "You see how bad he treats me?" she'd whine.

I didn't see that, but I did see and hear the same complaints from the women around me. My mother spent most of her spare time in church and the rest arguing with my father. When I was small, he came home from work every day and sat at the table while my sister did her lessons and I ran around crazily, trying to find an outlet for all my energy. He'd pick me up and ride me around on his shoulders. At night he was the one who tucked us in and sang some song in Spanish that I didn't understand but put me to sleep. After a while he didn't come home very much. Nobody rode me around on their shoulders or sang to me at night. Then when I was a teenager he didn't come home again.

"I knew he'd leave me," my mother told anyone who would listen. "At least he waited a while." She said she took his cheating for so long because that's what a woman does when she marries. "I took an oath in the church," she used to say

Later on, there were other men in our life, men she met in the factory, men who worked as dishwashers or waxed cars at the car washes, My mother was always happy at first with every new boyfriend, then there was the usual sound of good-byes, followed by her wailing and the crash of dishes being thrown at a closing door.

Some of the men she saw, and some that we knew through friends and family had wives and other families in Mexico but were lonely here and now. That was just the way it was, even though it was still frowned upon here and in Mexico, people looked away, pretending the other reality didn't exist. Some of these men left the U.S. after earning some money that they sent back home, lonely for family and missing the way things were down there. Some stayed in Mexico for good, and a few kept both sets of families. I had friends who had a few half-brothers and sisters across the border. My mother and her friends whispered about it all the time, along with naming the men who were cheating on their wives or girlfriends, information they usually got third hand but most of the time turned out to be true.

You could see early on that if anybody was going to live a different life than my mother and I, it was my sister, Lucia. She was always the smart one. No way in hell would she ever end up joining the service. Small-boned, delicate, and studious, with her hair tied back at the nape of her neck and her tinted wire-rim glasses, she kept her head down and concentrated on getting the highest marks in her class. She never wanted to play, to run the streets like me with the other rough kids playing disorganized games and not doing their schoolwork. Later on, she flat-out wasn't interested in boys and didn't care for makeup or sexy clothes.

"I have time for that stuff later, it's not in my plans right now," she told me as I dressed to go out with my friends, excited that I could now drink legally and sneak around with guys that my mother wouldn't let in the house. Her resolve's paid off so far. She's always worked a part-time job, gotten glowing recommendations, and stuck it out at college. I'm sure when she graduates college she'll marry some perfect guy she met in one of her classes. He'll wash dishes, help her with the housework, and later change the baby's diaper. He wouldn't dream of cheating. They'll honeymoon in Paris, cover the accent wall of their condo with their wedding pictures and later on, pictures of their grandkids. My mother will shake her head and think he's not masculine enough, but she'll be so proud that Lucia is fulfilling her duty as a woman and she'll probably expect to live with my sister as she gets older. That's how it's done.

My mother's on state disability now. She injured her hands and wrists spending years bent over some machine that ground out parts for assembly in stereos. All day long she connected those tiny parts with special tools, grasping, fitting, and screwing them together, her wrists swollen and aching every night. Then one morning she could barely move her hands, couldn't hold a coffee cup or a comb. They sent her to a fitness-for-duty exam. She didn't pass. Now she stayed home and when she wasn't watching *novelas*, gossiping with the women who lived nearby, or down on her knees in the church a few blocks over, she was arguing with her sisters on the phone.

The second day I was there, my mother offered to go with me to buy some decent clothes after she bundled up my uniforms and put them in a plastic bag. I knew she meant something with a skirt, short enough to show off my legs. "Men like to look at legs. Better show them before you get old and nobody wants to look at them anymore."

She told me she'd pay me from her disability check to cut my *trensas*. She said the braids made me look like a *campesina*, a fieldworker. I resisted cutting them. I'd spent countless time in Iraq, sitting and waiting, scratching my scalp and pulling the unwashed braids over my shoulder, burning the individual broken ends with a match. It was self-destructive and satisfying at the same time. I made a point of keeping my hair braided because I knew she didn't approve. Giving in was like letting her make me less of myself.

Things settled down after all the *tías*, *tíos*, and *primos* stopped coming around to see for themselves how I was when I returned. Two of my male cousins were still over there completing their last tour, and my youngest cousin, who never really learned to read and left school when he was fourteen, came home in a bag. "No," I told them. "I'm not enlisting again. I'm through with the service." Whatever I thought I was looking for, I didn't find.

I was sitting on the couch wrapped in a beat-up gray blanket that I'd dug out of the hall closet, watching *Dora the Explorer* reruns, losing myself in the cartoon, while the tightness in my muscles took a break when my mother got the call about my father and Ray.

Now my father lives permanently in Mexico, which he said was his real home anyway. He never applied for his legal residency here because he said it would be wrong and disloyal. He would always be a Mexican and a piece of paper would not make him an American. He had faith that one day his country would step up and overthrow all the corruption and take care of its people. His family had a small grocery there, and he said they needed his help to run it.

My mother, who was born here, only went to Mexico twice, the first time to follow my father and convince him to come back here and live with her again. I just turned fifteen and she left Lucia with me and traveled south. She was pregnant, almost in her last month at the time, and my little brother Ray was born there. I guess she was able to cross with him without a hassle then. The thought of her crossing with a new baby, risking both of them, was something I could never understand. I accepted it though because she was bringing him here.

The second time she went back to Mexico, she took Ray to see his father. Ray was five and my father said that he wanted to see his son but couldn't get enough money together to cross over, so she took Ray to him.

She said she left Ray there for a few weeks so he would get to know his father and she planned to go back and cross into the U.S. with him. Around then they started cracking down at the border and Ray, of course, didn't have a U.S. birth certificate, so she put it off hoping things would get better. They didn't. They just got worse when the new president was elected and started cracking down on immigrants. So, they waited some more, and two years passed. Ray was starting to forget his life here. He only knew my mother now by her voice over the phone.

When I first came home, my mother wanted me to call Mexico and talk to Ray on the phone, let him know I was his older sister, impress him by telling him I was in the military. So, I called and tried to talk to a little boy I didn't know. It didn't go well. He didn't speak much English, and I racked my brain, asking him a lot of stupid questions trying to get him to talk. All he said was "hi." He stayed silent when I asked him about his favorite cartoon and what grade he was in at school. I guess things are different in Mexico because he didn't seem to know what I was talking about.

I know my mother missed Ray and thought she'd made a big mistake by leaving him with his father. She started saying that if he grew up there he'd end up with no education and no way to get ahead in life. What she said made sense, but before I went to the Service, I overheard her arguing on the phone with my father, and I thought that it was probably more likely Ray was the link that tied her to my father and gave her a reason to keep some kind of relationship with him.

As soon as I got home, my mother let me know that my father

had a big problem now. He said the local gangs were demanding bigger and bigger payoffs every week to allow his family to keep the store open. He said that at first, they were able to make the payments even when the gangs increased their demand, but then the demands got outrageous. Finally, when they couldn't pay anymore, one of the collectors told them that the store would be burned down and maybe somebody would be killed.

Overnight, he said, his family shut down the market, and my father grabbed my brother and left for the United States. He told my mother he would try to get asylum here because of the threat from the gangs. When he finally reached the border at Nuevo Laredo, which was the only entry point for asylum seekers, he called my mother. Everybody coming to the U.S. for political asylum was being sent back to Mexico to wait for their hearings. My father was stuck with my little brother in the government building. He said he was afraid to leave because kidnappers were grabbing people as they returned to Mexico and kidnapping them for ransom. My father told her he was scared that he and Ray would be kidnapped as soon as they left the American side because he could see men who looked like kidnappers sitting in their SUVs lined up beyond the borderline. Then his phone lost reception.

Now, this brings me back to the next call, the one I overheard because I was sitting right there with my mother. She answered her cell phone on the first ring as soon as she saw my father's number. I know she hadn't been sleeping much since my father and Ray were stuck at the border. When she got the second call I heard her gasp and then put her hand to her mouth. Her other hand was shaking so badly she could hardly hold the phone.

"I don't have any money! What do you want me to do?" She was yelling into the phone and starting to sob.

I grabbed the phone, afraid of what I would hear. "Who is this?" My heart was pounding while I waited to hear an answer. There was a pause, the caller realizing that someone else was on the line.

"Who are you?" I yelled into the cheap cell phone that my mother had carried for as long as I could remember.

The answer hit me like a punch to the stomach. The voice spoke in English "Joaquin Barrios gave us this number to call. We have him and his son here with us. If you want to see them again, we need nine thousand for him and eight for the boy. If you call any police, I promise you'll never see them alive again."

I looked over at my mother, her arms were wrapped around her chest, and her eyes were full of tears. "What did they tell you?" She wailed. "The same thing they told me? My poor little Ray."

I stared at the phone, trying to make sense of what I'd just heard. Kidnapping was something you saw in the movies or on some television program. It couldn't be real. "How do I know you really have them there?" I could hear my own voice, a few words behind, coming through a speaker.

It was quiet; then, I heard a thumping sound and a voice that I barely recognized, frightened, shaking, full of dread. He was crying and I could her the terrible panic in his voice. I recognized the sound of his fear, different than any other. The distinct fear parents carry with them until they die, I'd seen it up close, smelled it radiating off their skin, mothers pleading for their sons' lives, watching soldiers hold guns to their child's head demanding to know whom they were helping, cocking the trigger when they didn't hear the answer they wanted.

"*Mija*, it's been a long time since I talked to you. Things are really bad here." His voice trailed off.

I blinked and tried to swallow past the lump in my throat. This was happening now, hours away from here by airplane. They were really in trouble. Fatal trouble if you followed the news on television. I'd fought one war over there and now I was back watching another one unfold, except there were no platoons of soldiers rushing toward the battle, just my mother and I on the other end of a cell phone.

I hadn't heard my father's voice for years now. When I was small, he always called me his little princess. For a long time after he was gone, even though I was a teenager, I wanted to hear him say that to me again. Something inside of me broke when he left. Something was missing, imperfect. It still is.

On the day I came back, my aunt told me behind a cupped hand that my father had another family in Mexico, another woman and two young daughters. My mother wouldn't talk about it. My aunt said my little brother didn't even remember my mother or my sister anymore. He certainly didn't remember me. Lucia said she caught my mother talking on the phone late at night and she wasn't yelling or fighting with my father anymore. Just crying.

"What's going on?" I could hear my own voice shaking as I waited for my father to speak.

There was a brief silence, and then his voice again, slow and sad, almost dull. "They want nine thousand dollars for me and eight thousand for Ray."

"You mean to let you go?" I could feel the anger starting, tightening the muscles in my arms and legs, my stomach stirring, followed by nausea. "Are you all right? What about Ray?"

"We're okay. Ray's pretty scared. Look, I know none of you have any money. But that's how they play this. I'm sorry." His voice broke and she heard sobbing coming through alternating with static.

There was a sudden sound of shuffling, and I heard the voice of the man I spoke to first, rough, clipped. "That's enough! You heard him. I want that money by tomorrow. I told you where you'll meet the guy I send to pick it up. If you don't show, I'll shoot them. It's no big deal to me. One more or less."

My mother wiped her tears with the back of her hand. She pointed to a pad of paper sitting on the corner of the kitchen table with some writing on it. "Please," she yelled in the direction of the phone in my hand. "My son is just a baby."

There was no answer except the silence that meant the man on the other end had hung up.

"I can't believe this," I said, suddenly my legs felt cold and numb. "We need to call the cops."

"No cops," my mother shouted. "I need to try and get that money."

"How can you do that?" I yelled back. "Who do you know that has that kind of money just sitting around?"

"I'm calling everybody in the family. We'll get it somehow."

I could feel anger like liquid heat, moving up my body. My hands jammed deep into the pocket of my sweats, reached for my service revolver that wasn't there. "I don't understand how you could leave Ray there anyway. How could you do that?"

My mother sat down at the kitchen table and picked up the piece of paper, turning it over in her hands. "Your father wanted to see him. I wanted Ray to have a father!" She started to cry, trying to explain. "It wasn't like now. Everybody was still going back and forth."

"Some father! He didn't even want to live in this country. He left, and he has another family over there now for heaven's sake!" I glared at her. She turned her face away and stared out the narrow window to another apartment building next door that looked exactly like the one where we were living. Then she picked up her phone book from its place on the table, the phone book that had everybody in this family's address and phone number.

I watched her, for the first time I realized that I wasn't just sad, I was angry too. Did she still love my father after he left? Was that the reason she chased him all the way to Mexico and used Ray to try and get him to come back? Was he a cheater the way she said? I wanted to know, to understand why.

I tried to picture my father the way I remembered him, but all I could see remember was his carefully combed black hair. What I saw instead were the images of blood-spattered walls in the bombed-out buildings I'd left behind—body parts in the street. A drunk Navy SEAL was taking pictures of the twisted forms of a woman and her little boy to send home to his brothers.

My father was in Mexico. Life goes on, or maybe it doesn't. I still loved him or perhaps I loved someone I knew nothing about. Somebody who left us. I wondered if he called his daughters in Mexico princesses too.

I turned away from my mother and looked across the hall so she wouldn't see me crying. I pretended to study the pile of washed-out denim and thick fleece twisted up in the laundry basket on top of my bed.

My mother started phoning the family right away. By the next day, after begging and pleading on behalf of Ray, she had collected almost nineteen hundred dollars, including the three hundred and twelve I was saving to move out. I stayed out of the room when the kidnappers called, and she told them how much she had, but I could hear her crying and pleading. She wanted them to understand she just couldn't come up with any more money. They put my father on the line and gave her one more day to raise it.

She came up with another hundred dollars the following day and they called her again. They hung up on her when she told them how much she had. She sat down at the kitchen table and sobbed over and over that they were going to kill Ray. I hadn't slept much in the last couple of days. My nerves were raw, and I felt as if I was exploding out of my skin. "I'm going to the police," I told her. In my mind, my brother and father were already dead.

"No," she screamed. "That will finish them!"

"We need to bring in the cops now! You're going with me. They have to know that people getting sent back to Mexico to wait are being kidnapped. Somebody will pay attention!" I couldn't take being this helpless, like my mother, waiting on someone else to call the moves, not after Iraq. I couldn't feel dangerous one moment and vulnerable the next.

We started toward the car. I grabbed the keys because I could see my mother's hands were shaking as if an electric current was running through her body. Just as I was locking the door, her phone rang. She grabbed it from her purse and held it to her ear, her eyes wide with expected grief. It was my father. Something had happened. One of the kidnappers was shot by a *Fedérale*, probably because he didn't bother to split his take on another kidnapping. The other one, who was guarding my father and Ray in an apartment near the border, decided to let them go. He told my father he didn't trust anybody else to collect the money, and he was afraid the same *Fedérales* would come looking for him. My father told my mother to wire him whatever money she raised, and he would try to have a *coyote* take Ray across. He told her it cost seven thousand dollars, but he would try and make a deal somehow. It was too dangerous for Ray to stay in Mexico.

My mother went back inside and sat down at the table. She sat sobbing into her arms, folded on the tabletop, and kissed a picture of Ray that she took out of her photo album.

I was stunned. "Are you really going to wire him the money?" I demanded. "It doesn't make sense. None of it. And now he wants more money to pay a *coyote*?"

I remembered the fear in this voice but then I thought about how he left us alone here and didn't want to come back, not even for me. Now he wanted money to send Ray here by himself with men who crossed people for money and sometimes left them in the desert to die. So dangerous. If that was really what he wanted to do. How could you know? My mother and my aunts were right about men. I'd heard it all my life; you couldn't trust them. I couldn't trust what he said now. "I didn't know you were sending him money. Why didn't you tell me?"

She looked up, surprised. her face drawn and sad, her eyes swollen and bloodshot. "I always try to do what's best for Ray."

"Trying?" I shot back. "Between the both of you, you're going to get him killed down there." I thought of the little boy in Iraq, Mo, with his large eyes and long lashes, wearing clothes that were just dirty rags, who followed our company everywhere, eating what we ate, and sleeping wherever we slept. A car bomb killed Mo's mother and father a year before. One day, running ahead of us back down the mountain, he stepped on an explosive. The guys scrapped together his pieces and dug him a small grave. I didn't watch.

"You really are a fool," I yelled at her. "Don't send him any more money. He's just using you. He's never coming back. Don't you know that?"

"You don't understand," My mother spat out as she walked away to her bedroom and closed the door without looking back. I knew she would send the money, and more later if he asked. It didn't matter what I said, and it didn't matter if you could see he was lying. Wasn't he?

The next morning, she woke me early and told me she was going to Mexico herself "to straighten everything out." She told me, "You watch, I'll arrange to cross Ray myself."

I told her she was wasting her time. She should just forget about it. She was crazy to go. It was dangerous there, and really dangerous to cross Ray. He was just a little boy. Of course, she insisted on going. "You're wrong," she said. She needed to bring her son back, whatever it took.

I accused her of only wanting to see my father again. "Any excuse because you can't get over him being with someone else." She reached out to slap me, but I ducked.

After calling one of her sisters to borrow money for the bus fare, she took off and was gone for nearly a week. The apartment was quiet, but I was uneasy, even more than usual. I kept thinking that you can't be vulnerable without somebody taking advantage of you. Twice I dreamed that I was walking through the villages in Iraq at night by myself but this time I had no weapon.

The following Sunday, I was sitting on the tiny balcony in the living room, smoking a cigarette and blowing the smoke into the street. I watched as it started to grow dark, feeling as if my empty life extended no further than the apartment door. The old images I brought back from Iraq were weaker every day, evaporating in my memory. They were replaced by new ones of my father and Ray at the end of a gun. I was a different person than when I returned, complicated, unwieldy.

Just as it turned dark, a small figure emerged from the darkness, walking toward the apartment building. As it came closer,

I saw my mother bent over carrying her worn out overnight bag from the bus stop four blocks away. I watched her look up at the building and then slowly walk up the stairs. Alone.

I ran down to meet her, taking the stairs two at a time. Under the overhead corridor lights, I could see gray strands seeded through her black hair that hadn't been there before. She looked thinner and her eyes were sunken, surrounded by lines. I grabbed her bag and helped her to the couch. She suddenly seemed so much older to me, broken, but struggling to stay upright. For the first time in as long as I could remember, she didn't begin to whine when she spoke. She was strangely calm. I blinked back my own tears and listened.

I expected to hear that she'd payed money to some *coyote* and Ray would be snuck across any day now. But instead she said Ray wasn't coming home. He didn't want to leave his father. He loved him and wanted to stay with him in Mexico. They were so close. Ray was sure he didn't want to come to the United States, even after she asked him over and over and showed him some pictures of Disneyland that she thought would change his mind. He chose his father over the promised trip. She'd left my father the money she collected. Maybe Ray would change his mind later and my father could pay somebody to cross him. Anyway, they needed money to live on. Ray needed shoes. He'd outgrown his clothes. She saw that herself. "If your father spends it on something else then it wasn't meant for Ray to come back here. It's all in the hands of God," she told me. "And I know what you're thinking," She said, her eyes still on my face, "You don't believe in God, but you should. He's the reason you came back from that place, that war. You're healthy, you have your arms and legs ..." She gestured in the air, "And it's not that dangerous where they're living. Not that much cartel activity. Maybe not as safe as here, but people live there you know, just like they do anywhere. They manage."

I thought back to the ruined streets and crumbling buildings which were all the kids ever saw in Iraq. They played in those ruins, ran, chasing each other, threw stones, and laughed. The places were all too similar in my mind.

"Karina," my mom began hesitating with each word. "I need to tell you something. Your father's family owed a debt to some people over there. Those people hired some guys to try and collect it. It wasn't the gangs or the cartel trying to extort money like he told me before. He must have been scared though. That's why I sent him money, whatever I could, before you came back. He said he'd pay back the money I sent him when he had it. He didn't know when that would be. See, he's trying," she said.

I stared at her trying to understand what she was telling me.

"The good news is we don't have to worry about Ray because he's safe," she told me calmly. "But your aunt was right. Your father's married to another woman, and this woman owns a business that handles money wires from the United States. He's running the business for her now. He says he has no interest in coming back to the U.S. again. Anyway, he has two daughters and a wife there to take care of. I saw them," she finished weakly, tears starting to run down her face.

"What about the kidnapping?" I demanded, anger making me choke.

My mother shrugged and looked down. "They kidnap people all the time there. Everybody's struggling. They always need money. You know how it is. Get it any way you can. They call some girl's parents here and tell them they have their daughter. They're going to kill her if the family doesn't send money. That didn't change when you were gone."

"I didn't ask you what they do to everybody else. I asked you about Ray. Was it true or not?" My voice was shrill. I was standing on the edge and the earth was slipping away from me, faster, every time she spoke.

Her eyes met mine and I saw the dejection and sorrow there. "This is what it means to be a mother," she answered instead. "Only God can judge who's telling the truth."

I tried to call up the picture of the kind, smiling man who

used to tell me I was his little princess. Her words were like a giant eraser, sweeping away every memory and replacing them with something else I didn't want to believe. He hadn't told my mother the truth when she was sending him money before and maybe not about the kidnapping either. The good feelings I got remembering him slowly emptied out, packed up.

"I had to help him because of Ray." She started crying. "You don't know what it's like to have kids. That's how it is when you're married. You don't give up."

I didn't know if I was angrier at him or her. "It still your fault he left to begin with!" I yelled back. "You made it so miserable here. No wonder he wanted to go back!" I was suddenly exhausted, angry that they'd gotten to me, dragged me into it, made my shaky sense of getting back to normal fade away.

I stretched out on my bed and lay there for a long time letting the tears come. All the tears I didn't cry when my father left, tears for Mo, and now for Ray who was in a place far away and part of a different world where I didn't understand the rules for survival.

I must have fallen asleep because the next thing I saw were long manicured blue nails tapping me on the arm. "Hey girl, wake up. I didn't come all this way to see you sleeping."

I straightened up, rubbing my eyes. They felt gritty and swollen. I wiped my nose on the back of my arm. "Lucia, what are you doing home?"

"I heard through the grapevine that Mom got back today. I let myself in. I still have my key. Sorry I didn't come to see you sooner. How long have you been back?" She dropped herself heavily on the bed. "So, Ray's staying down there they say. I wonder what kind of a fuss she made. Must have been hellish," she laughed, and I sat up and looked at her. She looked so different, but then I hadn't seen her while I was overseas.

Lucia's perfect shiny black hair was chopped at different lengths and tinted lavender in some parts, green in others. She saw me staring and ran her hand through it self-consciously. "Do you like it?" She had on lots of black eyeliner and very red lipstick. She was even thinner than I remembered and the black ripped jeans she was wearing looked like they belonged on a seven-year-old. Her blue-tipped fingers were covered with large brassy rings.

"I'm not going to ask you how it was over there. I watch the news," she assured me, looking around. "Is Mom in her room?" she rolled her eyes. Her wire-rimmed glasses were gone. I reached over and we hugged briefly. She tugged on one of my braids then backed away awkwardly. It was the same as if I'd seen her just yesterday but at the same time the feeling was different. Kicking off her thick black boots she walked over to the dresser where she grabbed a photo of us together and one of Ray as a chubby toddler. "He doesn't look like us, does he?"

I'd never really thought about it before. He looked a lot like my father, lighter-skinned, a stockier build. "You know about the kidnapping don't you?"

"Are you kidding? Mom put it on blast. She was desperate for money. She called everybody. This was the biggest thing she had to complain about since I don't know when."

"Do you think they were really kidnapped? He sounded really scared. I mean I talked to some guy too. It sounded legit."

"Dunno, Dad was always sketchy."

"You think so?" I was surprised.

"Well, you were his favorite, so you probably didn't notice what I did. But it could happen you know. My friend Socorro said her cousin was kidnapped when she went down there, outside of Acapulco for a wedding. Some gang kidnapped her from a bar. She was just having a drink with her friends. Her mom brought in the cops and they cut her throat. They sent the video to her family."

We were both quiet considering this. I thought about how delicate Ray's little body was the last time I saw him, and I shivered. "Do you think Dad cheated on Mom like she said?" I asked.

Lucia examined her hands. "Don't they all?"

I didn't know how to answer. "She was sending him money. Did you know that?"

Lucia made a helpless gesture. "That's Mom. Dipped into her disability for him."

I sat up against the pillows and looked at her. Something was different, not just the way she was dressed, but the way she seemed so uncaring, so apathetic, but then she'd always kept herself distant from the rest of us I thought. Her perfect image itself kept me away. Her image was really all I knew. "How's school?" I asked.

"I haven't been going lately. Been thinking about stopping,"

"Why?" That shocked me, it was the last thing I expected to hear. Lucia was the golden girl. Her future was sewed up.

"Kind of pointless. I only like art history. What the hell do I do with that?"

"But aren't you ready to graduate?"

"I've got another year left if I stay."

"What about your job?"

"Oh," She laughed. "I haven't worked for a while. I make a little money singing with a few bands. Rock and some alternative. We're going to be playing at the Echoplex in a couple of weeks. You should go. I'll leave your name at the door, so you won't have to pay."

I stared at her, trying to digest all this new information. This new Lucia. "So how are you getting by?'

"I live with my boyfriend. He's paying for everything."

So much had changed when I was gone. Singing with a band, quitting school, living with her boyfriend. I didn't know her anymore.

"I need a favor," she curled up in the corner and crossed her legs. "I need to borrow a little money and I need it real quick. Is it okay if I smoke?" She reached in her designer bag and pulled out a crumpled pack of cigarettes and a small silver lighter. She struck a light and inhaled twice.

"Well I gave Mom what I had when she went to Mexico. I don't have a job now."

"Oh," Lucia's voice was disappointed. She squashed out her cigarette.

"What about your boyfriend?"

"Can't ask him. He's the last person I'd ask." She ran her hands over her narrow hips. "Actually," she lowered her voice, opened the door, and peered out, "Making sure Mom's not listening. Thank God! Karina, I need an abortion and I waited too long already."

"You?" I felt my heart stop. "You're pregnant?"

"Isn't that why women have abortions?"

"I just ... How did you let that happen—You?" I touched the small square bulge under my skin near my shoulder, I'd gotten the implant before Iraq. Then I'd mostly forgotten about it.

"Got careless I guess."

"Why can't you tell your boyfriend," I wanted to know. "You said he's supporting you anyway."

Lucia reached into her purse and pulled out her wallet. She flipped through the plastic inserts and handed me a photo. "That's Tiago. Hot, huh?"

I studied the tall dark-haired young man with a wide smile, his arms around Lucia as he stared down at her in the photo. She was looking straight ahead, lips pursed, posing for the camera. No mistaking that look. He was in love. I felt sad for a moment, but I didn't know why.

Lucia watched my face. "Yeah, he's perfect. You know he graduated from Berkley; he's going places with this start-up tech firm. They're opening a second office in New York and he can work remotely if he wants. I think they're promoting him to Supervisor of Sales."

"So," I began, "why can't you ask him then?"

"Oh, I don't want him to find out for heaven's sake."

"Why, would he leave cause you were pregnant? If he didn't want the baby he'd want to pay for an abortion, wouldn't he? I don't get it."

"Abortion? You've got to be kidding. He's already been

talking nonstop about a wedding for the last year. A huge wedding for all our family and friends, on the beach, maybe Hawaii. Everything first class for about two hundred people. Do you know how much that costs? He's talking about asking his family for a little help. They want to buy us a house. Can you imagine, a house somewhere in the Hollywood Hills or Los Feliz. That's where he's always wanted to live. You know he proposed the first month we were together. The boy's in love," she giggled.

"So, he's against abortion?" I asked.

"I don't think so, not in general. But not for us. He would be crazy happy if I was pregnant. We'd get that home even faster, furnish it all designer-like. You know he treats me like a queen, like a damn goddess or something." She shook her head and began picking at one of her long blue nails. "You can't imagine. His picture's in the dictionary under the words, 'perfect guy.'"

"So, you don't want a baby I guess."

"Hell no! No way I want to ruin my life getting stuck with a kid I don't want. Besides, I'm probably dumping him anyway. It all gets old you know. Anyway, I met somebody, this drummer with the Executioners. I've been seeing him for a while. It could be his baby, I don't know."

The room seemed so stuffy all of a sudden, like I couldn't draw enough breath. I stood up and pushed open the small window against the wall. A rush of humid smoggy air filled the room.

"You won't spill the beans to Mom, right? I mean, I know you wouldn't. She'd just die if she knew. And it's not even that big a thing, I've had two before. But people are so ..."

I met her eyes and she looked away, slinging her purse over her shoulder. "Glad you're back home Sis, somebody needs to keep an eye on Mom. I would have stayed here but she kicked me out."

"Yeah, I heard, the Section Eight problem. I'll be leaving too as soon as I find a job."

"Nah, it wasn't cause of Section Eight. That's what she says. She found some coke I was stashing. She was so pissed she threw me out. Can you imagine? She thought the coke was marijuana. She doesn't know the difference and she was still furious." Lucia laughed. I moved my lips in a half-smile and we hugged a little tighter this time before she left the apartment.

Later that evening, I pulled out my duffel bag and shifted the folded clothes to one side. On the bottom were a handful of recruiting brochures from the Marines. I grabbed them up to take home before I got on the plane, a kind of souvenir. I studied the smiling faces of the soldiers riding in Humvees, climbing rope ladders, or sitting in the front of rows of impressive computers, their fingers poised above the controls. I lived in that world once, and now thankfully, the gruesome memories of my last combat missions are hiding someplace in the back of my mind. I never call them out. Death in real time is not like death on television. You can't sit back and watch it happen when you know you are a part of it. I broke down my service revolver and pushed it up into the back corner of the closet. I don't think about using it anymore.

After my father left to live in Mexico, I still carried the memory of a man who was gentle and caring, a good man, who in spite of everything, loved his kids. I always believed he left because he couldn't put up with my mother anymore. Now after everything that's happened, I'm not so sure. Is he a good guy who got pushed around by things he could not control or just a very selfish man who'll use anybody to get what he wants? And Lucia, once she was flawless in my eyes. Now she blew up that illusion. My sister, the person who I admired more than anyone, lives a lie.

When I went to Iraq, I was looking for a stable family and a place where I fit in. I thought I'd found it because now I knew the good guys from the bad guys. After I was there for a while, I wasn't so sure. The only thing I did know for sure was that the soldiers in your platoon would have your back, no matter what.

But that's all you really knew about them. So, I guess in a lot of ways the platoon wasn't very different than my family. They saw life in a way that made sense to them, put orderliness in their world when there was none. Now I see we all do that, whoever we are.

Like my sergeant told our platoon in Iraq, when some of the villagers brutally killed two young men on the spot who might have been Al Qaeda sympathizers, "None of you are fit to pass judgment on them or call them murderers. These people live their life the way it works for them. You can't judge their life. You can only judge your own."

A week later, I asked my mother to go with me to Rich Brew for a cup of her favorite cappuccino. She was surprised at the offer and changed her dress and combed her hair for the occasion. I hadn't spoken much to my mother that week, other than to tell her I'm moving out as soon as I start working. She doesn't talk about Ray anymore, other than to say she spoke to him and he's doing fine. She's not crying every time I see her the way she did before. She even has a new boyfriend, an elderly man who wears his pants too high and who sits on the recliner watching television with her and drinking beer that she buys for him. I haven't heard them fighting yet.

I Still Like Pink

"So, what did she say?" Genevieve twirled the dial on her locker and looked back at Sandra as she pushed her algebra book to the back and pulled out her history folder.

"Well … I didn't exactly tell her everything." Sandra looked down at her new booties, soft gray suede trimmed with black leather. She picked up one foot and rubbed it against the other.

"So then, what did you tell her? I thought yesterday was the day you were telling her."

Sandra raised her head and looked at Genevieve. Sometimes, like now, Genevieve looked like a stranger, not just an ordinary stranger, but someone she didn't want to be seen with. From her head to her toes, Genevieve was one strapping butch who always managed to look homeless.

"I just told her, well, you know, that I didn't like boys. That's all."

"That's all?" Genevieve shook her head. She looked disgusted. "You didn't tell her about me?"

"No … not yet." Sandra sighed as they started walking down the hall together. She was glad the year was almost over and she'd be graduating soon. Pretty soon, she wouldn't see these long narrow halls that needed painting and the rows and rows of banged-up green lockers in these rundown buildings anymore. When she started high school two years before, it was in the "good" district in a "good" school, not too far from her home in Brentwood where there were pretty Spanish-styled houses surrounded by green lawns. But then, right after her grandmother moved in to take care of her, the school board changed the boundaries of the school districts. Since the street she lived on was now in a different district that required bussing, she took the bus every day for over an hour to an inner-city school. Here, there was nothing pretty and green, just blocks of run-down stucco apartments and boarded-up buildings, surrounded by dry weeds and trash. The school board said bussing encouraged diversity. She had to admit she'd met a lot of people here that she never would have met in Brentwood. That included Genevieve.

"So, when are you telling her?"

Genevieve was stubborn, Sandra thought, as she tried to figure out what to say.

"It's just that ... I don't know. It wasn't the right time, I guess." She pictured her grandmother's face, sullen, eyes squinting in concentration, as she chopped chiles and added them to the hot oil in the frying pan. She would be standing in the shoes she wore while she worked as a janitor, ugly black Oxfords that she didn't have time to take off. Her ankles would be all puffy and swollen. *No*, she thought, *she'll be so upset.*

The hallway was getting crowded with kids moving between classrooms, calling out to each other. Their loud laughter filled the halls that looked like long twisting green columns. Genevieve moved closer to her, the way she always did when there were other people around. At first, Sandra found it creepy, but that was before she knew Genevieve, and before she knew how she felt about her. Now she liked them knowing they were a couple and didn't mind when heads turned as they walked or when Genevieve put her arm around her during assembly or when they walked to the gym. People stared at Genevieve because she wore boy's clothes and lace-up boots, and her head was shaved on one side and purple-tipped on the other. She had a lot of piercings too, one through her nose and a few in her ears and lips.

Actually, though, the kids here didn't seem to pay that much attention to the two Latinas as they walked around on campus. There was much more exciting stuff going on: some guys selling drugs near the auditorium, a girl-fight down by the gym, a couple of white guys from some gang bullying a smaller skinner version of themselves. The teachers didn't seem to care either. As far as Sandra could see, they all looked worn down and didn't seem to have the energy to deal with all of the bad actors on the campus. The message was "leave me alone and I'll leave you alone." That worked just fine for everybody. It was like that in class too. As long as you kept your mouth shut and didn't start any trouble, they'd probably pass you.

Sandra looked around her thinking about how different this school was from the one in her neighborhood. All the trees, green lawns, and Spanish tiles made a big difference. Plus, most of the kids were white and drove nice cars. The parking lot there was full of them, Mercedes, Jeeps, Hummers, Lexus SUVs. She wanted Genevieve to see it, but Genevieve didn't want to ride the bus all the way to that side of town. So far, she hadn't invited Genevieve to her home. She could just picture her grandma's face.

She pictured it again when she heard Genevieve's annoyed voice, "So, I'm gonna have the car this weekend, finally. I can pick you up, and we can hang out or something."

Sandra tried to picture Genevieve in her pink bedroom, sitting on the pink bedspread. She could see Grandma staring, her mouth all scrunched up in disapproval.

"Or maybe I could drive down here to your house," Sandra said quickly.

Genevieve didn't answer. She shrugged her shoulders and looked over sideways at Sandra, frowning.

Sandra wasn't born in the nice two-story house with all the Spanish tile. Her father started a software company before she was born, made a lot of money when he sold it, and then bought another one. After he bought the second company, her mother picked out their house in a neighborhood where all the houses looked like Spanish haciendas surrounded by beds of red and pink flowers that bloomed all year. Sandra's mother had light brown hair and blue eyes and was from the south bay. She met Sandra's father in college and she said her family was furious because she married a Guatemalan. She always told Sandra she never lived in a ghetto neighborhood, and she didn't want Sandra to live in one either.

When she was younger, Sandra went to the birthday parties where ponies were rented for the afternoon to ride on the wide green lawns, and a five-star restaurant catered the birthday dinner. Gifts for young children were routinely iPads, X-Boxes, and expensive racing bikes. In the summer, families of her young friends went to Europe or Asia for their children's enrichment. Sandra tagged along with her best friend when their family went to Hawaii and came back sunburned and happy for the time spent, simply, on the beach building castles.

Then, when she was thirteen, things changed. Her mother got sick and then sicker. She stopped coming downstairs, and then they took her to the hospital. Her father explained it was stage-four cancer. Sandra visited her mother at the hospital, staring down at the frail body on the bed. Now her mother looked so different, her arms and legs were skinny, and you could see the veins underneath her skin. She was so pale. Sandra kept staring at her once-thick, curly black hair, now thin and dry, her scalp bald in spots. The nurse explained that her mother didn't respond when Sandra tried to talk to her because of the pain medicine, and her father told her that her mother didn't have very long to live. Right before Christmas, they called and said she had died during the night.

And now it was like she'd never been there at all. Sandra watched as her aunts pulled clothes from hangers and grabbed up designer purses to carry off. They all fought over the jewelry until it was decided to put away a few of the better pieces for Sandra when she got older. Watching all of this, Sandra didn't cry. The memory of her mother, who didn't have much time for her, did a lot of charity work and gave lavish parties, faded surprisingly fast, leaving just the scent of her flowery perfume behind. She hurried to the bedroom where her aunts were grabbing up jewelry and plucked up the remaining perfume bottles on the dresser. Back in her room, she opened each one and sniffed it until the familiar flowery odor surfaced from one of the pink cut-glass bottles. She wrapped that bottle in scarves and buried it deep in her drawer.

After that, everything happened so fast. Her father started seeing Amy, a blonde real estate agent who was trying to sell their house. Amy suggested that the market would be better if he waited to sell. Then he moved out with Amy, who made it clear she didn't want a ready-made family. They were going to rent the house and send Sandra away to boarding school, but her father decided that the house was a necessary tax deduction for now, so he would go on paying the mortgage and the bills and have his mother move in to take care of Sandra. That way, Sandra could keep living there and going to the same school and he wouldn't have to help his mother out with money anymore.

Lately, she was starting to forget the little things that she used to fix her father's image in her mind, like the way he wore his expensive suits or the smell of his cigarettes. The sound of his voice talking on the phone grew fainter and fainter in her memory until she barely recognized it when he called. She didn't see much of him these days, just sometimes on holidays, and he usually called on her birthday to make sure she'd gotten the gift his secretary sent. But she didn't complain. She had her own bank account, and he made sure that there was always plenty of money in it, and, of course, there were the credit cards. She could charge as much as she wanted. She guessed that made up for him leaving.

One Saturday, a few days after her father moved out, Grandma Velez arrived in a taxi with two suitcases that she unloaded from the trunk herself and a walking cane made from polished wood with a carved eagle on the handle.

Of course, Sandra had seen Grandma Velez before—a few times on Christmas and her birthday—but Grandma Velez lived in a different part of the city and spoke almost all Spanish, so Sandra couldn't understand her when she did see her. Her father didn't understand her very well either. He told Sandra he'd forgotten his Spanish because he never needed it after high school when he left the old neighborhood on a scholarship to Stanford. He said he never looked back, and that included speaking Spanish.

Grandma Velez spent most of her spare time vacuuming and dusting their big house after she told their maid they didn't need her anymore. She said she was embarrassed having a maid from her home country cleaning her toilets. She herself still worked as a janitor at an old folks' home every day except Sunday, when she spent most of the day in church. Sandra's father tried to get her to quit work, but Grandma Velez said she worked because it was what the Lord wanted her to do and she couldn't accept charity, even from her son. Sandra thought he was embarrassed because his mother was a janitor who didn't speak much English and he didn't want anyone to know.

Grandma Velez cooked good food, though, like platanos and chicken pipian that Sandra liked so much, and she made sure there were always clean clothes to wear, even though she gave away a lot of Sandra's clothes to the Goodwill because she said they were too "naked." One rainy day she taught Sandra how to knit, and for the first time, Sandra felt like she could do something useful. Grandma Velez donated everything she knitted to a children's orphanage in Tijuana. After a little instruction, Sandra began knitting hats for the little girls. She took on the project with more enthusiasm than she had ever felt for anything else. Knitting little hats and scarfs in different shades of pink took up all her time when she wasn't in school and kept her from thinking about both her mother and father gone from the house. She always kept her needles in her backpack, along with a skein of pink wool, and pulled them out whenever she felt anxious, which was most of the time. Grandma Velez was really impressed with how hard she worked, hugged her, and praised her. For the first time, Sandra felt like she mattered.

The only thing that was hard for Sandra to take was all

that church stuff Grandma Velez insisted on. Horrified that Sandra had no religious training, she first tried to get Sandra to go to church on Monday and Wednesday night in addition to Sundays. Sandra fought back, insisting that she had too much homework on the weekdays and she managed to be sick almost every Sunday morning. It only worked sometimes. So, usually several times a month, she found herself sitting in the pews of the Catholic church listening to the priest warn against the many sins that her grandmother considered "the devil's work." Without being told directly, she knew that what she felt for Genevieve, and what they did together, was a sin.

"I'll come by Sunday, okay?" Sandra asked Genevieve, thinking about the last time they were together, feeling the warmth that started in her lower body and traveled across her breasts that suddenly made her feel flushed and tingly.

Genevieve steered her toward the lockers on the south wall. "You know I work at Grill and Go on Sundays. Every Sunday."

Sandra took her arm and squeezed it. "You could call in sick and we could go somewhere." The last time they were together, they went to Rollie's house, a friend of Genevieve's. He lived with his older sister since his parents had put him out when he told them he was trans. Rollie was easy-going, and for the price of a joint he didn't have to share with anyone else, he was willing to give up his room for a couple of hours.

"What do you say?" She asked again, her attention drifting.

Genevieve scowled. "You know I can't, they'll fire me, and they need the money at home. I don't have a rich daddy like you."

Sandra pictured Genevieve's house, small and crowded with two families: Genevieve and her mother and two brothers, and her sister and her two kids. She could hear the television blaring and the kids shouting while they ran through the cramped rooms. There were always empty take-out boxes and cartons on every surface, wadded up bags of chips, and half-filled plastic cups of melted ice sitting on the counters. The stove hadn't worked for at least a couple of months. Dirty clothes and clean clothes were stacked at opposite ends of the couch, and toys usually covered the floor.

Nobody paid much attention to Genevieve since she was almost an adult and brought money into the house to help pay the rent. Nobody asked her where she was going when she went out or told her she had to go to school or church. Nobody seemed to notice when she shaved one side of her head, covered her arms and the back of her neck with tattoos, or added to her piercings. Sandra felt nothing but envy.

Genevieve was Sandra's first. She'd stepped up and claimed Sandra, practically from the first time they'd met, on the second day the bus from the westside parked in the school lot, and Sandra in her designer jeans, pale pink sweater, and leather boots stepped off. There was Genevieve, in baggy men's clothing that looked worn and anything but stylish. She had a way of filling up space wherever she was so that nobody else tried to claim it. Genevieve was Sandra's direct opposite; she knew her place in the world. She liked it, and it was where she wanted to be. She was sure of herself and everybody else. She was never afraid of anything or anybody, and the world made sense to her. She wasn't like Sandra and didn't give a damn what anybody else thought about her. "Bring it on," she always said. "Sticks and stones can break my bones, but words? ... Fuck no."

But words did frighten Sandra, angry words and criticism made her want to shrivel up until she was so small she couldn't be seen. Shouting and cursing made her tremble. She told Genevieve that she was used to the quiet of her house and all the empty space. When she felt threatened by too much going on, she looked for someone to protect her. Before Genevieve, there was no one. Grandma Velez was too old and weak to count.

Sandra sometimes wondered how Genevieve managed, living the way she did, in that house that looked like it was falling apart. The very walls were pushing out from the pressure inside, where the tiny living space was stretched too far and filled with the sound of yelling, cursing, and blaring music. Then there was Genevieve's sister, the loudest and rudest one living there, always making nasty remarks that made Sandra cringe. She felt sorry for Genevieve because she had to be just like a grown-up, worrying about making money, with so many things to take care of. But at the same time, she envied Genevieve for owning up to being different. Genevieve told her she came out when she started middle school. It had been a startling confession when Sandra was still confused about what she felt and couldn't imagine talking about it to anybody.

"I really like you. Let's play together, only us. We won't let anybody else play with us," Sandra recalled jealously telling her first girl crush in the third grade. The girl's name was Patricia, and Sandra remembered her fine blond hair and blue eyes. Patricia wore big round glasses, and maybe that was part of the attraction. Sandra thought that the glasses made Patricia extra special. She made it a point to sit next to Patricia in class and followed her everywhere at recess, walking behind her when they left the school grounds. Sandra even gave one of Patricia's friends five candy bars to give her Patricia's phone number, and Sandra started to call her every night, wanting to tell her how much she loved her. Patricia always hung up on her as soon as she knew who it was, and the last time she called, Patricia's mother got on the line and threatened to tell Sandra's mother and call the police. Sandra hung up immediately, terrified. All she knew was that she wanted to stroke Patricia's shiny blonde hair and hug her. She thought if she ever got a chance to hug Patricia, she'd never let her go.

Patricia didn't feel the same way. She had another group of girls she hung around with, other little white girls with pale skin and light hair who didn't look like Sandra. They didn't include Sandra in anything they did. "Go away, you weirdo!" Patricia would yell after her as soon as she spotted Sandra lurking in the background. Sometimes the other girls would chase her away or throw rocks, and Sandra would skulk away alone, sometimes crying.

The teachers all had a good laugh when they saw Sandra chasing after Patricia but stopped laughing when Patricia's mother complained to the principal. Sandra's mother was alive then, and they called her into the office to "talk about the problem." Sandra didn't remember much about the conversation except that they told her she had to stay away from Patricia, not follow her anymore, or even speak to her, no matter how much she loved her. Her mother told her if she didn't obey, she would have the police put her in jail where she would stay in the dark and only have bread and water. Terrified, she backed off and watched Patricia from afar, in dismay.

In middle school, Sandra made a few more friends. She liked it when it was just the girls doing things together, like going to the movies or having slumber parties. The slumber parties were especially fun because they styled each other's hair in different ways, copying the photos in magazines, and put on makeup, trying to look like the models smiling back at them from the television screen or their cell phones. They slept next to each other in sleeping bags, so close that she knew she could reach out and stroke the skin of the girl next to her, if only she had the nerve. She stayed awake most of the night, long after the others fell asleep and watched them, aching to draw herself into their skin and hear their hearts beat. While she lay there watching the girls sleep, she felt a longing for something she couldn't explain. Somehow, at least, she was in the right place.

When they reached high school, the girls started talking about boys more than they talked about anything else. Some of them had taken the plunge themselves and gave detailed descriptions about how you had sex with a boy. Sandra colored red, thinking that the descriptions of a boy's penis were disgusting and the pain from him pushing it inside of her was a horrifying prospect. Just the thought of kissing a boy made her skin crawl. She promised herself it would never happen to her.

After she started getting bussed to her new school, Sandra saw less and less of the girls she'd grown up with. Shy and uncomfortable, she couldn't quite bring herself to approach the groups of girls at her new school. After checking out her trendy outfits, purchased at Nordstrom's with her father's credit card, most of them eyed her from a distance and left her alone. She wondered, sadly, if it would be different if her mother were still around, but then Genevieve took her under her wing and everything changed.

"Let's ditch the rest of the day!" Genevieve suggested, all of a sudden. "We have the whole rest of the day. I don't want to spend it here."

Sandra looked around nervously. "Where do you want to go?" She thought that maybe they could go to somebody's house where there weren't any parents around. She shivered, thinking about what would happen when they were alone. "I have to be careful my grandmother doesn't find out."

"I thought she didn't speak English?"

"She doesn't," Sandra answered, "but you know how the school calls home."

"Only if you don't bring a note. I'll write one for you. I'll say you had cramps and had to go home." Genevieve laughed.

Sandra looked down the hall. The crowd was thinning out. She'd only skipped school a couple of times before, and both times were in her old school. She'd spent the day at the mall and her grandmother never found out.

Together, they ducked down the side corridor leading to the gym and the rear entrance to the school. It usually wasn't monitored after school began in the morning and all the students had passed through the metal detectors.

"I have to get back to catch the bus home," she reminded Genevieve.

"You'll be back," Genevieve grabbed her arm and steered her down the stairs and out the rear entrance. They hurried along the side of the chain-link fence that enclosed the school. Sandra snagged her soft pink-striped sweater on a loose spike and stopped to pull the thread loose. She stood staring, dismayed at the hole it had made in the cashmere, rubbing the cloth between her fingers as if it would make the hole close up.

"What are you doing now?" Genevieve hurried back to where Sandra was standing, stopping beside her and looking down at the sweater.

"It's torn," Sandra explained, still staring at the hole.

"For heaven sakes, you must have a million pink sweaters, and your daddy will always buy you another one." Genevieve looked down the street for cops. "Let's get out of here. We don't want to get stuck. The cops will pick us up."

"I like pink, what's wrong with that?" Sandra shifted her backpack, remembering that she had a skein of pink knitting in her bag with the needles and the yarn. She was knitting another pink scarf in a hotter shade.

They crossed the street and kept walking. It was starting to get warm and sticky, the way it did most days in LA. The air itself looked kind of fuzzy as if the heat rising from the sidewalk had pushed the oxygen away. They passed a few liquor stores and a laundromat before the street dead-ended and they trudged up the road to the park.

Sandra looked around. The park here wasn't green and manicured like the park near her house—no wide expanses of trimmed lawn or flowerbeds. The dirt path was littered with broken glass bottles and cardboard food cartons. Large blackbirds that looked like crows fought over a package of half-eaten French fries, flinging them back and forth, while their shrill caws echoed on the pathway. From where they stood, she could see the bathrooms were locked down with a thick iron bar across the door.

"I have something," Genevieve said, as they climbed up a hill on a set of stone steps to a tree trunk that had partially fallen. "Sit down," she gestured as if this was her living room at home, and the log was her couch covered with food wrappers and folded clothes.

Sandra giggled and carefully eased herself down, stopping to brush dirt off her suede shoes. "What do you have for me?"

Genevieve reached into her backpack and pulled out a bottle of *Modelo* and then dug down into the pocket of her baggy jeans, hanging below a wide leather belt with a big brass clasp, and pulled out a small, tightly rolled joint.

Sandra clapped her hands and reached up to kiss Genevieve. The first time she'd tried weed, it had been with Genevieve. She liked the soft feeling of weightlessness it brought, the feeling that nothing was really that bad in the world. She stretched out her hand and took the bottle of beer. "It's warm," she complained.

"Of course, it's warm; it's been in my backpack since this morning." Genevieve lit up the joint, shaking her head. "Beer's beer. It'll get you high either way."

Sandra found a spot that wasn't completely covered in dirt and dried leaves and sat back on the log, trying not to dirty her light beige pants. She inhaled deeply, waiting for the warm feeling to flood over her. Genevieve took the joint and dragged on it a few times before handing it back and reaching for the beer.

"Want some?" she asked.

Sandra made a face and shook her head. Genevieve threw her head back and took a couple of long swallows. They looked at the traffic streaming past on the road below. The cars were just toys strung out like beads on a bright-colored necklace that wound through the city below. After a moment, Sandra stopped feeling anxious and leaned back to melt into the fallen brush that piled up against the log.

Genevieve nodded her head, looking around. "It sure is nice up here—nobody bothering us. No lame teachers giving me demerits, and nobody screaming that I got their order wrong. No nasty little kids yelling and fighting. That's for sure." The sun was stronger now, burning through the haze. "You know," she said matter-of-factly, "my sister's pregnant again. Another damn kid to worry about. She can't figure out how to stop them from coming!"

Sandra turned her face back to the sun. She wondered again how Genevieve managed to live with all those people. "Can't your sister move out and get her own place?"

Genevieve looked shocked. "Live somewhere else? That's what family is for, to help each other. Right? Anyway, she'd miss us if she moved out, and she pays part of the rent."

Sandra shifted, feeling uncomfortable. "I just thought that there'd be more space that way."

"We don't need any more space," Genevieve sounded exasperated. "You rich people are used to living in those big mansions, you never even run into each other. Who wants to live like that?"

Sandra thought about how quiet their big house was; Grandma Velez barely spoke to her, and only if she was making sure Sandra went to school or telling her to go to church. If it weren't for the television playing *novelas*, or MTV, there wouldn't be any sound at all. Genevieve was right; she liked the quiet. Still, it was lonely there, even if there was so much space and all the furniture was beautiful and expensive. But try as she might, she couldn't picture Genevieve in her house. She just didn't fit in with the way everything was arranged, neat and orderly, always precisely in its place. No way could she bring her home even if Grandma Velez wasn't around.

Genevieve finished the last of the beer and twirled the bottle in her long fingers. "Bet you can't hit that tree."

"With the bottle?" Sandra stepped back. "It's dangerous to throw glass."

"Come on, try it! Do something crazy for once!" She pushed the bottle into Sandra's hands.

Sandra looked down at the glass and back up at Genevieve. Genevieve's face was puckered and scowling. She didn't like it when Genevieve was angry with her. Sighing, she reached back and swung the bottle over her head, letting it fly in a high arc. It didn't get as far as the tree but landed on a rock where it smashed, filling the air with the crisp sound of cracking glass.

Genevieve laughed and took the last hit of the joint. "I need to teach you to throw. Didn't you ever play any sports?"

"No, not me." Sandra reached into her backpack and fingered

her skein of knitting, touching the sharp point of one of the needles. "I never liked running, getting all sweaty for nothing." She put the backpack on again and leaned back against it for comfort.

"Is that why you always get excused from gym?"

"I don't like to go, so my grandmother gives me a note. I write it for her. She says she doesn't care if I go to gym. I'm not getting an education there."

Genevieve rolled her eyes. "That's stupid. You can learn things playing sports. I get my best grades in gym class. So anyway, am I coming over this weekend or what?"

Sandra looked down. It wasn't really a question, Genevieve was insisting. She felt her face get red. It wasn't that she was ashamed of Genevieve, or was she? It would have been easier if Genevieve looked and dressed like the other girls she'd been attracted to, girls that looked more like her, with pretty faces, who wore their hair long and their skirts short. When she thought about it, Genevieve didn't really look like a guy though, even though she tried so hard. Maybe she could take her shopping and get her some decent clothes that didn't look like they'd come from a thrift shop. She could just charge them on her credit card the way she always did. Her father would never know. But somehow she couldn't bring up the suggestion to Genevieve. She didn't want to make her angry or hurt her feelings. Not when she knew how much Genevieve cared. She really did love Genevieve, she thought. She gave Sandra a certain feeling that she never felt with her mom and dad or anybody else for that matter.

"You shouldn't throw glass like that. Don't you know better?"

The voice was harsh, threatening, with kind of an accent, Sandra thought, turning to see who was talking. The voice was coming out of the clearing, along with three guys who were walking toward them, slowly, taking their time. They were young, she saw right away, maybe her age, dressed in baggy jeans and long white T-shirts. Their heads were shaved and they had tattoos on their necks and arms. The tallest one walked ahead of the rest. Sandra noticed he was wearing new tennis shoes, OG Air Jordans, she thought, the expensive ones, that all the guys wanted, and a blue hat turned around on his head.

As they came closer, the two guys walking behind looked her over, their eyes roaming across her body, but the one walking in front didn't take his eyes off Genevieve. Sandra noticed his eyes were light and huge. They looked like they were popping out of his narrow face.

He stepped ahead and stood directly in front of Genevieve, his hands in his pockets. "What the fuck are you supposed to be?"

Genevieve stood up to her full height, and Sandra noticed that she really wasn't very tall, maybe just a little taller than she was. Strange, she'd always seemed so imposing, but now these guys towered over her.

"I asked you a question, bitch. Why are you wearing those clothes? You're not a man!"

"What's it to you?" Genevieve answered, looking past the three to see if there were any more.

Sandra felt a chill go through her body though the sun was beating down in the clearing where they stood.

The two guys who'd been walking behind moved up. They stood next to the guy with the hat directly in front of Genevieve. Sandra could see they were shorter and thinner than the guy who was talking to Genevieve. One of them pointed at Sandra. He had a line of devil's heads tattooed on the right side of his neck. "Now that's a nice piece of ass. Real pretty. I'd like me some of that. What do you say?" He stuck his tongue out and licked his lips.

The guy next to him had both his ears pierced and wore large brass washers in each. He laughed and rubbed the front of his pants. "Didn't know we'd get lucky today." He moved closer to Sandra. "Let's go back behind those trees. I have something real good for you."

Sandra shrank back. Her heart was pounding. Why did she

let Genevieve talk her into coming here? Her father always told her this neighborhood wasn't safe. "Never leave the school except to get on the bus," he'd said.

Genevieve stepped in front of her. "You stay away from her, or you'll be sorry!"

The one with the devil's head tattoos laughed a short laugh like a snort and then spat on the ground next to him. "You gotta be kidding me, you ugly dyke."

Sandra stared at Genevieve with her hands on her hips facing the first guy who'd just called her a name. He shifted his eyes to take in Sandra shaking his head from side to side. Sandra could hear her heart banging against her chest and cold sweat starting at the back of her neck. All eyes were now on Genevieve. Nobody was watching her. Maybe she could run down the hill and get away before they caught her. She looked back at the path they'd hiked to get to the clearing. Just one step, she thought. I'll run like hell.

Just then, her arm was jerked behind her back and another thin wire-muscled arm covered in tattoos, wrapped around her body. Sandra screamed and tried to push away from the body behind her, but it held her like a vise.

The face of the boy with the skull tattoos leaned around her and grinned. "Where do you think you're going? We haven't had any fun yet."

"I said, let her go. You'll pay for this." Genevieve's voice was angry and shrill.

Sandra dug her carefully filed nails into the arm that was holding her and felt it swing away.

"You fucking bitch!" tattooed-skulls roared. His fist sent her spinning when it connected with her mouth, and she fell back, landing on her backpack. staring up at the thick green foliage that covered the clearing like a woven green canopy. Her head was reeling as blood began dripping from her mouth. She could see Genevieve struggling with the two other guys who were trying to get her down on the ground.

The one with the hat yelled out, "Get over here! Leave that skinny little twat alone. Help me with this one. I'm gonna teach this queer a lesson she won't forget!"

The skull-tattoos backed up and went back to help the other two. The one with the hat was unbuckling his pants. They had their backs to her.

"Run, Sandra, get out of here!" Genevieve was yelling and sobbing. Sandra saw them all standing over her, and one of their fists hit her in the stomach. Genevieve doubled over and the one in the hat pushed her to the ground.

"You sure she ain't a dude? I'm not fucking any dude."

Sandra stood up on shaky legs that felt like liquid or as if they were attached to her body with rubber bands. She could hear Genevieve screaming. She looked at the open space down the hill. Run now! Something in her head was shrieking. The sound pulsed through her whole body. But she couldn't run. Her feet stuck to the carpet of dried leaves and twigs. She couldn't leave Genevieve here. You just didn't leave people you cared about alone when things went bad. I'm not like my father, she thought. Wasn't that what family was for? To help each other. That's what Genevieve believed.

Spitting out the blood that filled her mouth along with what felt like pieces of a tooth, she grabbed her backpack and pulled out her knitting needles. She felt the turn in her stomach and braced herself for the crash. Then she ran at the one with the hat. His back was to her, and his pants were down around his ankles. He was kneeling over Genevieve while the other two were fighting to hold her down. Sandra ran up to him, raising the needle high and then bringing it down, sticking it deep into his back as hard as she could.

Hat-boy fell forward, screaming in pain as his legs buckled underneath him. The two holding Genevieve dropped her, looking back in shock at the long metal needle sticking out of their friend's back. Skull-tattoos stood up and tried to grab his friend's arm and drag him up. He quickly pulled his hand away when he saw the blood running from the wound in his friend's back and started moving away. But he wasn't fast enough.

Sandra ran at him yelling, "I'm not letting you hurt my girlfriend!" and stuck the second needle in his chest as he turned at the sound of her voice. He doubled over, grabbing his chest, hollering in pain. The third one, no longer holding Genevieve, was already running back into the wooded area.

Genevieve pushed herself off the ground in a single move and stood up shaking. Her face was streaked with dirt and drying tears, and half of her hair was tangled in a twisted knot of leaves and twigs. "Run!" she screamed at Sandra, grabbing her hand and pulling her along behind her. And they ran, Genevieve with her long strides, pulling Sandra with her full backpack slapping behind her until they reached the exit to the park.

"I was so scared. I thought they'd kill you," Sandra sobbed between gasps. Looking back, she saw the other two guys staggering off toward the wooded area they'd come from. The clearing in the park where they were sitting minutes before was suddenly still. A slight midday wind began blowing through the clearing, pushing away the gray haze. A few birds began perching in the tops of the taller trees soaking up the warmth. It looked like a scene out of a dream.

Genevieve hugged Sandra and reached into her backpack. "Call the cops. I don't have my phone."

Breathing hard with shaking hands, Sandra dialed 911 and told the operator it was an emergency; some guys attacked her girlfriend in the park. Genevieve grabbed the phone and yelled that they probably needed an ambulance too. The voice on the other end told her a unit was on its way.

When the call was over, Genevieve put the phone back and put her arms around Sandra, pulling her close. The tears came then, running down her face, hot and tasting of salt, while Sandra sobbed into Genevieve's striped shirt with the holes in the sleeve.

Sandra looked up at Genevieve's pale, blotchy face, tears

drying on her cheeks, and then she stared at her hand, the one that held the needle, where the sharp pain from her clenched fist was now just a dull throb. She could still feel the needle pressed into her palm and a burning sensation in her shoulder where she'd raised it above her head before bringing it down to strike.

Grandma Velez was off today, Sandra suddenly remembered. She told Sandra they were cutting back on her hours. That morning Sandra saw her asleep on her single bed covered with her favorite Indian blanket. She was probably still at home cleaning. By now, she'd be scrubbing the bathrooms. That was the way Grandma Velez always spent her mornings when she was off. Sandra grabbed the cell again, holding it to her ear with a shaking hand, listening to the ringing. It went on and on. She swallowed her disappointment and felt her eyes filling up again.

And then, her voice hesitant, questioning, "*Bueno?*"

"Grandma! It's Sandra!"

"Sandra?"

"Yeah. Grandma, I just wanted to tell you. I'm in some trouble here. The police are coming, and I don't know what's going to happen, but I think everything will be all right. I'm going to call Dad and let him know. I just wanted to call you first. I'm here with my girlfriend. Her name is Genevieve, and I'm going to bring her home to meet you as soon as I can. She's the best person I know, Grandma. I know you don't understand everything. I wanted to tell you before about me, but anyway, I love you."

There was silence on the other end. Sandra saw the police car pulling up, and Genevieve walked over to meet them.

Sandra started to click off, then she heard the words, faint, but sure, "I love you *mija*."

She smiled and took a deep breath. Then straightening up her shoulders, she walked over to Genevieve to face whatever would come.

Later, sitting in the emergency room, and after that, at the police station, Sandra planned to tell her dad not to drop off Genevieve, to take both of them to her house, so Genevieve could finally see where she lived. Her dad would probably look at Genevieve and think she was strange, judging her, the way he did with the punks, the goths, and sometimes the kids who weren't white. But she would stick right by Genevieve and hold her hand when she introduced her. Then when they got home she would go and get Grandma Velez. She would tell them to all sit down and she would introduce Genevieve to her grandmother and tell her she was her girlfriend. She would tell them how Genevieve tried to save her when they got attacked in the park and how she put herself at risk to help Sandra. She would tell Grandma Velez that she loved Genevieve for the beautiful person she was inside. The important people in her life needed to know who she was.

He Shuffles When He Walks

Mariana set the mop down carefully and studied the long corridor, tiled with soft rose-colored pavers. The dog must have tracked in dust from one of the decks, probably the one on the west, and she'd need to mop and wax it again. The morning light shone on a small puddle near the corner by the balcony, most likely coffee spilled by the Señora. The Señora's hands always shook until midday when she'd taken all her pills and had a few drinks to calm her nerves. That was when she bothered to get out of bed at all.

Sighing, she took off her tennis shoes, the ones she'd pulled out of the Goodwill bag that the Señora told her to leave at the bottom of the entrance to the estate. They were too nice to give away—Nikes, hardly worn—and the ones she had from the Discount Daily were worn down completely. The Señora did not even notice she was wearing them. Why would she? She had two whole closets full of shoes. The closets themselves were as big as the apartment she shared with her son, her niece, and her two kids.

So many shoes! She shook her head, mystified. Just last week, before the big party, she took them all down from their shelves and out of their plastic containers, dusted them, and then rearranged them. They were sorted into groups according to what occasion they were to be worn for: party shoes, boots, sandals, casual shoes, tennis shoes, and slippers. Then they were sorted again by color. After that, she sorted the purses the same way. It took her a whole day to finish, and she just finished in time to clean the rooms again for the party.

Mariana pushed the dust mop down the corridor and peered into the partially open bedroom at the top of the stairs where the floors were covered with thick carpet. The Señora wasn't moving in the huge mahogany bed surrounded by velvet pillows. The cut glass decanter of vodka was still full. She must still be asleep. Probably those pills she took. Sometimes she slept all day and was still sleeping when the Señor came home. The shades were drawn and the heavy silk drapes shut out any small streaks of light that tried to slip through.

She hurried down the stairs, two, at a time, and began waxing, watching the pavers begin to shine as she rubbed. Pausing, she pushed open the doors of the rooms she passed. Six bedrooms, four baths. That didn't include the living room, the den, the dining room, the guestroom, and the kitchen. Of course, there were the three patios that faced beyond the hills, where she could sneak a smoke sometimes and even a drink when nobody was around. Her favorite thing to do was to step barefoot on the redwood planking while she looked out at the skyscrapers gleaming in the sunlight so far down below. There was the aqua-blue Olympic-sized pool that clung to the side of the hill surrounded by a bed of jagged yellow rocks. Thick green ferns, large pastel-colored flowering plants, and heavy-leaved foliage hung over the rocks and parts of the water, making it look like a lagoon, the sort she'd only seen in pictures. They never invited her for a swim, but then, she told herself, she didn't know how to swim anyway.

Today there was no time to go out on the deck. No time to make herself a sandwich with the expensive bread and the black stuff they kept in a jar in the refrigerator called "caviar." No time to imagine that this was her house and that she owned everything in it. Grabbing her bucket and cleaning sprays, Mariana hurried up to the second floor again. The Señora was ringing the buzzer and it echoed through the house. She wanted her morning coffee. The house was always silent this time of day. Still, usually, it was silent anyway, except for the cleaning crew, the ones that did the heavy cleaning, or her trainer, her manicurist, or her hairstylist. Their voices were the only sounds she heard, at least until the Señor came home. Then all the televisions were turned on and each room had a voice of its own.

She made sure the rooms were always swept and dusted, the beds made, and the shades drawn the way the Señora liked. There were no children in the house. The Señora was too old now. Besides, she couldn't have children and didn't believe in adoption, or so the Señor said. The Señora, well, you couldn't know precisely how old she was. That was probably because of the surgeries, and because she stayed so skinny, only eating lettuce without any dressing, and getting the rest of her calories from the alcohol that she kept in the cabinet downstairs.

The Señor? He still looked just like he did when she came to work here sixteen years ago. She was young and pretty then, in this country only a few months. A friend recommended the job when she quit here and went back to Mexico. Of course, the Señor was younger then, tall and handsome in his gray business suits, his hair gleaming silver, combed back from his tanned face. He played tennis in a white shirt and shorts that she was in charge of washing. She washed his clothes separately then and air-dried them so they wouldn't wrinkle. The Señora sent her clothes out to be cleaned.

The Señor had a son. He'd never lived with his father, and she knew the Señor was never married to his mother. She'd only seen him one time by accident. He was sitting in the car with the Señor, who forgot something at the house and returned to pick it up. She'd heard that the Señora didn't want him around, that she was jealous of his mother. Maybe it was true. She'd heard it from Layla, and you couldn't believe everything she said anyway.

The son was staring out of the window of the Cadillac when she saw him that time. He looked right at her, right in the eye. He was blond, like the Señor, but there was something else so familiar about his face, the shape of his eyes, the plump lips. So familiar. The way he pushed his hair back from his face. So much like someone. Who? She frowned, pushing back the thought. She never saw him again.

Mariana hurried to the kitchen and poured a cup of black

coffee into one of the English china cups the Señora prized, slid a saucer under it, and loaded it, along with a white linen napkin onto the polished mahogany tray. Then she hurried up the stairs.

The Señora was sitting up when she opened the door, and she took the cup without saying a thing, turning immediately to gaze out the window.

"Good morning," Mariana said as cheerfully as she could, setting the tray down and turning on her heel to leave. Her eyes immediately went to the large photograph on the bedside table. It was a picture of the Señor taken around the time she'd started working here. His silver-blonde hair was longish and fell over his forehead, and his sun-tanned skin looked like it would be warm if you touched it. Large blue eyes smiled at the camera, inviting her to stop and stare into them. Her face flushed, and for a moment, she could hear his deep voice murmuring and feel the strength of his arms.

Mariana looked away and hurried out the door, taking the steps two at a time until she reached the bottom. The Señor was older now, but just as handsome. Sometimes he smiled at her when he said "hello," but usually not. She wondered if he remembered at all or even thought about it ever again.

It was only that once, she reminded herself lost in thought. She was a lot younger then and recently married to Julian, but still curious about the world and this new place where she'd landed. Men still whistled on the street then, and she liked to pretend she didn't notice, all the while enjoying the attention, her cheeks getting red and the warm flush running down her body.

The Señor always looked her over back then and smiled. It looked like a smile of appreciation. Julian never studied her like that. She'd known him since she was twelve and they'd made the dangerous trek to the United States together. It was more about how they could help each other, and Julian never looked at another woman. At least not then, and you couldn't argue with that.

So Mariana smiled back at the Señor, welcoming the way his blue eyes roved over her body, and she liked it when they passed each other in the hall and he rubbed against her for the briefest of seconds. Would anything come of it? She liked to believe it. Sometimes she imagined that she lived in this fine house and all the things inside, including all the beautiful clothes, were hers. The Señora was younger then too, but hardly ever spoke to her once she'd been given instructions on what was expected of her every day. She'd mulled over those instructions again and again, on her long bus ride back to East Los Angeles.

It was warm that August night when it happened. The Señora was out of town with some friends in Las Vegas. Mariana helped her pack for the weekend. There were several suitcases stuffed with clothes. She remembered thinking the Señora would have to change clothes a lot to use everything she packed. She was planning to go home for the weekend, waiting to catch a later bus that wouldn't be sitting in traffic for the next few hours. The Señor had just returned from taking his wife to the airport. They were both in good spirits when they left. The Señora was actually smiling, and it wasn't because something she'd ordered in the mail had just arrived.

The Señor entered by the back door when he returned, and smiled at her, giving her a quick off-the-shoulder hug, as he shuffled over to the dining room. Mariana knew he'd been born with that shuffling walk from a small birth defect that got worse when the weather was damp like today. She often thought that he was perfect except for that little defect. He motioned her to sit at the table. She told him in a mixture of Spanish and halting English that she was going home, but he just shook his head and pointed to the antique dining room chair.

So, she sat down, and he poured her a glass of wine from one of the bottles he brought up from the cellar. The wine tasted so good, not like any wine Mariana ever had before. He poured her another glass, and then another. They finished that bottle, and then he brought another from downstairs. The Señor talked

163

the whole time, showing her pictures from the last trips they'd taken. She felt warm and relaxed and a little sleepy.

Reluctantly, Mariana got up from the table. Julian would be getting off his shift at the factory and coming home soon. She should be there, or he would worry. The Señor took her by the arm and gently led her toward the stairs. He was kissing her neck and murmuring things that she didn't understand. He led her up the stairs and into the bedroom where he and the Señora slept. He unbuttoned her blouse and began to kiss her. Part of her wanted to stop him, but he was so handsome and she was floating, feeling so happy and free.

His hands were moving now, and she heard him moaning and saw her clothes laying in a pile on the floor. Somehow, they were lying on the bed, and he was covering her with his body. Mariana heard him call out, and then it was over, and he rolled away to the other side of the bed. She remained there for a long time, not sure what to do next. When she heard him snoring, she sat up and put on her clothes.

It was late when she finally got home and opened the door to their second-floor apartment. Julian had already been home for a while and fixed himself a plate from the leftovers in the refrigerator. He asked her why she was later than usual, and she told him she'd had to help the Señora get ready for Las Vegas. Julian didn't question it. She thought he felt something was off, but she wasn't sure why. Just my conscience, she told herself. But after that night, he insisted they make love more than ever before. He seemed so much in love.

Mariana didn't see the Señor much after that. He was always traveling somewhere or at the office. When they did see each other, he nodded briefly and turned away. The first time it happened, she was hurt and tears spilled down her eyes. She hid in one of the bathrooms until she could stop crying.

A few months later, Mariana woke up and barely made it to the bathroom. She threw up all morning, and most of the mornings for the next few months as the pregnancy progressed.

Julian was proud and happy about the baby. He called every-body back home in the evening when the rates were cheaper.

She worked up until a day before the baby was born. He arrived early in the morning, after what seemed like hours of pushing. His soft, peach fuzz hair was the first thing she saw. Julian held him first, a small bundle with light greenish eyes. You could see how proud he was of his son. He smiled from ear to ear when he held him and named him Javier after his father.

Javier was a colicky baby right from the start. He cried day and night, even though Mariana gave him *manzana* tea, the way she'd learned from her mother. Her sisters were surprised every time they visited and heard him screaming away. No other baby in the family had ever been that vocal. He didn't want to nurse, which surprised and upset her. Every time he pushed her away, she felt hurt and rejected. Luckily he fed from a bottle but didn't like being held to close. He squirmed when Julian held him, flail-ing his arms and legs, as if he were a spider stuck in a web.

When Mariana started taking him out of the house in the stroller Julian bought for her, people always stopped and told her what a pretty baby he was. They also asked her if he looked like her employer, assuming that she was his nanny. "No, he's mine," she would say indignantly for the fifth time that day. Of course, he didn't look like her. He didn't have her olive skin and black straight hair. His eyes weren't dark brown. They were greenish. His fair hair was a medium brown and it curled in soft ringlets. He had long arms and legs too. Even his fingers and toes were long. She was pretty sure he wouldn't grow up to look like her, short in stature. Small. He looked even less like Julian.

As Javier started to grow, she caught Julian staring at the baby, his face puckered in concern. He held him in his lap while he squirmed to get free and studied his small fingers and toes. Then he took her hands and held them up to Javier's. He looked from one to another and then dropped the baby's hands and turned away.

When it came time to feed Javier solid food, she prepared

the mashed rice and beans that her family always fed the babies, but he spit it out and refused to eat. His babysitter, Rosa, who spent the day taking care of him while she cleaned the big house on the hill for the Señora, complained that he was losing weight, and looked at her with contempt. That day she went to the market and spent the rest of her food budget on high-end baby food, labeled "homemade without preservatives." She tasted it, and it was disgusting, but Javier gulped down spoon after spoon, happily, and began eating well.

Julian started going out at night with his friends to drink after work. Mariana was too busy taking care of Javier and putting her messy apartment back together at the end of the day to mind. Besides, Julian seemed to stay away from Javier when he was home. He seemed to stay away from her too. When she finally got Javier to sleep, she sat alone in the stillness of her apartment, letting the memories return. She wondered what the Señor was thinking and what he was doing. He knew of course that Mariana had a baby. The Señora sent her an expensive playpen from a baby shop in Beverly Hills as a gift, but Julian didn't approve and wouldn't let her use it. The playpen ended up folded into sections in the hall closet. She didn't argue with Julian.

Javier started to crawl, languidly cruising around the living room, he sometimes stared up at her curiously, as if he wondered who she was. When Mariana spoke to him in Spanish, he turned his head up and listened, but he never tried to repeat the words himself, the way she thought he would. Rosa said she spoke to Javier in English because she started night school and knew quite a few words. Javier picked up the English words immediately. He began speaking in sentences and sometimes she couldn't understand what he said.

Later, Javier would whine whenever Julian tried to hold him or play with him. He stared at Julian suspiciously as if he didn't trust him. Julian didn't take the rejection well. "He doesn't like me because I'm dark," he told her. "He doesn't like dark people. You can see for yourself."

Actually, she could see. But she was so proud of the little boy who looked like an angel in a painting; proud to carry him around, and know he was a part of her. "He's just a baby. He doesn't know anything," she told herself.

Julian surprised her by asking her to quit her job and find another house to work in. He wouldn't give her a reason, just that he didn't like her going there anymore. She told him that good jobs were hard to find these days, and the Señora paid her well and on time. Besides the work wasn't all that hard, and they let her leave at 4:30, instead of five. They argued that night, and Julian went out and didn't come home. She didn't miss him. Her baby was all that counted.

Julian lost his job a week later. He said they'd accused him of stealing some tools and it was really the owner's son, but they always blamed the Mexicans. He had trouble getting another job after that because they always called his old boss for references. He started going to the Home Depot parking lot in the morning to stand with many other men looking for a day's work, hoping some white man needed his house painted or his yard cleaned. The men rushed the truck whenever a white man cruised through the parking lot looking them over, like so many cattle at an auction. Sometimes Julian was hired, but a lot of the time he wasn't. Dejected when he wasn't chosen, he spent the rest of his day hanging around with his friends who didn't have work either. They pooled their money and bought liquor. Julian came home either drunk or sick, spending most of his time in the bathroom. He avoided Mariana. There was a defensive wall around him, and he hunched his shoulders in shame. He couldn't provide for his family and she was self-sufficient without him.

When Javier was two, Julian met another woman, the sister of one of the men that met at Home Depot. He snuck around with her for a while and then one cold rainy weekend, he came home early from a day spent pulling weeds on the grounds of some business park and told Mariana he was leaving to be with the other woman. It only took a matter of minutes to deliver the message. She wasn't surprised. Not the way things were going. He didn't even look at Javier as he walked out the door.

Then they were alone, just herself and Javier. He was a sturdy child, with soft floppy sun-touched hair and large greenish eyes. His skin and hair were turning darker now and his nose a little broader. But his features were still Anglo, she told herself. He was used to being with her now and his eyes followed her around the apartment, always watching. Without Julian sometimes helping out with money, they had to move, so she found a family with a back house for rent. It was perfect for them, and Rosa liked the arrangement more than before. Julian came to visit them a few times and then stopped. He said his new girlfriend didn't want him over there.

Then Javier was walking, a slow lumbering baby walk. He shuffled from side to side on his baby legs. She watched him coming toward her, arms outstretched. He'll outgrow that shuffle she thought.

When she was cleaning the Señora's house, she sometimes saw the Señor. He looked at her now, instead of avoiding her eyes. He said, "Good morning," and "Good evening," if he happened to be around. He wasn't friendly, but he was polite. Whenever he was around, she watched him, looking for him to give her some sign that he remembered they'd once been together, but he never did.

The Señora just seemed to grow crankier as time passed. She kept ringing her bell, demanding this and that. She criticized everything that was done in the house and yelled at all the deliverymen. The Señora spent more time awake now and sat at her computer ordering clothes that were delivered in large cardboard boxes every day. Mariana dutifully carried them upstairs for Señora's inspection.

One day the Señor stopped Mariana as she climbed the stairs and took the packages out of her hands. His face was red with anger. He took all the packages into the bedroom and started yelling at the Señora. She didn't understand all of it, but it seemed he was angry because the Señora spent so much money on clothes that she didn't wear. He said he was getting older and he couldn't work as hard anymore. The Señora would have to cut down on expenses. He told the Señora that she had to return the clothes.

As she helped the Señor carry the boxes back down to the gate, Mariana studied his face. He was getting old! She hadn't noticed before. He must be around sixty. She wondered if she should tell him, introduce him to Javier. What would he say? What would the Señora say? The Señor would probably deny it and they would fire her. They wouldn't trust her because she'd waited so long. They'd probably think she wanted something from them. She didn't. She'd raised Javier herself, without help from anyone, and what would Javier think, knowing this rich powerful man was related to him? She wondered if everything would change. Maybe the Señor would take Javier in and he could live in this lavish house. No, that didn't seem likely. Maybe he would give him money. That way Javier could go to college instead of straight to work.

She thought about it the rest of the day. Javier had no feelings for Julian anyhow. He barely remembered him, and only as the man who left his mother. She'd thought it over many times before. Javier had a right to know the other part of his family. All kinds of benefits came with that, and every mother wanted the best for her son. Javier had never asked any questions, but maybe if she told him he'd go directly to the Señor. If the Señor questioned it, there was always a blood test. She told herself she was the powerful one this time because she had her son.

Javier was almost seventeen now. He worked part-time, and it seemed he was going to finish high school. Mariana was proud that she'd been able to work all these years in the same house in this country so Javier could finish school. Maybe he could even go to college and get a good job someday. How could she be sure that telling him would make things better in his life. Mariana told herself she couldn't.

Maybe Javier would resent her for not telling him sooner, for making him miss out on a better life all this time. Maybe he'd compare their life to the Señor's and be ashamed that Mariana was a house maid. What if he didn't want her around? He was all she had. She couldn't bear that. Let it go, she told herself. You don't have to say anything now. Nobody's asked.

But sometimes she worried, watching Javier as he walked across the room or hurried down the hall. He walked quickly with an obvious shuffle that never went away. Nobody else seemed to see it, but she did.

Today was Saturday, and Javier was asleep on the old green fold-out couch in the living room since his bed was taken. Mariana rented out the extra bed in the hall alcove to an old man who worked nights in a factory. The old man was sleeping now and snored like a bull. Mariana noticed one of her son's legs hung over the edge of the couch. She pulled a blanket from the closet and covered it. He was sleeping so peacefully, she thought. Measuring his breaths. Julian was stupid to leave his son, but Mariana didn't understand the changes she could see in Javier's behavior, and she wished that Julian was here to help her stop them.

Javier lay on his side, his arm partially covered his face, the deep copper of his skin glowing against the faded green couch cushions. Sometime during the last week he'd buzzed off all of his hair, the lighter brown hair was gone, and now only dark stubble showed against his scalp. Mariana didn't like his head shaved. "You look like a *cholo*," she told him angrily when she saw it. It wasn't only the hair that bothered her. For the past year or so, he'd managed to add even more tattoos, obvious ones that were very large and looked like they were rising up from his skin.

"They do some great work down in Long Beach. Don't they?" Javier said proudly last night when he saw her staring at the twisted red and blue drawings after he took off his shirt.

Mariana was horrified. She'd been too busy to notice how many tattoos he had. "No more," she yelled.

Javier just smiled and gave her a hug.

"Where are you getting the money for this?" she demanded.

Javier didn't answer. "Everybody has tattoos," he told her. To prove his point, he grabbed the remote and punched in MTV. "See that?" He pointed at two young white men wearing wife beaters and low-slung pants, their entire bodies and arms were covered in bright colors and patterns. "Do you know how much those guys make?" He shook his head in wonder at the thought. "See, they're white too, not *cholos*." He added.

"I don't care," Mariana shot back. "It's different for white guys. Everything is different for white people. That's how they expect to see us, all covered in *tatuaje de pandilla*. You're just asking for trouble. Something bad will happen to you if they think you're a gang member. Don't you hear the news?"

"Relax," Javier laughed. "You know I'm not in any gang. "You like to worry. That's all."

Mariana folded her arms over her chest and thought about how angry Javier's *abuelo* would be if he saw him like this. At least Javier was still in school. She reminded herself of that every day.

Now in the morning light as he slept without his shirt, Mariana could see that the tattoos covered both his arms and the sides and front of his neck. The small tattoos on his chest that used to be covered by a T-shirt were now the center points for the picture of a large eagle surrounded by coiling snakes and strangely shaped letters that she couldn't read. The coiling snakes had flickering tongues that wrapped around his neck and ran down to his wrists. Two-inch letters "J", "A" and "V," for Javier, were tattooed on the front of his neck. Small X's were tattooed under his eyes and on the sides of his face.

Mariana turned her head away wondering why her son wasn't taking advantage of his clean-cut good looks. Why did he want to look like a Mexican gangster? She watched while Javier's skin tanned to a deep bronze from the sun while he worked construction with his cousin Pablo last summer. Then she fretted silently because his color didn't fade when the weather turned cooler. At least he had his light hair and eyes, she thought. But now as time passed, his eyes seemed to be turning from hazel to a darker brown, and whatever hair he hadn't buzzed off was nearly black. And those tattoos! She shook her head and wondered what she should do. Maybe it was all in his fate and he was meant to look the way he did all along.

When she went to park her old Honda at the top of the hill above the Señora's house the next day, she saw a large red Jeep was parked in her usual spot. Mariana glared at the shiny vehicle and wondered who owned it. Now she had to drive down to the bottom of the hill and walk back up. The walk, when she had to make it, always made her back and legs hurt. Today her back would hurt before she even started the heavy vacuuming and floor polishing.

As she walked up to the house, she saw the Señor's Mercedes parked in front. What's he doing home? She wondered. It was a weekday and he was hardly ever there on those days.

Mariana let herself in the front door and looked down the corridor into the cavernous living room covered in imported tile from Spain. She could hear voices echoing. Somebody was arguing. She tiptoed over the entryway and flattened herself against the wall so she could hear more.

It was the Señor and another man, but she didn't recognize the other man's voice. The Señor was angry. She could hear that much, and she had only seen him that way a few times before. She watched as he paced back and forth in front of silk-cushioned carved wrought iron furniture.

"Don't think I'm going to help you out again! If you want to act like a punk, you better do it on your own dime. I'm not posting bail again, Brandon."

Mariana stiffened. Brandon was the Señor's son. She remembered the name. She looked up the stairs and wondered if the Señora was listening to this. Did she even know Brandon was in the house? She wasn't going to like it when she found out.

"You can stay here for now, if you don't want to go back to your mother's." The Señor's voice was loud and he sounded frantic. "But you need to go back to school or get a job. I pay a fortune for that damn school, just to have you flunk out, get kicked out. You're not going to lie around all day and do your damned drugs. How am I going to explain it to her?" Mariana watched as the Señor gestured toward the staircase leading up to the second-floor master bedroom.

The voice belonging to Brandon responded. "Don't know. Tell her what happened I guess."

"You think I want to tell her you got arrested for dealing drugs and burglary? What the hell were you thinking? She's going to be furious you're here, you know. And you want me to tell her that?"

"Well, that's what the charges were." Brandon spat back. "If you don't want me here and if you're afraid of her, I've got friends. I can go there." Brandon challenged.

Brandon's voice was so familiar.

The Señor's face was red, and he was pulling his tie loose from his collar. "I know you think I'm made of money, but I worked hard for all this. I'm not throwing away any more money on a two-bit punk, even if you are my son!" The Señor was yelling and pointing. "Do you know how much it cost me to get them to drop the other charges? Who I had to suck off with contract awards? I had to deal with the City, after I paid for your shyster lawyer, and I'm not through paying. What would you do if I didn't have influence around here? Sit your ass in some cell till you rot. That's what!"

"I'm not sending you to rehab again, either. How the hell can someone get kicked out of that? With all the money I paid, they didn't even want to keep you there." The Señor's voice dropped, as if he suddenly remembered where he was and who could hear. "And the gun charge? Where did you get it? Why do you need a gun? It's those no good *cholos* you're hanging around with! You have every advantage! I made sure of that. I pay for it. Do you know how much money I've given your mother all these years? Do you?"

Mariana watched Brandon shrug his shoulders and slump in his chair. She could hear her heart beating and she covered her chest self-consciously as if that would quiet the vibration.

"Go get your damn suitcase!" The Señor yelled. "Take it to the downstairs guestroom, and then come back up. I'm going to find you another private school. No son of mine is going to be a drop out!" The Señor walked away, taking long strides. When he got to the second floor, he walked to the end of the corridor and slammed the door.

Mariana stayed rooted to the spot, not wanting to move. Not wanting them to know she was listening. Brandon wasn't in any hurry to move though. He put his feet up on one of the ornate tables and lit a cigarette. After inhaling, he flicked his wrist that rested on the arm of the sofa and the ashes dropped onto the teak wood floor. Mariana gasped and covered her mouth. She looked at her watch. She needed to start working even if it meant cutting through the living room. She took a deep breath and started forward passing a few feet from where Brandon was sitting.

She kept her head down but snuck a quick look at the figure on the couch. It was amazing! Brandon resembled her son so much. His skin was lighter than Javier's, rosy and almost translucent, and his hair was almost blond, but it was also shaved down close to his scalp. From what she could see, his arms and neck were almost completely covered with tattoos. Seeing the tattoos made her heart sink. As she stepped past him, he looked up and she saw he had light-colored eyes. The color Javier's were before they changed to a darker brown. They're brothers, of course, she thought, a sudden uneasiness tightening her chest.

Mariana worked doggedly, absently waxing the same areas of the floors twice. She found herself thinking about Brandon most of the day, wondering about his mother and what his life was like away from here. It sounded like the Señor provided for him well, he'd stepped up as a father she thought. But Brandon didn't seem to appreciate it.

At noon Mariana peered out the French doors facing the street and looked for Brandon's red Jeep, but it was gone. She felt oddly relieved. The house was quiet again. Driving home, she wondered again, how different Javier's life would be if the Señor knew. He could swim in that big pool and go to private school, drive a nice car instead of the beat-up Honda, but oddly she couldn't think of much else.

The next day Javier drove her to work, it was some kind of school holiday he said, and he wanted to borrow the car. She told him it was fine. They rode in silence, until Javier announced that he was thinking of joining the Marines.

"Why?" Mariana wanted to know dismayed. "I want you to go to college. Get an education! That's what I work for."

Javier just sighed and didn't answer. He tapped on the wheel impatiently. "I'll pick you up at 4:30 right?" He leaned over and gave her hand a squeeze. "Bye Mom, catch you later."

Mariana nodded, upset with this latest development. Brandon's red Jeep was parked at the curb and Javier took a long look at it as she got out of the car. She could see the envy in his face and it worried her.

Brandon was home all day. The Señor was trying to find him a new school and it involved both of them sitting at the computer and making many phone calls. Mariana served cup after cup of black coffee at the Señor's direction and emptied the black onyx ash tray that kept filling up. The Señor was set up in his office, but Brandon preferred to stay in the den where he sprawled in a leather chair and played video games until the Señor yelled; "Get in here! I want you to take a look at this one. The bastards are charging an arm and a leg!"

The Señor introduced Brandon to Mariana a few hours later and told her Brandon would be staying here in the guestroom. Mariana fixed them both lunch, cold cut sandwiches made from grass-fed beef and ham and gluten-free potato salad made from cauliflower. The Señora had all the groceries delivered from a high-end market across town and printed up weekly menus in case Mariana had to prepare any meals for her husband. As far as Mariana could see she never ate anything herself.

After lunch Mariana returned to washing the linens and Brandon went out to swim laps in the pool. She watched him from afar through the kitchen window nervously and noted that even his legs were covered in tattoos. After an hour or so he stretched out in one of the deck chairs and appeared to go to sleep. Mariana kept watching. His pale skin underneath the tattoos burned pink in the sun. He didn't tan like her Javier.

At four o'clock Brandon wandered back into the living room, leaving wet puddles on the freshly waxed floor. Biting her lip, she went straight for the mop and followed behind him. While she was cleaning the entryway, the Señora walked slowly down the stairs. Mariana raised her eyes in surprise. The Señora was dressed in a knit dress and wearing one of her pairs of Manolo Blahniks with thin gold straps that wrapped around her ankles.

She looked over in the direction of the huge flat screen television that dominated one of the south-facing walls. Brandon was deeply engrossed in the video game he was playing and only looked down to check the control. The Señora stopped in the center of the staircase and stared at him. Her mouth puckered in distaste and she leaned over the railing and called out, "Shouldn't you be doing something constructive instead of sitting on my couch all day? If you have to be here, I'd suggest you stay in your room, so I don't have to see you whenever I come through here."

Brandon didn't look up. "It's my father's couch, he paid for it, just like everything else. You can't say shit to me."

Mariana reddened, feeling embarrassed for the Señora whose eyes were wide with surprise, the skin on her face and neck looking flushed and mottled. She's not used to being talked to like that, Mariana thought. Brandon was certainly very rude. His mother, whomever she was, hadn't taught him any manners. Javier never talked to adults like that. If he ever did, he would feel the back of her hand across his mouth.

She watched the Señora's face settle into an angry scowl. *She hates Brandon,* Mariana thought. *He's another woman's child.* The Señora would hate Javier too. She would never let him into the Señor's life if the truth ever came out. First, she'd have to deal with the Señor to prove Javier was his son and then with the Señora's anger and resentment. Poor Javier would be in the middle of it all and he'd probably turn against her too. Mariana shivered. Her instincts had been right. Don't tell!

"I'm meeting friends for dinner," the Señora said, turning to Mariana, "In case my husband asks." The house was silent except for the sound of her heels clicking on the tiled floor and the slamming of the heavy front door.

Mariana walked back to the kitchen and leaned against the counter. She felt suddenly exhausted and realized that she had been worrying nonstop since she first saw Brandon here.

The doorbell rang at four thirty before she had time to take off her apron, grab her purse and go downstairs to meet Javier. She finished putting the dishes in the dishwasher and started toward the living room. Javier was never early. It must be somebody else, she thought.

"Your son's here!" Brandon called out.

Mariana grabbed her purse and headed for the living room. Javier and Brandon were standing on the front deck talking. Brandon was pointing to the red Jeep, and Javier was nodding his head. Seeing them standing together brought a cold chill up her back and she could feel her heart begin to beat faster. Javier was pointing to the tattoos on his arms and she could see by his face that Brandon approved. She wondered if they saw how similar they looked to each other. It didn't seem that they did. She watched them deep in conversation. They didn't see her come in. She stood there for what seemed like the longest time watching them talk.

Finally, Mariana called out. "I'm ready to go, Javier."

"Oh?" Javier looked up distracted. "You can take the car Mom. Brandon and I are going to hang out here for a while. We'll probably go get something to eat later."

"What?" Mariana listened to the words shocked. She turned to Brandon. "Did you ask your father?"

"Why?" Brandon looked at her puzzled. "I come and go like I please."

Mariana turned to Javier, "I don't think … You have school tomorrow, and aren't you supposed to work a few hours tonight at Reese's Burgers …" Mariana began and stopped.

Javier and Brandon stared at her. Javier frowned, looking embarrassed, he handed her the car keys. "I'm calling in sick. Here's your keys. I'll see you later." He turned away and followed Brandon down the corridor.

Mariana's heart pounded and she felt a sudden chill. Javier was almost seventeen. In Mexico he wouldn't be a teenager, he would be a man, working full-time, probably supporting himself and the family, making his own decisions. But here, Javier was still a schoolboy. He lived with his mother and he'd always obeyed her, treating her with respect. He knew how she wanted him to act and what she wanted him to do without even asking. Before today.

Mariana drove home her eyes stinging with tears. Something had shifted today, tilted her whole world, and now there was nothing to hold on to, nothing to ground her and keep her from falling. She was sliding away from everything she knew, everything that was familiar and comfortable. She must have dozed off staring blankly at the television screen because when she woke up, she saw it was three o'clock and Javier was not curled up on the green couch where he usually slept.

"An accident!" she thought. Something bad must have happened. Javier had never stayed out this late before. She grabbed her phone and dialed, but it went straight to message. She got up and looked out the window but the world outside was dark, peaceful and untouched, except for an occasional low-pitched bark from the dog next door, and the sound of a car traveling down the street toward the freeway. Mariana kept trying to call Javier on her cell phone but gave up at five o'clock. She thought about calling the police but that was risky since she was illegal. You never knew what trouble they could bring. They might want to see her social security card or her driver's license, both of which were fake. She considered the hospitals and decided that she would start calling as soon as it was light. She made herself a small pot of coffee and tried calling again.

Just as she heard Javier's message start up again, Javier walked through the door. She smelled him before he even stepped into the cramped apartment: sweat, cigarettes, marijuana, and stale beer.

"Where have you been?" She demanded. "I called and called, and you didn't answer."

"Oh," Javier yawned when he answered. "Battery's dead" and pointed the blank screen in her direction.

"Were you with Brandon?" She wanted to know.

"Yep," Javier answered.

Mariana looked at his face; it was grimy and streaked with sweat. His usually white T-shirt that she laundered herself looked like one of the rags used to polish furniture in the Señora's house.

"Where did you go?"

"Just chilled. Here and there, you know." He collapsed on the couch and she saw that his skin had a greenish pallor. She stepped closer. Javier smelled of vomit.

"I didn't give you permission to go out last night you know."

Javier shrugged and turned his back to her curling up on his side.

"Aren't you going to school?"

"Nah, too tired."

"I don't like you missing school. Only when you're sick."

"I'm sick! Okay? I have a fucking headache." Javier snapped, and rubbed his eyes which were bloodshot and watery.

She stepped back, shocked. Javier never talked to her this way. "You drank too much. I know that much and you're under-age too. What if the police catch you? I don't want you hanging around with Brandon anymore. It's not good because I work for his father."

"Brandon's got a pretty sweet deal," Javier mumbled, his face in the sofa cushion. "Nobody bothering him, nobody tell-ing him what to do, his own credit cards. He can buy whatever he wants too."

"He's not a good boy," Mariana felt the tears leaking from the corners of her eyes. "He's in trouble, I heard it."

"Well if he is his father will take care of it. He told me his father knows all kinds of people. He can fix anything. Brandon never has to worry."

"What happens if you get in trouble hanging around with him?" Mariana dabbed at her eyes with the bottom of her apron.

"I guess you'll have to fix it then," Javier told her sarcastical-ly and covered his head with the green velour pillow.

The next evening Javier came home to take a shower and she served him rice and beans that she made yesterday. He made a face as he looked at the plate. "Is there anything else? That's all we eat around here." he complained. "I don't want any of that."

For the next few days, she didn't see much of Javier. He wasn't there when she returned home and didn't come in until almost morning. "I was with my friends," he told her curtly when she asked. Then he curled up on the couch to sleep and turned away from her.

Mariana kept a careful eye on Brandon while she was at work. He still wasn't in school and slept most of the day locked in the guestroom. The Señor came home early on Wednesday and forced him to get up and go out to the pool so that Mariana could clean the room where he was staying. She held her nose as soon as she opened the door. The bedsheets were twisted and filthy and liquor bottles covered the floor. Brandon had burned holes in the carpet with his cigarette ashes. The Señora would go crazy if she saw the room this way. Mariana sighed as she went to tackle the bathroom next.

On Thursday morning, she left her car with Javier because he said he needed it for an errand for one of his classes. She was relieved to hear he was going to school since he'd missed two days already this week, and his boss from the fast food restaurant where he worked part-time kept calling her number looking for him. At eleven o'clock she heard the thud of the brass door knocker banging against the heavy wooden front door, followed by the shrill sound of the door buzzer echoing through the first and second floors. She ran to answer it and Javier was standing there.

"Here, I brought you the car. I don't need it. I'm chilling with Brandon today." He looked in the direction of the pool.

"What about school?" Mariana was dismayed. For the last couple of days, she thought Javier had stopped hanging around with Brandon. Now he was coming back to this house, a place she didn't want to see him.

"What are you doing here? Why aren't you in school?" Mariana wanted to know.

Javier looked around, straining to see past her into the cavernous entryway. "Don't know. It's boring. It's not like I'm going to college or anything. Just a waste of time. My friends don't go. They went and got jobs. Now they have money to spend."

"You spent all the money you earned on those horrible ..." Marina pointed her finger at the tattoos covering his arms. "If you don't go to school, you'll just have bad jobs all your life."

"Well I don't want to work in a greasy restaurant anymore, so I'm not!" Javier told her. "I quit there. Got better things to do!"

"Better things? You mean being here?"

Javier didn't answer. Mariana stepped back and watched her son walk away toward Brandon's room. He didn't walk with the steps of someone who was cautious, a little unsure, like the guests that came here to visit the Señor, once in a while, the guests she made little sandwiches for, cut freshly grown strawberries into halves, and brewed gourmet coffee or organic tea. He walked as if he had lived here always.

Sometime when she was cleaning the den, Javier and Brandon went out. Brandon's red Jeep wasn't parked in front of the Señor's house in the early afternoon and it wasn't there when she started up her Honda and drove home after work.

She wasn't surprised when Javier didn't come home that night, but she stayed on the green couch waiting just in case until she fell asleep. It was light when she got the call.

"Mom, you need to help me. Something went down last night, and I got caught up."

"Caught up?" Mariana struggled to understand.

"Yeah," the voice on the other end was sobbing.

For a moment, she hesitated. It was Javier's voice, but it was the first time she'd heard him crying in a long time. She was awake now and tense. "Where are you?"

"Downtown. County."

"County?"

"Jail. I'm in jail!" Javier yelled into the phone.

Mariana felt a cold chill move down her body. This was the fear she'd carried in the back of her mind ever since Javier was small, the fear that one day, no matter how hard she tried, she would get a call like this. Her mind raced. Javier was legal though, born here in White Memorial. No matter what he did they couldn't deport him.

"What happened? What did you do?"

"I can't tell you on the phone," Javier sniffed. "You can't come to see me till I finish getting processed. It's not my fault what happened. It's the damn cops. They're all racist mother-fuckers. All of them!"

Mariana started crying. "*Mijo*, Are you all right? Are you hurt?"

There was a long pause. "They beat the shit outta me. You gotta get me outta here! Get me a lawyer! I didn't resist arrest. They're lyin!"

Mariana held onto the couch for support. "What should I do?"

Javier gave her two numbers to write down. "Here's the phone number for information and my booking number," he told her. "If you call there, they'll tell you when I'm going to be arraigned. They set bail that day."

"Arraigned?" Mariana whispered to herself. The word sounded terrifying. "Bail," She knew what that was. Her stomach lurched. "How much money is the bail?"

"I don't know yet. Call a bail bondsman. I've got to hang up." She heard him take a deep gulping breath and then there was silence on the line.

Mariana stared at the number written on the back of her prescription receipt. *What if I can't understand their English?* she wondered as she punched in the numbers. *What will I do?* Her hands were shaking, and her tears made the cell phone screen blurry. There was a recorded message, and she was relieved when it directed her to a Spanish-speaking prompt. Following the directions, she carefully typed in the numbers that Javier gave her. Since he was arrested and taken into custody on a Friday, he wouldn't be arraigned and formally charged until Monday. His processing would be complete though by tomorrow and he could have visitors.

Mariana felt a blinding headache beginning behind her eyes and moving around her head like a rope that someone was squeezing tighter and tighter. She stumbled back to her bed and did what she'd only done twice before in all the years she'd worked there, she called the Señora and told her she wouldn't be coming in to work today. She apologized in her best English. "*Gracias Dios,*" she said as she put down her phone, because the Señora wasn't awake yet, and she was able to leave a voicemail.

Mariana stayed in her room for the remainder of the day, tossing in her bed, trying to fall asleep and shut out the sound of Javier's voice asking for help. How did this happen? She'd done her best, worked hard and spent every penny she earned on Javier. She made sure he ate well and went to school every day. She bought him new clothes at the beginning of each school year. Since he didn't have a father to help, not even Julian, it was all up to her. He was doing well, too, she told herself. She'd never seen him with anybody from a gang even though their neighborhood was full of *cholos*. Of course, there were those tattoos, but white boys had them too. All you had to do was look around. What happened to Javier? Why did he get in trouble? she wondered doggedly, shifting from her stomach to her back, the pain in her head was the same either way.

She was up early the next morning. The headache was almost gone. The recording said Javier could have visitors, so she could see him today, to make sure he was all right, to let him know that she would do whatever he needed. But was that safe? She rubbed her eyes and remembered that ICE was arresting people coming from court. Were they arresting them at the jail when they went to visit their families? She thought she remembered someone she knew getting deported that way. Hadn't her friend Layla told her that?

Mariana sighed and twisted her hands. If ICE picked her up, she'd be deported for sure and she had no money to try and get back. Then what would happen to Javier? Who would take care of him? Still, she couldn't just leave him there alone. It all must be a mistake. Javier was a good boy. It would get straightened out she told herself. Mariana ran the scenario over in her mind. How could she help him if there was no money for bail or for a lawyer? He would have to get a public defender, she thought. That's what people with no money did. She took a ragged breath. Javier was scared, and she was his mother. Of course, she'd go and see him! She needed to tell him she loved him, and that he was her beautiful son, that everything would be all right. That's what mothers did. She felt a pang of guilt for worrying about herself.

The next day Mariana was one of the first visitors in line at Central Jail. She stood next to several Black women pushing small children in strollers and a few toddlers who followed along still bundled in their pajamas. They were ushered into a large room with benches along the wall and several vending machines. An older child, about eight, wearing an oversized Kershaw baseball jersey, ran up to the first machine. "They have Flaming Hot Cheetos!" He yelled in excitement, dancing from one foot to the other.

His mother grabbed him by the arm, pushing him down onto the bench besides her. Mariana bowed her head and listened to him crying, while he wiped his nose on the sleeve of his jersey, grateful that she'd never taken Javier to a place like this when he was a child. After a while, a man in uniform came out and gave them some papers to fill out. Luckily, there was a Spanish version on the one side, and it asked for her driver's license. Mariana hesitated and then filled it out and returned it to the man in uniform sitting behind a glass partition. The sheriff told her to sit down and they would call her when they located Javier.

By nine o'clock the room was full and all of the benches were occupied. Smaller children sat on the floor at the feet of their parents. Women trailed in wearing house slippers and pajama pants. A few wore halters that barely covered their breasts, unabashed at the rolls of fat that hung below. Mariana stared at them open-mouthed looking down at her slacks and long-sleeved shirt.

A few boys who looked about ten, dressed in basketball shorts and tank tops, chased each other barefoot around the strollers, laughing and throwing a wad of balled-up paper back and forth. Music boomed from a large radio and some of the older teenagers called out to each other and bopped their heads in time to the beat.

The room was mostly full of women, Mariana noticed, women with children, young women alone or with friends, and older women by themselves, faces drawn and eyes downcast, mothers like herself. She hoped their sons were here by mistake too. Here and there, a young man sat by himself, waiting, probably somebody's brother or relative she thought. There were only a few white people in the room. Didn't anybody come to visit the white prisoners? she wondered. Probably there weren't very many. The people she saw getting arrested on *Cops* were always Black or Hispanic.

As the time passed, the room grew noisier, the din from dozens of conversations enclosed within the waiting room walls. The air was heavy and damp, filled with the ripe smell of children's unwashed bodies. How did Javier end up in this place? She shifted in her seat wanting to use the bathroom but afraid of losing her space. What if they called her and she wasn't there? She might miss a visit with her son.

Mariana watched the clock on the wall as the hands moved by slowly; one hour and then two. The babies in the strollers cried. The mother of one of the smaller babies wrapped in a dirty pink blanket, lifted up her blouse and began to nurse. Mariana blushed and looked away. The toddlers, bored and tired of sitting, began to whine and one of them sitting near her feet fell asleep on the cold tile floor. His mother was talking on her cell phone and didn't seem to notice. Mariana wanted to pick him up off the dusty, sticky floor and hold him, but she was afraid to approach the Black woman to ask if she could. She didn't think she'd ever talked with a Black person before. She sat and looked down at the floor and pictured Javier's round baby face smiling up at her as she looked down into his crib. She could see him riding the tricycle she bought him one Christmas. All they needed in that world was each other.

After a while, Mariana noticed that almost all of the other people had been called and sent into another room. She waited for another hour. Finally, she went up to the check at window again to ask about Javier. A small bald-headed Asian sheriff with wire-rimmed glasses told her impatiently they were still trying to locate him in the system since he was a recent booking, and they would let her know when they did.

At three o'clock, when her stomach hurt because she hadn't eaten, and her back ached from sitting on the hard, plastic bench for so many hours, another sheriff motioned her to the window and said Javier was waiting behind glass partition number ten on the other side. She could talk to him by using the phone on her side of the wall directly in front of the partition.

Mariana walked through the door, her heart beating quickly, the blood pounding in her ears. The room contained rows of partitions separated by Plexiglass sheets. A phone was attached to the wall of each partition under a sign showing a stick figure picking up the phone to speak. She hurried over to the partition marked 10 and looked for Javier. There was nobody there, so she waited ten more minutes, standing in front of the glass. Then she saw him, limping toward her window in an orange jumpsuit, leaning on crutches and motioning her to pick up the phone on the wall. Mariana stared in shock and grabbed the phone as she started to cry. Javier's eyes were black and swollen, and his face was covered in cuts and bruises. The left side of his scalp had been shaved and black stitches ran upward from his ear and across the side of his head. His right hand was in a thick white cast.

"Oh my god! What happened?" she covered her mouth to stifle the sobs choking her voice.

Javier tucked the receiver under his left ear with his free hand and looked up at Mariana. "I had a problem last night," he answered quietly, and then looked down at the floor.

Mariana blinked back the tears, watching his mouth as he talked, his swollen lips covering his broken front teeth.

Javier looked around quickly as if he didn't want to be heard. Tears started running down his face and he whispered into the phone so that Mariana had to strain to hear what he said. "I've got to get out of here. I can't take it. I want you to get a lawyer. Bail me out!"

Mariana gaped at the boy behind the glass. Her son. Gone was the happy, easy-going teenager she remembered sleeping peacefully on her couch, the one who always gave her a hug and hung around in the kitchen while she fixed him something to eat. He'd been replaced by a man she didn't know, a different man, with features only similar to Javier's, a face that looked aged, distorted and ugly, brown eyes that were now sunken and haunted, the eyes of a terrified and broken man. "What happened to you?" She asked again, the shock starting to register.

Javier lowered his voice. "I was just chillin with Brandon and he told me this guy, Kyle, owed him some money, so we went across town to collect it. Brandon gave me his gun to hold. We went to Kyle's house and parked in the driveway. Kyle came out and said he didn't have the money. Brandon said he was lying and threatened to hurt him if he didn't pay up. Kyle told us to get the fuck out. Then Brandon told me to show Kyle the gun. So, I pointed it at him to show him we meant business. When Kyle saw it, he came running at me to take it away. I don't know what happened, I guess I got scared and pulled the trigger. Kyle went down right away, I hit him in the chest and then a bunch of Kyle's friends came out of the house and jumped us."

Mariana listened, shocked. "Brandon gave you a gun? You shot a gun? Why *Mijo*? Why?" she moaned clutching her chest.

Javier kept talking, the words from his swollen mouth muddled and hard to understand. "That's not all. A neighbor heard the shots and called the cops. They got there when we were fighting and they tried to grab Brandon, but he got away with a couple of Kyle's friends, and they couldn't catch them. They called more cops and sat two of the guys on the curb. Then they all came over to me and started hitting me with their sticks. They beat the hell out of me, broke my arm and my ankle. I was the only one those pigs were beating on. They didn't touch the white guys."

Javier gestured at his cast. "One of them got me down and grabbed me around the neck. He said, 'Where I was raised, they kill Mexicans.' He started banging my head on the ground and the other cops were just standing there watching. I threw him off and punched him in the face. Then he fell back and hit his head on the bumper of Kyle's jeep. He just lay there and bled all over the driveway."

Mariana clutched the phone, pressing it to her ear. The

sudden silence on the other end was so loud it filled her head. She squeezed her eyes shut, trying not to imagine the horrible things Javier described. "What happened to that policeman?"

Javier's voice dropped even more, "They said he's in critical condition … but Kyle, the guy I shot … he's dead." Javier leaned against the wall and sobbed into the phone. "It's bad, real bad, I know. It all happened so fast. I'm sorry Mama. I didn't mean it."

"What about Brandon?" She heard herself ask dully. "You said he was there with you. What happened to Brandon?" She pictured Brandon's face, his light blond hair, and the way he had of looking at you with complete disrespect through his blue eyes that were so much like his father's. She thought about how both Javier and Brandon were the same in so many ways right down to their tattoos. But it stopped there. People would always see Brandon as white and her son as Mexican, just the way the police did when they beat him.

"They're looking for him, and the rest of the guys," Javier finally answered. "When they find him, his dad will get him out. He'll fix it. Brandon told me he's done it before. You've got to help me get out of here!"

"But you were the one with the gun! You said you shot that boy and you were the one who pushed the policeman and he got hurt. That's what you just told me."

Javier nodded his head slightly, agreeing, his red swollen eyes were bewildered and unfocused. He gripped his metal crutches tighter to his body, and looked up at Mariana, "He might not die though Mom. Maybe not. He might make it; some people are saying so." His whisper was louder and fiercer.

Mariana could hear the painful hope in his voice. Maybe only one dead, not two.

"Murder," she said slowly. "That's what they're going to get you for, murder. Maybe two murders."

Javier wiped his eyes on the sleeve of his orange jumpsuit and looked away. "What are you going to do?" His voice pleaded with her to make it better.

Mariana looked past her son at the rows of men in orange jump suits holding phones and the people on the outside talking to them. She remembered how she'd argued with herself about telling Javier who his father was. She'd gone round and round with all the possibilities. All the problems that would come her way. The Señora and her anger, and Javier himself, because he might turn against her. The chance she'd lose her job. She'd decided not to in the end. Javier had her, his mother, and that was all he needed.

The sound of a shrill whistle coming over the loudspeaker stopped her thoughts and she watched as one of the sheriffs began walking down the visitor's row, pointing to his watch, and motioning to everybody to hang up their phones.

"I guess I've got to go now," Mariana slowly released her death grip on the phone, her eyes stayed fastened on Javier.

Javier looked down the row as the visitors hung up their phones. His eyes darted back to her, wide with fear. "Mom, when are you coming back? When are you going to get me out of here?"

"Soon, *Mijo*, soon. I love you. Goodbye." She choked out the "goodbye."

Mariana waited in line with the others to sign off on the visitor's log and then in another line to use the bathroom. The walls in the bathroom were covered in strange spidery-looking black letters, just like the walls everywhere in the neighborhood where they lived. The faucets in the sinks were missing and the toilet didn't flush. She looked for the trashcan and saw it was overflowing with used diapers. As she left the building, Mariana looked around one last time at the visitor's waiting area. She and Javier were now just two more of the black and brown faces on both sides of the glass, faces that belonged to people propelled by circumstances they couldn't control. And no matter how much she loved her son, she had no way to save him from this place.

As Mariana drove away, she recalled what she learned in

church, that the saints already had a plan in place for everybody's future before they were even born. If that was true, then she couldn't have stopped Javier from meeting Brandon, and she couldn't have stopped their friendship, because brothers had a particular bond all through their lives, but so did fathers and sons. She had no power to help Javier now, all she had to give her son was her love, and Javier needed a lot more than that now. Javier needed a bond that came with power and influence, and more importantly, privilege. Mariana changed direction and picked up the freeway. She headed toward the Señor's big house. She would wait for him to come home today. She had something to tell him.

He Didn't Call Back

Minerva bent over the crib and tickled the plump little foot that stuck out of the covers. The small shape lying on its side stirred and pulled the foot inward. She ran her fingers along the curve of the tiny back and slid her hand under the covers to let her fingers sink into the butter-soft folds of baby skin. She glanced at her cell phone and noticed the time. Frowning, she shook the small shoulders under her hands and the little girl stirred, raising her head. Mando was supposed to come over after work when the factory closed. She'd told him she'd fix something for dinner, so she needed to figure out if she had any funds left on her card and what she was going to cook.

Sighing, she picked up her daughter, already whining, and walked the few steps to the tiny kitchen area in the single apartment. Placing the baby in the plastic highchair from Goodwill, she opened the minifridge and pulled out a jar of pears. The pediatrician said that Maya was supposed to have vegetables and meat to eat, but she didn't like them, so Minerva stayed with the canned fruit and *galletas* that Maya liked to suck on with her bright pink gums. She looked over at the two-burner stove, remembering that she needed to clean it before tonight.

Minerva spooned some of the pears onto a pink plastic spoon. The baby took the spoon in her mouth before spitting the pears back, so they landed on Minerva's black blouse, right where the buttons gapped over her chest and dripped down to her bare midriff. "God damn!" she jumped up and grabbed a towel to wipe herself off. "Little bitch," she mumbled to herself. Maya threw back her sharp little chin and laughed at her mother's antics.

Jerking her daughter out of the highchair, she checked the

kitchen table, which was really more of a storage shelf for Maya's baby food and formula when she had it. There was still a liter bottle of Pepsi left from the last party. Good. She wouldn't have to buy another one for tonight. Mando liked to mix his drinks with it. He got so upset when there wasn't any left.

She sat Maya on the fold-up bed that served as a couch during the day and scrubbed at the sticky stain on the front of her blouse. After she'd scrubbed it so much that her bra was soaking wet, she gave up and tossed the dishrag in the sink along with the dirty dishes sitting in gray water. The one room was messy. She needed to sort the dirty clothes and put the clean clothes away in the broken dresser in the corner. She needed to dump the trash. The plastic diaper pail was overflowing with Maya's dirty throw-ways. It was starting to smell really bad, and she knew the smell bothered Mando. He wasn't used to it because he'd always left as soon as his girlfriend got pregnant. He didn't much care for Maya and didn't like to come over if she was awake.

The toys needed to be put away too. Grandma Maria bought so many, maybe because Carlos, Maya's father, wasn't around. Still, you couldn't say anything bad about her son, even if he was still locked up at Wayside.

She turned on the small color television from the swap meet. It worked most of the time, and some days it was the only thing that kept her company. Minerva switched on some cartoons and propped Maya up with some pillows, hoping she'd sleep again until she got to her mother's place. Stepping into the alcove that was separated from the main room by a shower curtain, she sat down on the toilet and heated her curling iron. From where she sat, she could reach the opposite wall of the shower with her out-stretched hand. Rolling the curling iron expertly through her hair, she studied her face in the mirror and decided that she need-ed to buy some more makeup as soon as her check came. She ran her hands over her stomach. It was almost flat now, and so were her boobs, except they'd been aching for the past couple of weeks.

Looking at her chest in the mirror made her frown. Mando always gawked at those girls on the cover of the car magazines with their boobs hanging out of their blouses. She comforted herself with the thought that she was much prettier than any of them and her hair was lighter too. Naturally, she thought.

Before she walked out of the alcove, she dug into the plastic clothes basket against the wall and pushed her hand to the bottom where the bottle of pills lay snuggled in her old underwear. She uncapped the lid hastily with hands that were beginning to shake and poured a few pills into her palm. Cupping some water from the faucet, she threw back her head and swallowed. The pills didn't work right away, but she knew that as soon as they did, everything would go soft and warm. She would feel the glow rising from the pit of her stomach and spreading slowly through her chest, filling her head. When the glow started filling her up, time stopped. Sometimes she was lost, for how long she didn't know. Maya would cry herself to sleep. Sometimes she didn't know if it was just a few hours or all day. Sometimes they both woke when it was dark. She thought she should feed her baby, but she was so warm and safe in her cocoon. The outside wasn't welcome. Maya would cry herself to sleep again.

Mando brought the pills home from his doctor after he broke his leg. They were for pain, he told her. He stopped taking them after the first week because they made him constipated. She tried one, and it was love at first sight. Mando kept getting new prescriptions because she liked them so much, even though his leg healed a long time ago. When she was high, he did things, things she wouldn't let him do to her otherwise. But she knew it only from a distance far away and from the bruises and cuts he left on her body. She had some good luck though, her mother Donna took the same pills. She could always get more from her.

Maya was whimpering again. Probably she should have stopped to feed her. "Oh well," she said out loud and filled a bottle with a little orange soda she had left over. Maya grabbed the bottle and began to suck greedily. "Thank God," she whispered and plopped the small body into the flimsy umbrella stroller with the right rear wheel that didn't move.

Awkwardly, she eased herself and the stroller with Maya in it down the steep steps. Sometimes she had visions of losing control and falling down the cement steps with Maya rolling ahead of her, striking her head on the cracked stone. The image made her shiver, but she couldn't bring herself to take the stroller down first and then go back up to the apartment to get her baby.

As she rolled out to the front of the apartment, the guys sitting under the shade of a blue canopy drinking Forties whistled and called out, "Hey baby, you look fine. Wanna give me some? I'll put another baby in you. You can count on me."

Minerva held her head high and ignored them. It was broiling hot in the middle of the day and they had nothing to do and nowhere to go. No jobs. No girlfriends. Nothing. At least Mando had a job, she told herself, even if he wasn't that good-looking. He should try to fix himself up, she thought. Get a few tattoos or shave his head or something. He looked like a dud.

She walked up the street to Sunset Boulevard and headed west, pushing the stroller unsteadily on two worn front wheels. So much change had happened so fast since she was a little girl playing down the street in Echo Park. It was all different now. Cleaner, she thought, and full of white people. All the old neighbors had moved out. They couldn't afford the rent once the new people they called hipsters bought the buildings. The tiny apartment she lived in that was carved out from the back of one of the rear houses on her street was safe for now. That was because her mother Donna used to go out with the owner, Mr. Fernandez. She guessed he still had the hots for her mother because he never said anything about raising the rent. She'd be in trouble if he did. Her check didn't stretch any further than covering what he already charged and the gas and electric. She always ran out of money by the end of the month and had to borrow from her mother, which was where she was going today. Luckily, she could usually persuade her mother to give over a few dollars, especially if she told her she hadn't fed Maya for a day or so.

The heat was sticky, and the smell of dried pee hung in the breeze blowing along the sidewalk. She passed cafés with curbside seating where young people in torn jeans and expensive tennis shoes lounged in their seats, staring out at the sidewalks through dark sunglasses that cost as much as her whole county check. A few of them stared at her, their eyes lingering on Maya, and then returning to her. She wanted to give them the finger but kept staring straight ahead. Fucking white people. They all thought they were better than her.

She passed a taco stand where the smell of *barbacoa* flowed out from the take-out window, and a small *panadería* where the smell of baking bread made her take a deep breath remembering she hadn't eaten since yesterday. Next to the taco stand were some small shops. One sold comic books that cost a fortune, and one sold old clothes they called "vintage." She couldn't understand why anyone would want to buy old thrift shop clothes. They were only a little cheaper than the clothes they called, "designer" on the corner of Sunset near Hollywood. She thought the clothes were ugly. Nobody she knew would wear them. But the white girls who shopped there wore them proudly, socks with high-heeled sandals, plaid skirts with polka-dot tops. What the fuck!

"*Quieres pan dulce?*" the little old woman with the tightly coiled gray braids thrust a plastic bag in her direction. Her eyes were hopeful as she moved closer to the stroller, stepping away from the shade of the building. Minerva looked down at the woman's hands and saw that the nails were broken and black-rimmed. She stepped back, pulling the stroller with her as Maya reached forward, her eyes intent on the bag of sweetbread.

"No!" she snapped, shoving the bag back in the direction of the woman and pushing the stroller toward the center of the sidewalk. Walking faster, she turned to cut through the park. Near one of the picnic tables, an older man sat facing the barbecue pit, gesturing toward the sky. His lips were opening and closing rapidly, showing large white teeth that gleamed in the sunlight. He was intent on a conversation he was having. Minerva wondered who he thought he was talking to.

She began a slow jog with the stroller, thinking that somehow seeing that the man who always looked like he lived in the park was like reassuring her that some things stayed the same. Lately, with all the new people moving in and the rent going up so high, everything was different. You hardly heard Spanish spoken around the neighborhood anymore. Huffing along, she pushed the stroller up to the end of Clinton Street and to the back row of apartments on the right-hand side. Then she carried Maya up the stairs to the last apartment at the back of the corridor. She paused at the door and then knocked loudly. "Mom, are you up yet?" There was no answer from inside. Minerva knocked again, harder, watching Maya's big eyes widen at the loud sound of her voice. "Mom wake up! Answer the door!"

After a few more moments, the door opened a crack, and a woman peered around it. She was dark-skinned and slim. Maybe in her middle thirties. Everybody said they looked like sisters, and not like mother and daughter.

"I told you I was coming by to borrow a little money." Minerva pushed past the woman and stepped into the darkened apartment. Compared to where she lived, the place was large and almost roomy, although it reeked of cigarette smoke and spilled beer. Maya smiled, recognizing Donna. Minerva turned up her nose.

"Mom, your house stinks!"

"Well, I'm trying to quit. It's not easy, you know."

"Did you smoke when you were pregnant with me?" Minerva stuck out her lower lip. When she was pregnant, they gave out pamphlets warning of the risk to your baby.

"Of course, I did. I keep telling you to call me Donna, and

don't you train her to call me Grandma, either!" With a shake of her head, the woman leaned over and stubbed out her cigarette in the ashtray in the middle of the coffee table.

Minerva sat down on the faded velour couch that was starting to tear in the center and on the arms and put Maya down at her feet. The little girl pulled herself up by hanging onto the coffee table and dumped a cup of cold black coffee onto the rug.

"God damn it, can't you even watch your kid?" Donna yelled, bending down to pick up the cup. "You know," she said as an afterthought, "I don't have as much money as I thought this month. I had to pay my court fine, or they'll revoke my probation. I told you that, remember?"

Minerva looked over at her mother, who was pulling plastic rollers out of her hair and teasing it back from her face. She had to admit her mother was pretty, especially when she put on a little makeup. Being pretty helped her get nice tips, and that made up for the little money they paid her to serve drinks. When she was little, Minerva liked to wait up for Donna when she came home from work, just to count the loose change and bills she brought home. Minerva couldn't remember when her mother didn't work in a bar. She said she had to because the welfare didn't give them enough money to live on. Minerva figured it was probably true, but her mother told her a long time ago that she liked to be in bars all the time anyway because everybody was drinking and happy. When Donna drank, she forgot about all of her problems: the overdue rent, the cheating boyfriend, the *comadre* who wanted to kick her ass for flirting with her husband. All was good when she was drinking.

Donna reminded her that she was afraid she might lose her job waitressing because some hipsters had bought the bar to turn into an "entertainment venue." She wasn't exactly sure what that meant, but she thought it probably involved young white people wearing all back and heavy boots, acting crazy as hell, yelling and screaming, dancing to music that sounded just like a lot of loud hollering. The worse part she told Minerva was that when they drank too much along with all their drugs, they usually threw up all over the bathroom.

Donna pulled on a short, tight skirt and a purple top. Minerva watched while she patted on foundation and outlined her eyes in stark black. While the eyeliner dried, she rubbed on blush and colored her mouth with Red Persuasion, the latest trendy lipstick color on display in all the drugstores. Then Donna carefully put on false lashes, a few at a time, until her eyes peeped out through a heavy black fringe.

Maya was tired and lay quietly on one of the green suede couch cushions, her eyes half-closed. Minerva thought about how she used to dress up and wear makeup herself before she got pregnant. She wondered what would happen when Carlos got out. Would he still like her? Some of the guys changed when they came back. Then what about Mando? He was okay and he kept her in pills. But Carlos was cuter and his body was covered with tattoos, the kind that made the other gang members take notice. The girls all wanted Carlos, but she was the lucky one.

Donna came out of the bathroom, smoking a joint. She offered it to Minerva, who reached for it before she felt a wave of nausea hit. Jumping to her feet, she ran to the bathroom, barely making it in time.

Donna came in as she was wiping her face with a wet towel. "You pregnant or something?" Her voice was accusing. "I thought I told you to go to the clinic and get some pills. They're free, you know."

"I'm not pregnant!" Minerva yelled back, pushing her sweaty hair off her face, suddenly thinking about her tender breasts. She didn't want to tell her mother that Mando wouldn't let her use any pills and he wouldn't use a condom.

"What for?" he shouted, every time she brought it up. "Are you some kind of whore? Are you doing it with everybody? You only do it with me, and you don't need no pills then. Do you?"

Donna stared at Minerva's flat stomach. "You're stupid if you get pregnant. They don't give you that much more welfare, and you'll be stuck with two babies. I didn't want to be the one to tell you this, but I heard that Mando's been seeing this new girl. Moved here from South Central. I think she's Guatemalan. Supposed to be really pretty. Real light-skinned."

"Oh, shut up. That's just a lot of bullshit. *Chismosas!* He's coming over tonight anyway." She didn't say that she hadn't talked to him since last week when he said he was coming over tonight. She left messages and texts, but he never answered. So what? That didn't mean he was with somebody else. If he were, she'd find that bitch and kick her ass!

She stormed back into the living room, glaring at Donna. For as long as she could remember, Donna had been harping on her about using birth control pills—just like she didn't have two daughters herself with no father in sight. She tried to abort Monica when she was fifteen, and she never got along with Monica either. Monica didn't even talk to her mother now. They said it was because she had Donna's half-white blood in her. White people were cold like that. It was different with Minerva. Donna had thought that Minerva's father was going to stick around—said he loved her—but he left too, which led Donna to always say not to trust any man.

But still, Donna always had plenty of boyfriends. Minerva remembered them coming and going when she and Monica were just little kids. All kinds of guys, but mostly *cholos.* Donna liked their style, so manly, ready to fight for anything, anytime. Nobody dared to make a move on her when she was with them. The apartment was always full of Donna's friends. They came by at all hours, and sometimes she moved the girls out of their bed in the middle of the night because some couple wanted to use it. In the mornings, Minerva would count the people sleeping over, on the couch and the overstuffed chair that leaked foam padding, on the rug, and even sleeping in the kitchen chairs with their heads on the table. She watched them drink and smoke in the evenings. They played their music so loud it drowned out the sound of the small television Donna set up for the girls in the bedroom, so they'd have to give up trying to watch their programs and go to asleep.

When Monica was twelve and Minerva was eight, Donna started going out at night. "I'm taking the party with me," she said. Minerva understood that she went to bars so she could drink and dance. "I'm going to find me a real boyfriend. One with money," she told them. Sometimes potentials came home with her and stayed until morning. She watched them go while she ate cornflakes before going to school.

A few years later, Monica moved out with her boyfriend, and then it was just Minerva and Donna. It was lonely for Minerva by herself at night. Then Donna went to jail for selling drugs, and Minerva went to live with Monica, who worked long hours at a factory, and when she was home, she fought with her boyfriend because he brought girls to the house when she wasn't there. He finally moved out and took the television with him.

Monica got a new boyfriend who didn't want Minerva there. He was creepy and kept staring at her, so it was back to her mom's apartment again. Donna went back to work at nights, and Minerva was alone every night until she met Carlos. The rest happened fast, maybe because Carlos was a lot older. She wasn't sure exactly how old, but old enough to drink at a bar with his own ID. He was happy when she got pregnant and started selling crack in a different part of town where he could make more money. He told her it was for the baby. Then he got into a fight with another gang banger and stabbed a guy. He would get out on parole eventually. Everybody was pretty sure.

"Mom, can I have a few bucks till my check comes in. I need some, you know ... food for her." She pointed to Maya, who was fast asleep.

Donna sighed, reaching for her purse. "You know I told you when you asked that I'm short cause I have to make my court payment. Can't afford to have my probation revoked again."

Minerva thought the way she said the words almost sounded like they were memorized, but she kept quiet and looked at the floor. She didn't want to get into it with her mother. It never helped to argue. Besides, Donna usually came around.

Donna dug into her wallet and handed Minerva a ten-dollar bill.

Minerva reached over and cupped it in dismay. She didn't bother to ask for more. Donna probably didn't have it.

"What do you say, ungrateful one?"

"Huh?" Minerva was still staring at the crumpled bill. There wasn't enough money on her card to buy anything good to cook. Maybe she could buy enough hamburger meat to serve Mando. She'd skip the milk for Maya. As long as she had a little sugar or something sweet to flavor the water she put in her bottle, she'd be okay for another day or so until her check arrived and her card was loaded.

"Thanks. Well, I guess I better get going since you're going to work," Minerva offered.

Donna stepped into the bathroom and resprayed her hair. "Guess so. I'll help you down the stairs." Minerva picked up Maya and walked to the door. Donna grabbed the folded stroller and started after her.

"Okay, Mom. Call you in a couple of days," she reached around and gave Donna a quick hug. She felt more unhappy than usual when she left her mother. Donna almost hadn't made it last time she OD'd, but luckily one of the guys that bought dope from her wouldn't give up banging on the door when she didn't answer. The manager finally broke the door open with minutes to spare. Minerva tried to imagine not having Donna anymore. Then there would be nobody in her world. You couldn't count on Monica. She had her own problems and never called anybody. Sighing, Minerva loaded Maya into her stroller. The little girl woke up crying and Donna found a small piece of candy in her purse and gave it to her to suck on.

Minerva started back down the street, heading east this time. She stopped at the small market a few blocks from home and purchased a small amount of ground beef and a scooper full of rice from the bin near the freezer section. With the change that was left over, Minerva bought a Mexican soda for herself and poured some in Maya's bottle to quiet her down.

Back at her apartment, she showered and washed her hair, then filled Maya's bottle with soda again and put her back to bed. She cooked the hamburger for Mando very carefully, turning it over and over again to make sure it was perfectly browned. She couldn't help remembering what her mother said about him seeing someone else. No, it wasn't true, she told herself. Still, she took extra pains with the rice, which came out perfectly.

Then she sat down to wait. The food grew cold. She called Mando's cell, but he didn't answer. She knew she'd almost used all her minutes for the month. Finally, she turned on the television and tried to concentrate on one of the old sitcom reruns she sometimes watched. Tonight, it didn't make her laugh. She scraped the cold rice into a bowl for Maya and put it into the minifridge. Maya would have something to eat tomorrow.

Then it was ten o'clock. Minerva left another message for Mando. Then she walked into the alcove and opened the tiny cabinet where she kept things like baby oil, deodorant, and aspirin. She pulled out the over-the-counter test she'd purchased last month. The caption on the front said that the test results were rapid. All she had to do was pee on the stick and watch it turn color.

She tore open the plastic wrapper and began to squat down, arranging the test stick under her. She checked the time on her cell phone. It was twenty minutes after ten. Minerva straightened up and pulled up her panties and jeans. She didn't need the test. She already knew. Some things were certain. Maya would wake up hungry and crying in the morning. Her check would arrive in a couple of days, and one day her mother would shoot up too much of whatever she was taking, and she'd be alone. Minerva checked her phone for the last time. She knew she would have heard it ring, but she checked anyway. He hadn't called back.

Sighing, she dug around in her pile of paper bags and pulled out an old *Glamour* magazine that Donna must have given her. She sat down and peeled back the first glossy page and stared at the face of a model with double thick eyelashes and swollen red lips. The model stared back at her, insolent, daring her to act. Minerva did. She threw the magazine against the wall as hard as she could. The thud was satisfying. It would have been better if the pages ripped too. She felt tears in her eyes. She was as pretty as that model. Why wasn't she in that magazine instead of stuck in this tiny apartment with a baby and another one coming? It was so unfair! She brought her face close to the mirror. Donna always told her, "Beauty opens doors."

But it hadn't opened any for Donna. She still hustled drinks in a dirty bar and tried to keep away from the customer's hands.

Minerva figured her looks got her boyfriends. She hadn't been without a boyfriend since middle school. If it was true Mando was leaving her, there'd be another one. She wouldn't ever be alone. At least there was that. She noticed suddenly that the television was really loud. The people in the front house would be knocking pretty soon. She wondered how Maya slept through it. So much sound coming from that little set.

But there was another sound coming from across the room where Maya slept, she could hear it now that the television was turned down, a raspy dry sound, breath being drawn in sharply, followed by a gurgling, choking sound. Maya!

She ran to the portable playpen her daughter slept in, her heart suddenly beating double time and her nerves raw and jangling as she looked over the side. Maya lay on her back, her body twitching and jerking. Her face was bluish in color and covered with sweat and her black curls were plastered to the top of her head. "Maya!" she screamed, but the little girl did not turn to her. She turned her head to the side and began coughing, a dry retching sound. Minerva reached down and picked her up, she could see a clear liquid pouring out of her mouth. "Oh my God! What's wrong?" She pulled the little girl close and rocked her as Maya kept gagging, her body jerking and twisting every time she coughed. Minutes passed, but the time seemed to stand still. Minerva patted Maya's back, bouncing on her toes as she walked back and forth in the little space with the sound of her daughter gasping and choking. When she pushed her daughter's wet hair off her forehead, she saw her translucent skin was a deeper shade of blue. Her body was hot and feverish.

Fear suddenly made her stop moving, stop bouncing up and down. Her legs went limp as she watched Maya's face. The little girl wasn't moving as much, her jerking had slowed.

Minerva clutched the little girl to her chest. She needed to do something, fast. Minerva looked around panicked. She didn't drive, and even if she did, she didn't have a car. The lights in the front house were off, so the neighbors weren't home. She grabbed her phone and dialed 911. She saw the numbers painted in white stretching and expanding in her head as she punched them in her phone. Sobbing, she told the dispatcher that she needed an ambulance. Then she sat down on the couch and rocked the small body that had almost stopped moving.

She didn't remember the ride to the hospital. The trip played through her head in a blur of motion as they flew through street after street traveling on mostly red lights. Then they were in the emergency room, and they were wheeling her daughter away on a stretcher, while she was led over to a small cubicle, where a woman with red hair and purple scrubs asked her questions. "How long had her daughter been sick? When did she start running a fever? Was she exposed to any contagious diseases?"

"No, she was fine this afternoon." Minerva tried to think. All afternoon she'd been thinking about Mando, wanting so much to see him that night, then so disappointed when he didn't show. All she thought about was Mando. She couldn't think about anything else or anybody.

"Do you have your benefits card?"

She did and took it out of her purse with shaking hands.

The waiting room in the County Hospital was crowded for a weekday night. The seats closest to the big screen on the wall were taken first and additional plastic chairs were set out in the hall. By seven o'clock each night, all those seats were taken too. Small children who were not too sickly or carried in their mother's arms sat on the floor and stared vacantly at the screen. Worried looking mothers sat with the other children wrapped in blankets.

Emergency patients as well as outpatients used the services of the hospital, so there were people waiting to see friends and relatives alongside people with runny noses and sore throats, while others were bleeding or had broken bones. Those with gunshot wounds were channeled to the trauma center at the back of the hospital. This hospital had, just a few hours earlier, admitted a newly married teenager still dressed in his wedding tuxedo with a screwdriver sticking out of his head. Minerva stood alone, scared and sick with worry. She looked at the other mothers with their children and wondered how they could stand to be here. She propped herself against the wall and waited.

Tears kept dripping down her cheeks and she wiped them away with the back of her hand. She loved Maya so much, more than anything, but she realized it was probably the first time she'd said that to herself. Most of the time Maya was a problem in her life, a burden to be tolerated, a child that she had to make excuses for. Carlos didn't really want his daughter once she was born. He had other children and couldn't support them. And Mando … well, Maya wasn't his, and he made a point of telling Minerva he didn't want her around either.

Poor Maya, Minerva always tried to get her to sleep before the guys showed up at night. If she woke up crying, there were problems. You never knew what kind of mood a guy could be in. Sometimes they were loving, wanting sex, but they might also be moody or angry, and ignore her completely. She knew she had to be prepared for either and not expect too much. She wondered when she learned that. It seemed she always knew it.

The last time he was there, Mando left when Maya started whining to get out of her crib. Maybe that's why he hadn't called her. Carlos hadn't asked about her once since he was locked up, and when she complained to her mother about it, Donna told her to get used to it. "Nobody wants a woman with kids. Especially kids that aren't their own." She'd already been there. Minerva remembered being locked in the bedroom with her sister when Donna had company.

"You just have to figure out how to get the kids out of the way when they're around or else you'll be lonely without a boyfriend the rest of your life." Donna said.

Minerva knew that everyone saw a woman without a man as a failure, "not a real woman at all." It was something Donna told her to keep in mind.

"But Carlos is Maya's father," she argued with Donna, wondering about the fathers she saw walking their kids to kindergarten and holding their hands as they passed her street. Maybe Carlos would be different when he got out. Except for sex, he really didn't pay that much attention to her. She was lonely when Carlos was around, and still just as lonely when she took up with Mando. She supposed she loved Carlos, and now Mando. You always loved the boyfriend you were with. Especially if he was good looking. Didn't you? They'd never said they loved her, she thought.

But when she was with her daughter, Maya, just the two of them, and she wasn't waiting on pins and needles for her boyfriend to come around, she was calm, happier. She wasn't worrying about Carlos or Mando getting angry at Maya, screaming at her, and leaving to be with someone else. She wasn't worrying about some bitch someplace else, scheming to take her guy.

Maya was the only real family she could count on. Minerva could hold her small perfect body and stare at her in wonder. Maya, a beautiful doll that came to life as soon as Minerva heard her first cry. Maya would always be there, calling her Mama, looking up at her, and touching her face so gently, even if the guys came and went. Sometimes she dreamed it was just the two of them, alone, living on some beautiful beach where the day was always sunny, and Maya stayed the baby she was, looking up at her laughing.

But now she didn't know what was going to happen to her baby. She looked around. Most of the mothers were alone with their children, a few had men sitting with them. To her right sat a young couple, maybe a little older than she was. Minerva immediately identified them as wetbacks by the woman's Indian features and her faded polyester clothes that looked like they'd been picked from a rag bin. She wore her long braids tied in back of her neck. She was crying, holding a tissue to her red, swollen nose. The man's clothes were covered with white plaster dust that had hardened on the front of his shirt. Minerva noticed that his work boots were badly scuffed and full of holes. There were two large overflowing suitcases sitting at their feet. The man and woman sat together, the man's arm around the woman, holding her to him. The baby's blanket was partially unwrapped, and she could see huge glassy black eyes peering out. Looking at the young woman, Minerva thought how much better off she was than that woman. She had better clothes, and a place to live. She was much prettier than the woman ... but she kept staring, watching as the man sitting with the woman held her close and tried to comfort her. But that woman, as chunky as she looked, had a man with her, the child's father it looked like. Minerva didn't have anyone. Nobody to comfort her and say it was going to be all right. That woman had something she didn't. Something she should have, her child's father. She kept staring at the couple as she tried reaching Donna. Suddenly she wanted her mother badly, but Donna was still at work. The bar wouldn't close for another few hours. She tried Mando again, but his phone went straight to message. Her sister didn't answer either, but Minerva had heard she was into drugs now, and Minerva was suddenly overcome with a sense of loneliness like she never had before. She looked around and wondered why she was here alone.

A nurse exited one of the swinging doors and told her she

could go back to the ICU where her daughter was. She followed the tall figure wearing pink tennis shoes and a big afro around a corridor and into a large room partitioned with curtains. Maya was in the second bed. Her arms were covered with white squares of tape and the tubes under them were connected to bottles hanging from poles, standing like guards around the sides of the bed. Machines were set up next to the poles, and Minerva looked at the whirling needles and colored lights, bewildered. Maya was covered with hospital blankets, and Minerva could only see her face, so pale it blended into the white sheets.

Minerva began to cry harder, looking at the little body in the bed, and wondering where she could touch her, put a kiss on her face. Anger started to rise up and fill her chest. Anger for all the times she'd pushed Maya aside, ignored her, neglected her, for Mando, and before him, Carlos. Wanting so badly to please them though they were never there for her. She leaned over the bed and sobbed. "I'm sorry Maya. I'm sorry."

A young man wearing a white coat that flapped around his legs and a cotton mask that hung from his neck, tapped her lightly on the shoulder. "You're the mother here? I'm Doctor Bryce. Your daughter has pneumonia and severe dehydration. We're giving her antibiotics and fluids. We'll be keeping her here in Intensive until we see some change." He looked directly at Minerva's face. "It's a good thing you brought her in when you did. Otherwise it might have been too late. Do you have any questions?"

Minerva shook her head. The question was choking her. "I want to know, I mean, is she going to be all right?"

Doctor Bryce looked back at the bed and then up again at the monitors. He frowned. The residents here were used to giving news that brought unimaginable sorrow. Thankfully, he didn't have to do that today. "She's not out of the water yet, but she should pull through. We're running some tests, and we'll know more then. Are you planning to stay here?"

"I'm going to stay here until she can go home,"

Doctor Bryce looked away. She was so young. A baby with

a baby. "Leave your cell phone number with the charge nurse at the desk."

Minerva sat next to the bed; her eyes locked on her daughter. She shivered, thinking that if Mando showed up tonight, she wouldn't have checked on Maya, wouldn't have known how sick she was. By the time Mando left it would have been too late. Maybe she should thank him. But no, she hated him now! Hated him for not calling, for leaving her here alone, for the way he always wanted her to get Maya out of the way. For so many reasons, but she hated herself more.

Minerva found a patch on the back of her daughter's hand that was not covered with the tape that held the tubes in place. She thought about how she was angry and unhappy most of the time, but didn't know why, and she thought of how she kept it to herself, trying to make sure her boyfriend was happy with her. She kissed the small bare space of skin, and Maya moved just the slightest bit. That was a good sign wasn't it?

She watched the nurses hurrying down the halls from room to room, dragging carts and wheeling machines across the waxed floors. They all moved so fast, headed somewhere, bringing something to help someone. Minerva remembered playing doctor and nurse when she was little. She always made her sister be the patient, and the patient always got better. They played school too, and she was always the teacher. What happened? She wondered. I wanted to be those people when I grew up. I wanted to go to work dressed up, wearing nice clothes, and high heels, driving a nice car. But now I'm here.

Tears started up again and she tried calling Donna. This time Donna answered her cell. She just finished work and was headed to another bar. Minerva started to tell her she needed her mother, but she stopped thinking Donna would probably give some excuse, and Minerva couldn't stand to hear that now. Finally, she choked out her fear that Maya would die, and then she hung up.

She must have fallen asleep, sitting in the chair by her

daughter's bed, because the next thing she knew one of the nurses was shaking her arm. "Wake up! I have some good news. Your daughter's fever is going down, her color's back and her vitals are stable. The doctor started her on a different antibiotic, and she opened her eyes a while ago."

"Thank you! Oh, God. Thank you!" Minerva stammered, as she started crying again, never taking her eyes of the little figure asleep in the bed. Maybe Maya is getting a second chance, she thought, and maybe I'm getting a second chance too.

Undeliverable

If the air conditioning had been working that day, she never would have ended up in the extra bedroom looking for the large fan to cool the part of the top floor of the house where her study was. She was sure the temperature was around a hundred degrees, even here on the west side of town where ocean breezes managed to find their way around the tall buildings with long glass windows that lined Wilshire Boulevard and drifted through any open hand-crafted designer-windows in the large homes on the side streets.

The extra bedroom was the fourth bedroom, the one nobody used. Since Matt and Tiffany went away to college, their bedroom doors stayed closed, and the beds remained freshly made, just the way she'd ordered when they left. The master bedroom belonged to her and Ricardo, or Rich as he now called himself, and had since he'd graduated law school. Around the corner from the master, which took up over half of the second floor, was her study. This was where Kim poured over recipes and prepared for her cooking show, Custom Cookery, that ran every Friday afternoon at four o'clock. Once she had the recipe she wanted, she usually took the stairs, two at a time, for more exercise, down to the kitchen on the first floor.

There, among the myriad of copper utensils and designer crock ware, she would prepare her "first draft" of the recipe, sometimes testing it on whoever happened to be at home. Lately, there wasn't much of anybody, and so the cook, housekeeper, and gardener usually sampled the first batch of whatever she prepared. Sometimes the surprise on their faces as they tasted the unfamiliar ingredients was enough to tell her that whatever she had created would be a big hit with her foodie fans.

The show was a big hit. It got high audience ratings, they told her. People were following her on Facebook and Instagram. It was funny how it all happened. Her daughter needed a "how-to" video for one of her classes. She suggested one of her old recipes for vegetarian lasagna. Tiffany filmed her cooking and it ended up on YouTube. Somebody from the network saw it, and they called her to come in. The next thing she knew, she had a weekly television show spotlighting vegetarian recipes.

She remembered opening her first check from the network in complete shock. Having never worked since she married, over twenty-four years before, she had no concept of how many hours it took to earn money these days and wondered why she always saw strikers on television demanding higher wages. Her check seemed reasonable for thirty minutes of airtime, plus another hour or so preparing for the show. It didn't occur to her that most people had to work a whole week for what she earned in thirty minutes. But now the network told her they weren't picking the show up next season. The ratings were still good, they said, but the sponsors wanted to capture a younger audience. Younger audiences were interested in virtual tours of the latest restaurants and bars, how other millennials behaved on dates, hook-ups, and catfishing. The same producer who had told her there was always room for another cooking show when he hired her, now told her there were more than enough cooking shows on all the networks, to say nothing about the ones on cable. Unless she could come up with a way to make her show more exciting for the sponsors, he couldn't carry her for another season. He joked that she could try cooking in the nude, or better yet, have a good-looking young couple cooking in the nude. She didn't laugh and tried to hide her disappointment, and later, her panic.

"You'll think of something else to do," Rich assured her when she broke the news. "Be creative. It'll come to you." He was still telling her that as he said goodbye most mornings when she didn't go to the studio and slept most of the day.

Sighing, she pushed her damp hair off her forehead and re-twisted the light blonde highlighted ponytail with soft pinkish streaks that her hairdresser had insisted she start to wear. "It's youthful," he kept telling her, hands on his hips. Along with the square black fingernails and the ripped jeans, she looked every bit a millennial, if you didn't notice the fine network of lines behind her sunglasses. Anyway, Rudy, the makeup man from her show, always did such a fantastic job for the camera where her appearance really counted.

She switched on the light and looked around dismayed. Furniture that nobody used crowded the floor. Chairs were stacked on the top of tables and dressers. A tall bookcase stood against the window crowded with Rich's track and basketball trophies and high school memorabilia. She'd persuaded him to move it from their bedroom, hoping it would end up in the garage, but here it was. Boxes were stacked along the sides of the room, five or six high. She couldn't remember what was in them.

In the corner, she saw a couple of space heaters, bringing back memories of their first apartment in East Hollywood. It had no air conditioning or heat, and sometimes no hot water if she forgot to pay the bill. She smiled to herself. Rich was just a poor law student then. He lived on his student loans and his clerking jobs at law firms in Century City. She took art classes at LACC and tended bar in a dive joint on Hollywood Boulevard. The job itself made her seem worldly and exotic to all her girlfriends, even though she knew the only reason the owner hired her without any experience was because of her oversized boobs. Rich stopped in sometimes. Maybe he was checking on her. She never gave him a reason, though.

Back then, Rich was young and eager. He wanted more than anything to make sure everybody important enough to have his ass kissed knew his name. He'd chosen politics back then for his career. He was by no means a conservative on any issues. She was sure of that when they started going out because she was never attracted to opposites, like her girlfriends, who only went with men who were nothing like them. She was a poster child for the free-wheeling liberal women of her day. People considered her a little too wild, someone who slept with too many men. They said she drank too much and probably smoked weed too. They were right about all of it.

Rich was labeled a radical Socialist, given to criticizing the government at every turn. He organized protests and marches on and off campus. His favorite topic was the disenfranchised poor and how the system kept them down. He always spoke of the "Chicanos," a group he was proud to be a member of, as hardworking, proud, and industrious. Just like his parents. They'd spent the better part of their years picking crops in places where they wouldn't be welcome if they weren't working. He said they saved all their money and paid for a large portion of his college education. He reminded everyone that they never wanted anything for themselves and were happy to hide in the shadows as long as he had a good education.

Her father was a middle school teacher and her mother worked in a bank. They both hoped she'd go to college, but they had no money saved, so she paid her own way for some classes in junior college before she met Rich, who was in his second year of law school. After that, she lost interest, or maybe she just lost her way. She wasn't sure. Anyway, the future was infinite, and you could always go back to school once you figured out what you wanted to do. So far, she wasn't particularly good at anything, except maybe tending bar, and later cooking. You didn't need college for that. Years back, she wondered about what it would be like to go back to school, but by then, there were the kids and the house to manage. All those years passed, and now the show that had fallen into her lap by accident was almost over. She still couldn't think of anything she was good at doing. She knew she had the privilege of having what everybody called a "great life," full of advantages and privileges that the rest of the "ordinary people" didn't have. You couldn't complain about that.

Rich always went on and on about how Chicanos, like

himself and his parents, were mostly dying out now and being replaced by a different kind of immigrant. This, he said, marked the beginnings of a new humanitarian crisis. He advocated long and loud on the floor of the State Senate for immigration reform and humane treatment of refugees. Sometimes she helped him sponsor huge fundraisers for immigrant children or people seeking asylum here in the U.S. The fundraisers were well-attended by mostly white people who let the help (mostly undocumented Mexicans) park their Land Rovers and Jeeps up the hill from their large sprawling Spanish-style home. Dressed in contemporary distressed bohemian, with skinny jeans and tunics, clanging large pieces of ethnic jewelry, they donated thousands and thousands of dollars to whatever cause he sponsored for the poor and marginalized.

But back then, when nobody knew him, Rich was always available to hand out flyers in the park and stop every passerby. He mainly stopped the white ones, to discuss the immigrants' plight, praise the unions, and slam the big corporations, whose greed he said was ruining the country. He donated all his spare time, when he wasn't pursuing his law degree, to "the cause." She'd seen him give a large chunk of his meager salary from working as a file clerk in a law office to a local immigrant organization to help the arriving population.

Everybody reminded her all the time how lucky she was to have a husband like Rich. She'd heard it since the day they were married. He was perfect. He was handsome, generous, caring, empathetic, a decent father, and an impressive provider. He'd even managed to forge through her father's prejudice.

"He's a foreigner. I didn't raise you to marry a foreigner." Her father shook his head in amazement when they bought their house high above the city. Until he met Rich, his only experience with Mexicans was limited to hiring a couple of guys from Home Depot to drywall his garage.

She pushed aside a stack of boxes and peered out of the grimy window toward the gardens facing the rear of the house.

"This place needs dusting!" She made a note to get Carmen, who came in to help the regular maid do the heavy cleaning once a week, come up and get to the windows right away.

Cleaning off a dusty square of glass, she peered out at the lush green tropical plants that they had imported last summer. They hadn't done so well at first, but now they were thriving in the unexpected humidity, along with the Protea and some other plants whose name she had forgotten. They stretched upward in brilliant reds and oranges, their petals spotted and striated with darker, softer colors in geometric patterns.

She could almost hear the stream trickling along the path that separated their property from the rear of the tennis court that belonged to their neighbor. She watched the water slowly skirt around the large river rocks that the gardeners had carried in, one by one, and the pool by the small waterfall under the Japanese redwood bridge. Rich was complaining that money was a little tight lately, and maybe a large part of the garden area would have to go because it cost so much to maintain between the gardeners and all the necessary watering. She really didn't understand this, but she knew better than to question him about money. After all, he earned it and could spend it how he chose. Besides, he never asked how much she spent, and she spent a lot now that the kids were gone and the days were long and empty, except for the one day she worked on her show.

Well, she didn't see the fan anywhere. It must be buried back here. Her hip brushed against an oak dresser pushed back along the wall next to the window. Looking down, she saw that the top drawer was partially stuck open. Something was jammed in the hinge. She pulled on the glass handle and an envelope, large and square, fell out from the space where it sat lodged in the drawer hinges. The addressee's name had an "x" through it, two bold red lines that crossed each other. Next to the "x" was the word "Refused," also written in the same bold red strokes. Stamped across the front of the envelope was the word "UNDELIVERABLE."

She stared at the envelope frowning, not recognizing the name with the x through it, "Allison Rice." Who was this person? The return address said it came from Rich's district office. What was it doing here? His official mail never made its way back here. She checked the postmark. It was over six months old. Frowning, she pulled down a chair from the stack to her right and slowly sat down. Her heart suddenly beating faster, she opened the envelope and pulled out several sheets of paper and unfolded them. Instead of the usual thin, bought-in-bulk copy paper, he used for mailing his constituents; this paper was a creamy thick beige. Expensive.

She was surprised to see that the envelope was addressed by hand, and for a moment she almost didn't recognize the tiny, tightly woven letters that slanted to the right. It was Rich's writing. She hardly ever saw it anymore since everything coming out of his office came from the word processor and through his secretaries.

She began reading, a cold, clammy sweat breaking out on her forehead.

Dear Allison:

I waited for your call or even a text from you this whole week, but you aren't answering. I know we shouldn't have argued the way we did. I don't know why I get so angry, but I'll try to explain. First, though, I just want us to go back to the way things were between us. I can still remember all those times we snuck away to be together. Making love to you has always been the highlight of my life. This has been the loneliest week of my life. I can't face another week like this one. I told you that I would be getting a divorce very soon, now that my youngest is settled in college, and I won't have to carry expenses for the house. I'm ready to do it now, and I don't want you to think I've been stringing you along all this time. As much time as we spend together, you should know how much I love you.

Right now, it doesn't look like I'll have my old job back at the firm after this term is up. Don't worry, though, I put money away for us all the time. And when we sell the house, I can buy her out pretty cheap. The house is in my name only, and I don't think she'll fight me for it.

I thought I'd go back to my practice, but there were a few problems with a couple of Mexican clients I represented, and after all this time, the court decided in their favor. It'll be a while before I can get my license back, but in the meantime, I'll try something else.. I was tired of law anyway, tired of kissing the asses of those retarded people I worked with. They're worse than the clients.

I couldn't say it in court, but it's just bad luck that I represented those dirty Mexicans. They're all lying, thieving sons of bitches, always looking for an opportunity to cheat somebody or take advantage. I really hate the race. All of them, even my parents. They were stupid, only good for digging in the dirt. I wish they would stop them all from coming into this country and breeding. We don't need anymore of these maggots. They're dirty and ignorant, and they're all on welfare as far as I can see. They have a ton of kids, and we're choking on the scum they produce that we have to pay for. They get everything free, and there aren't any decent jobs for anybody else anymore. Hitler had the right idea. Too bad they weren't around then, he could've exterminated the whole race and made me happy. If I could, I'd round up all their children now and burn them before they grow up and become maggots like their parents. I already have someone on the inside who's going to have those clients I represented deported. I even dreamed after the trial that I took a rifle and shot up their home, killed the whole family and the neighbors.

I know you're angry because you found out about that problem I had with the DA in that paternity suit, and that's why you're not taking my calls. But it's all been taken care of. It turns out I'm not the father of her kid, and I don't have to pay support. I told you she was nothing to me, just a dumb *broad I met one night at a club when you were gone shooting a movie. Maybe I did see her a few times after that, but she told me she was on the pill. Between you and me, I wouldn't have paid child support anyway. Why should I? She's the one who opened her legs.*

If my kids want to keep going to college so bad, they have to borrow the rest themselves. I'm done supporting everybody.

I miss you so much. I just saw your photo in Essence *now that we get it. I can't believe I have a girlfriend who looks like you.*

You said you didn't want to see me again, but I know that's not forever.

Please know I love you and want to marry you.

—Rich

She sat up straight and the dusty cane chair creaked when she stretched. She stared at the boxes stacked against the opposite wall and swallowed but couldn't get past the lump rapidly closing off her throat. Tears stung her eyes and then spilled down her cheeks. Her legs felt like jelly, and she wondered if she'd be able to stand. The room spun and her stomach churned bringing up the taste of burning, bitter acid.

She closed her eyes wanting the letter to disappear. In her head, she could see the words "I'd round up all the children and burn them," large black letters stretching in size, tattooed inside her head, making it feel as if it would explode. Was that more awful than his relationship with this woman? The woman who'd refused the letter? And another woman thought he was the father of her child. Who was this man?

He must have brought the letter home because he didn't want anyone to see it. Like any politician, Rich had enemies everywhere; people were waiting to drag him down and watch him fall. Rich always said he had even more enemies than most of the others because he was Mexican, and everybody was against Mexicans. That's why he had to stand up for them, he said. Make sure they were treated fairly. You couldn't trust white people, he said, ignoring the fact that she, his wife, was a white person.

This Allison person, how long had they been together? He said he would marry her. How had all this been going on without her knowing? And he said he hated Mexicans. Talked about genocide. How could that be? The problem with his clients and the lawsuit. Now he wouldn't have his license. He wouldn't be practicing. He was going to do something else he said, and there was no money for the kids' college. None of it made any sense.

This person couldn't be the same man she'd married, the one who boasted about being a "full-blooded" member of his race, the one who spent his whole career trying to make things better for others. He was loved by everybody he worked with, always had been. The clients loved him too. She'd seen the worship and respect in their eyes, one of their own, so educated and so important. A high-ranking man in government, an elected representative. What would they think if they knew how he really felt about the people he represented? How much damage could this do? Why, she wondered, would he put all these feelings into a letter to this woman—share all his secrets? He must have trusted the woman to keep those secrets. He certainly hadn't trusted his wife.

It felt suddenly chilly in the stuffy closed-in room, where the air was moist and thick and seemed to have stopped moving in today's heatwave. It wasn't really a physical cold that made her body tremble and her hands shake. It was a cold that was slowly released from her heart, pushing out the warmth and security that had lived there all these years. She heard herself whisper, "I used to think I would love someone, and they'd love me back my whole life." There was nobody there to hear.

She touched her forehead, where lines were starting to mark her pale, freckled skin. He'd said he was selling the house and it was in his name, but it was their house.

She ran out of the room and down the hall to her study. Grabbing the cell phone off her desk, she located the icon for his number and tapped it. The phone rang, loud and raspy. As soon as she heard it, she clicked the call off. No, she didn't want to listen to his voice. Whose voice was it anyway?

She sat back in her burgundy leather chair part of a set imported from Spain. The rest of the chairs were in the den downstairs surrounded by more designer furniture from some store on the Westside, whose name she couldn't remember. All of this—everything in this house, her clothes, the cars—thinking about them suddenly made her weary. She didn't know she was so tired. And the parties and fundraisers, one after the other. All a lie. Nothing was real, not her marriage, and not the man she married—a man who hated himself.

The petals had been torn off the rose, and the stem stood alone, exposed, ugly, and unwanted. The funny thing was, she didn't want the rose any longer, even when she pictured it the way it was before, with soft, beautiful petals. The picture was fading to be replaced by the image of an ugly stem with prickly thorns.

She walked to the large stained-glass French doors opening onto the balcony. The city sprawled below her bathed in the glare of the hot yellow sun glowing through grayish smog. She felt a rush of sadness making her eyes tear and her body chill, as she looked out at the city that she'd only seen from great heights for so long. She was a stranger there now, just as much as Rich was a stranger to her, to everyone out there. But she was free now, free of all of this, free of him, and the hate that he held onto. She folded the letter into a small square and tucked it into the bottom of one of her lingerie drawers.

Three weeks later the public outcry started. You probably saw the clips on television. Channel five got hold of the letter first. Lucky break for them. State Senator Rich Munoz asked one of his assistants to send out a letter he'd written to the water district directing them to make a policy change in recording water surpluses. His assistant was leaving early that day and delegated the assignment to the newest intern. Somehow the new intern sent out the wrong letter, the one that Rich saved without naming it, and forgot to erase after he printed it. It went out to Personnel and they didn't know who was supposed to receive it, so they sent it out to all the department heads. And then the letter went viral.

The funny thing, Kim thought, was that she hadn't shown anybody the letter herself, hadn't talked to anybody about it. Rich did it all himself. Well, she thought ruefully, he always liked to handle his own publicity. This was his best pitch yet.

Public figures making spectacles of their lives make the best news, particularly if the story is the foulest form of gossip about an adulterous sex scandal and hidden bigotry. With a juicy piece of gossip like this, everybody could get a shot at pointing their finger and calling out corruption and racism. Preferably both.

Portions of the letter were read on television first by a slim blonde newscaster in a tight print dress with blow-dried hair and double-layer eyelashes. She read slowly with emphasis, expressing Rich's feelings just the way they were written. Kim always changed the station when the blonde woman fluffed out her hair and started reading for the cameras.

A second anchor interviewed the ACLU about the impact of the letter and the Chicano Coalition about racism in state government. A few women's organizations called a press conference and told the reporters that women would be coming forward in the future to talk about the sexual harassment they experienced when they worked on Rich's campaign and how other women felt about what they heard on the air. Kim shuddered. This was new too.

If you didn't catch the story on TV then you must have seen it on the cover of *People*, while you waited to pay for your organic milk and gourmet nuts and fruit mix. If you opened *People*, there was a story about Rich's ex-wife and a second smaller interview piece about his former girlfriend.

Or maybe you were like the rest of the people who saw the

headlines while you were scrolling down your Facebook feed, drinking coffee and reading the comments. And were there comments! Some people wanted criminal charges filed against Rich, because they said his resignation wasn't nearly a big enough step toward combating racism in America. Others compared him to Hitler or Mussolini and shared the post along with photos of the local police using what looked like chokeholds to make their arrests on street corners in blighted areas of the city.

Some people marched and called for all of the members of the executive branch of the state government to resign immediately, and for the attorney general to start an investigation into their official conduct.

A few citizens groups composed of Latinos picketed the state capital and called for state officials to come out. When they didn't, some of them threw rocks and bottles in the direction of the capitol building. The police chief came out and pleaded with the crowd. "This individual is just 'one bad apple,' among all of our good, hardworking public servants." Most of the crowd didn't agree.

As more networks picked up on the letter, there was even talk of a television show. Dr. Phil wanted to bring Rich in and have him face off with a militant Chicano rights organization. Kim's closest friend Gracie wanted her to hold off for Oprah because everybody watched Oprah and her opinions were absolute gospel. The producer of Kim's cancelled cooking show was interested in a doing a "tell all" about the lie Rich had lived and how he had duped his family as well as his constituents. A literary agent left six messages in an excited voice, talking about a book deal she could put together with Harper Collins. They were SO interested. She wanted to hire a ghostwriter to tell Kim's story and to get started right away.

Through it all Rich was on administrative leave. He didn't call or come around. She'd declined all of his calls after she read the letter. She noticed things now, like some of his clothes and toiletries were missing and his favorite luggage wasn't stacked on the top shelf of his closet. He must have been planning to leave before all of this blew up.

Kim sat in her chaise lounge on the second floor trying to make sense of it all. She hadn't moved much, just from the chaise lounge to the bed and back. She let the maid go, tired of her curious stares. Tired of her asking, *"Donde esta El Señor? Que paso?"*

More television channels were covering the story since it was first released. In fact, it seemed wherever she looked, she couldn't help but see her face and Rich's next to photos of their home perched on the hilltop above LA.

Her son Matt came home from school last week and hired two security guards to keep the traffic moving up the hill as the gawkers drove by the house, stopping in the middle of the narrow one-way road to make sure they were taking pictures of the right house with their cell phones.

"What a bastard!" Matt swore as he strung barbed wire around the garden entrance that was out of the security officer's line of sight. She kept the shutters drawn now and no longer saw the view of downtown Los Angeles and Catalina Island.

After the news was out for a while, she even got a few calls from some female friends recommending attorneys that they told her were "high-power divorce lawyers." She wrote down the names numbly. "You need to take him for everything he's got," they insisted after asking her if what they heard was true.

Tiffany called crying. "It's all over Facebook. Dad's a racist and he has a girlfriend too. Didn't you know? How can I face my friends?"

Kim didn't know how to answer her. She drank diet soda all day with just a little vodka and stared at herself in the mirror. There were more lines, especially around her mouth, and her neck was starting to get saggy she was certain. Her roots needed attention too. "I look like an old hag," she told herself. Feeling exhausted, she lie down on the bed and tried to think about what to do next. Sooner or later she'd have to talk to Rich, she thought. There would be a divorce, she wanted that, but she admitted to herself that she also wanted to wake up in the morning and find out that none of this really happened.

Then there was this nagging curiosity about this "Allison" person. Who was she? What was she like? And of course, why was she Kim's rival anyway?

Kim mulled over the possibilities. She had to be young and beautiful. Rich wouldn't be wasting his time with any woman her age. Dragging herself out of bed, she dumped the contents of her first lingerie drawer on the bed and pushed the slick lace bras and panties apart. Remembering it was in the last drawer with her summer lingerie, she dumped that one too and grabbed the letter. Turning the envelope around in her hand, she studied the name and address and any information on who this Allison was. Allison lived on the west side close to West Hollywood, and she was an actress. Of course, all the young women living here called themselves "actresses." Still, the letter mentioned she was in a movie. She hurried over to the computer and typed in the name. The screen came alive with "Allison's" who were actresses. She stared at the faces, blinking. They were all young, pretty, and wholesome, maybe in their twenties, except Allison Janney, and she was pretty sure she was the wrong Allison.

Kim held the envelope closer to the light and turned it over. She was suddenly overcome with a need to see this woman, to satisfy her curiosity that there was a reason for Rich wanting to be with her, to be in love with her. A reason she could understand. That would make it acceptable, let her know she'd run her course. The need to know took root, firing up her body with a jolt of energy she hadn't felt in weeks.

Kim ran to the shower and turned on the water full force. Twenty minutes later she combed out her wet hair and changed into jeans. She called down to the security officers who opened the front gate. One of them ran ahead and started moving the few cars that staggered in a meandering line, snapping pictures of her house.

Kim quickly put on her sunglasses and started the engine of her Mercedes SUV. Taking a deep breath, she made a U-turn and headed into traffic down Western, toward Santa Monica. Fifteen minutes later she turned onto a narrow street bordered by two-story apartments on both sides. It was an older neighborhood and the apartments looked like they were built in the sixties, the underground parking facing the street. They're ugly, she thought, remembering she'd lived in worse back in the day.

Rich always felt more comfortable in that part of town. "My kind of people," he would laugh. "The young and the hip. They're the pulse of our nation."

Parking across from the address, she shut off the engine, suddenly feeling naked and exposed. Now what? "Just one glimpse," she whispered to herself. "That's all. Just to make sure."

Kim found herself crossing the street. Allison probably doesn't even live here now, she thought as she stepped up the concrete platform to the mailbox. People living in these apartments moved in and out all the time. But she was wrong, Allison lived there. The name on the mailbox proved it. Apartment two. She looked to her left and saw that apartment two was just one stairwell over on the first floor and the large front window in the living room faced the walkway between the apartments. It was late afternoon. Allison would probably be at work. No, she was an actress. She didn't have a nine-to-five job, Kim told herself.

She waited for somebody to come out to the mailbox and see her. What was she doing there? She was snooping, they'd call the police. More embarrassment. But nobody came out. Finally, she took a deep breath and slowly walked past the first window. She took a quick peek, you could see the entire kitchen and living area through the partially open blinds. It looked like there was nobody home and she felt strangely relieved. She started walking past the second apartment and turned her head to look in at the last minute. A woman sat half-turned on the sofa facing the television. She was holding a hand mirror toward the light from the window and applying something to her face. She was so engrossed in what she was doing that she didn't notice Kim staring at her. Kim kept her head turned until she reached the concrete divider demarking the third apartment. It was enough time to get a good look at Allison, if that was who she was. Allison was African American.

Kim kept her head down and walked to the back of the complex before exiting the garage to the street. Shaking, she opened the car door and collapsed inside, her heart beating faster than it had in such a long time. Could that be Allison? She hadn't expected Allison to look like that. Allison wasn't as young as she thought. She was pretty, in an average woman sort of way, with short hair and medium-dark skin, but not what Kim expected. Not the good looks you expected in an actress. And Rich wanted to marry her! No, that couldn't be Allison, she thought. She started the engine, remembering something from the letter she hadn't paid attention to because she was so upset. Rich had mentioned *Essence*. She'd heard of it before. She grabbed her phone and quickly looked it up. It was a magazine. An African American magazine. That woman had to be Allison.

Kim wasn't sure what to think now. She wondered what Rich felt about African Americans. She'd heard him make a few nasty remarks. Here and there. But then, she'd heard a lot of people make those remarks after they looked around and made sure they were only speaking in the company of a white person. But what did Allison think about the letter and all of Rich's hateful remarks? She was a person of color. Was it different because Rich had only spewed his hatred of Mexicans? Maybe Allison felt the same way. Kim remembered Rich telling her, "Blacks don't like Mexicans. It's like they're fighting over the same piece of pie. They look down on us. Blacks think there's nothing lower than a Mexican," he'd say, shaking his head. But then it seemed he thought that way too. Maybe, she thought a little hopefully, reading about his hatred was the reason Allison wasn't talking to him or maybe it was only because he told her about the possible paternity case against him.

Kim drove back home her head speeding along from thought to thought. Now that she'd seen Allison, she felt better, but puzzled. Allison wasn't a skinny blonde supermodel type after all. So, what was the attraction? She couldn't figure it out. And then she felt herself blush, was she so surprised at Rich's choice of girlfriends because she considered herself better than Allison because she was white? She'd argued long and hard against white woman's privilege, but then so had Rich.

Matt was in the kitchen when she stopped to get a glass of water on her way upstairs. It was strange doing all of those things herself after all these years of calling on Consuelo, or Maria, or Carmen, whomever happened to be waiting on her at the time.

"Hey Mom, Anything to eat?"

Kim stopped. "I've got a headache," she started and then stopped. She hadn't cooked for her children in so long. That had stopped when she got so busy handling all of their social commitments. Rich was never home and cooking for the kids was tiring and seemed so degrading at the time. "Sure," she said, "What would you like me to cook?"

Matt walked over to the refrigerator and studied the contents. He turned back and smiled, "How about a hamburger and some fries. Real fries like you made a few times when I was little."

The next morning, Kim opened her eyes slowly, willing all of this to go away. The house was empty and cheerless. So empty that the smallest sound resonated through the rooms. Yesterday she thought she could hear the security guards down in the kitchen whispering as they made peanut butter sandwiches for lunch. The sound of a toilet flushing on the lower level exercise room seemed to travel directly to the second floor. All of the sounds coming from some place outside of the bedroom seemed to be pulsating in the noiseless house, moving closer and closer to the sanctuary of her room. She needed to leave this space, to shut the door and not look back.

For a moment she thought she saw Rich stepping out of the

walk-in closet, holding one of his bespoke suit coats, but it was just a shadow from the lace curtain flapping in the breeze. Tears started in the corners of her eyes. She peered out of her balcony windows, there were only two cars slowly cruising by her house. Maybe the novelty was wearing off.

She wiped her eyes and fixed herself a cup of coffee while she studied the names of the divorce attorneys her friends gave her. They were all located in Beverly Hills or Century City. They were all male. She crumpled up the list and turned to her computer. After scrolling through several pages of listings, she found what she was looking for: a female attorney, with a Spanish surname and a small office that also handled immigration matters.

One week later, Kim sat stiffly in the lobby of the small office on a main street in East Los Angeles along with several older women carrying paper bags full of documents and a few teenagers who sported hoodies and tattoos. The women spoke softly together in Spanish, but the two young men with shaved heads wearing wife beaters chattered away in a combination of Spanish and English. They were there, she heard, to fight deportation orders.

After she told the attorney, Ms. Sanchez, who she was and who she was divorcing and showed her the letter written to Allison, she saw the young woman wearing a ponytail and canvas flats start to smile broadly. "A client like you comes along once in a lifetime. We're not going to have any problem. You'll come out of this smelling like a rose, and the publicity will do my practice good."

Kim was doubtful. She kept expecting a fight, but Rich only tried to contact her once. The call came late on a Saturday evening. He let her know he'd been served and he was furious. "What the fuck are you trying to do? You're not getting away with this. I'm not going to let you leave me penniless!" he screamed into the phone.

"You're not supposed to contact me," Kim told him calmly. "You need to get yourself a lawyer." Then she hung up.

Two days later local television channels were broadcasting the latest news: authorities were investigating Rich's handling of missing government funds while he held office. There was evidence that substantial sums of money had been transferred to a private account somewhere offshore. Like the contents of the letter itself, the news hit all of the media.

Kim's lawyer, Ms. Sanchez, gave a press conference in front of the Los Angeles Courthouse after the news broke. "On behalf of my client, my office is investigating whether there was also illegal conduct in hiding community assets involved in this divorce proceeding."

Rich didn't fight her the way she feared. He was agreeable now, even turning over the assets he tried to hide when he was served. It seemed he was up to his neck in investigations and disciplinary actions coming at him from all directions, to say nothing of the press and the creditors, who emerged from every corner once his name was on everybody's tongues. He was renting a small condo and working in a real estate office waiting for his disbarment proceedings.

The house was up for sale, and so was the furniture and the cars. Tiffany and Matt came home to pack their things, watching as furniture was loaded into moving trucks.

Tiffany took it the hardest. "I was so happy here," she sobbed while she packed up scrapbooks and stuffed animals along with her cheerleading uniforms and her prom dress. "I don't understand why everybody's so against Daddy now. People started posting hateful things about me too, saying I'm a rich spoiled bitch and a racist. That I'm pretending to be white. I don't even know them! It's so unfair!"

Yes, it's all unfair," Kim answered as she hugged her daughter and thought how she had imparted her own view of the world on her children when she raised them. They had a total lack of imagination for tragedy. But then so did Rich. He spent all his time trying to figure out what side he was on, and he didn't realize that everybody else had already figured it out for him.

Three years later, Kim walked across the narrow concrete walkway from her house to her five-year-old Toyota wagon. As she got closer, she saw that the front two tires were balding, and the left rear tire was low. Sighing, she made a note to take the car in as soon as she could take her first draw on her new business.

"Wait! Wait!" Carmen yelled, waving her arms as she ran toward the car. Kim stopped as she opened the door.

Karla was right behind her, hopping on one foot as she tried to stuff one foot into a pink pair of high-top tennis shoes. "Don't forget to get chips, the kind with salt and vinegar," she told Kim, "and some flour tortillas. We hate corn."

Kim gave a thumbs up and drove away thinking about her tires. Money certainly was not plentiful the way it used to be. She'd forgotten how much kids cost to raise or maybe she never paid attention before, but her two stepdaughters reminded her and Miguel often, but gently. There were fees for club soccer, dues for the drama club, new outfits, highlights and manicures for school dances and parties. There were so many it seemed. She didn't remember paying that much attention to those things with Tiffany and Matt. In those days she just handed over her credit card. Rich paid the bills, or so she thought.

The house was finally sold when the divorce was final, after they repaired the earthquake damage that showed up on part of the foundation during inspection, one of the downsides of living in a multi-million-dollar home on an expensive hillside that eroded a little each year. Then there were the mortgages Rich had taken out on the property. She'd agreed to them, she supposed, and signed off without a question. He always handled the money. And, of course, there were the unsatisfied mechanics liens, so many of them from so much work on the property as they tried to make the transplanted greenery appear natural and the imported tropical plants survive. The lawsuits were settled with the proceeds of the stock sales, the cars, the RV, jet skis, the imported furniture, and boat thrown in. The attorneys said it was better to take the hit otherwise if they filed bankruptcy, the trustee would take control of everything.

She opened a separate account to stash a few hundred thousand for herself. You could never be too cautious. There was still enough money left over to give Tiffany and Matt some for college tuition and to make a substantial payment on the house she and Miguel bought for themselves when they married in a small ceremony in his mother's backyard east of downtown.

Her father stuttered in surprise when he met Miguel and shook his head doubtfully when she told him they were marrying, "You're too old, and you both have children already." Then he walked away mumbling something to himself that she couldn't hear.

Matt said, "He looks like a nice guy."

Tiffany rolled her eyes. "He's not like my friend's fathers. That's for sure."

Kim couldn't explain to herself how it all happened, except that she now believed that it wasn't important what race or color you were when you were born, but who you made yourself into that counted.

They met really by accident, when Miguel climbed the hillside steps to her house in Los Feliz to inspect the heating and air conditioning prior to the appraisal. He was shorter than Rich and his hair was starting to go. Almost all of it was gone now. He didn't have a college education or a public following and elevated ambitions, just trade school and a job that kept him on call sometimes seven days a week. He lived with his two daughters in a small apartment off Sunset, near Hollywood. He spent all his spare time with them. After talking to him for just a few minutes, she knew he meant the entire world to his daughters. Their mother died when they were little more than toddlers, crashing her car into a tree, her blood level testing high for a mixture of the drugs she used.

They spent two hours talking that first time, sitting in the front living room on the imported sofa which was only used for company during fundraisers. Miguel didn't know about the scandal. He must be the only one, she thought. He told her he had some of those "traditional Mexican beliefs," that gossip about the privileged didn't concern him and should be best left alone. "I really don't follow politics, but I do vote," he explained. "I know what a good leader looks like. How they should put the people first."

He was willing to listen to Kim though, and so after a couple of hours spent talking, they went to dinner, driving down the hill to one of those little Italian places that also served take-out. A place where Rich always said he couldn't allow himself to be seen.

After a while, Kim met his two daughters. She never pictured herself starting over again with two teenagers, but it was different this time. The girls were shy at first, wary of her, no other woman had played such an important part in their father's life. But they were coming around a little more every day, counting on her like they would a mother. "You're coming to my soccer game. Right? It's at four o'clock and I'm starting today," or "is it all right to have a sleepover next Friday night?"

Kim felt the heavy cloud of sadness and hurt that had latched onto her slowly break apart, until there were only thin filaments that floated further and further away until she couldn't feel them anymore. She supposed if you'd asked before she would have told you that if she married again, she expected to marry someone just like Rich, wealthy, successful, always upwardly mobile, not a man who made his living installing air conditioning and brought home a paycheck every two weeks that they carefully budgeted together.

Before Kim met Miguel, she most likely expected to live in another mansion somewhere, this time an even more imposing one, with more massive rooms, no less than five bathrooms, a bigger pool and tennis court, not the small stucco house with the neat little backyard where Miguel cut the grass every Sunday and called out toward the kitchen window, smiling at her, "It's so hot. Do we have any soda to drink?"

There were no more hair and nail appointments, except for a trim every month or so at Cuts to Go in the city's strip mall, first come, first serve. No massages, Pilates, and charity lunches and fundraisers with women who were most concerned with the spring clothing line.

But now there was the Breadbasket, a small bakery she'd opened in an abandoned space in a strip mall with a little of the money she'd put aside. Miguel was immediately enthusiastic. "You'll be a shoe in at this. I'll do all the renovations. I can make it look better than any of those bakeries in Beverly Hills." And he did, all the carpentry, cabinet installation, and painting. All by himself, every night after he finished his regular job. He whistled and sang when he hammered and painted, and hugged Kim tight, his entire face lighting up on the day they opened.

Some evenings when they just sat around, and Kim looked up from the television or from whatever she was reading, she found Miguel watching her. She saw his eyes shining and she could see in them how much he loved her. Her face would flush, and she would look down at the small and inexpensive gold band she wore on her finger and polish it against her clothes.

The finished outline of a "tell all biography" about her life with Rich was lying in the top desk drawer. She'd written it out while the divorce was underway. The agent that her lawyer referred her to told her that the market for an expose like this was just waiting, and it would take her to the top of the best-selling charts overnight. She could leave her ordinary life behind in a heartbeat. There was nothing stopping her at all. Nothing, except that she loved her ordinary life.

About the Author

Francine Rodriguez grew up in and around downtown Los Angeles and later worked as a Civil Rights and Equal Employment Opportunity Investigator in the Federal sector. All told, she has worked in the fields of law and psychology for over thirty years, and her experiences in these fields inform her writing. She has published two previous novels: *A Fortunate Accident* (Booklocker 2015) and *A Woman Like Me* (Booklocker 2019).

Her website is FrancineRodriguezAuthor.com